The Socialite's Guide to Sleuthing and Secrets

ALSO BY S. K. GOLDEN

The Pinnacle Hotel Mysteries
The Socialite's Guide to Death and Dating
The Socialite's Guide to Murder

Stolen Pieces

The Socialite's Guide to Sleuthing and Secrets

A Pinnacle Hotel Mystery

S. K. Golden

NEW YORK

This is a work of fiction. All of the names, characters, organizations, places and events portrayed in this novel are either products of the author's imagination or are used fictitiously. Any resemblance to real or actual events, locales, or persons, living or dead, is entirely coincidental.

Copyright © 2025 by Sarah Golden

All rights reserved.

Published in the United States by Crooked Lane Books, an imprint of The Quick Brown Fox & Company LLC.

Crooked Lane Books and its logo are trademarks of The Quick Brown Fox & Company LLC.

Library of Congress Catalog-in-Publication data available upon request.

ISBN (hardcover): 979-8-89242-026-6
ISBN (paperback): 979-8-89242-228-4
ISBN (ebook): 978-1-63910-858-9

Cover design by Kashmira Sarode

Printed in the United States.

www.crookedlanebooks.com

Crooked Lane Books
34 West 27th St., 10th Floor
New York, NY 10001

First Edition: March 2025

10 9 8 7 6 5 4 3 2 1

*For Mom and Dad:
you're my favorite.*

Chapter 1

It's a curious thing to know exactly where you are and still be lost. For example, I was at lunch.

On Sunday afternoons, the Pinnacle Hotel turned the opulent Gold Room from ballroom into restaurant, open to guests and tourists alike, who could order from a prix fixe menu and listen to the piano while they sipped champagne and chatted about the upcoming week. Maybe even dance about the room with a romantic partner, if one was feeling up to a waltz. A thing of dreams for many.

A nightmare for me.

There were too many people here. It was better up in my room, alone with my pets. But, alas, I had made a promise, and I intended to keep it.

"Do cheer up, Evelyn," my dear friend Henry Fox said. He raised a glass of champagne and winked at me. "I'm here, after all."

If anyone else had said it, it would've sounded arrogant. But Henry was a movie star who had recently opened to rave reviews on Broadway. Getting him all to myself had been nigh but impossible the last two and a half months.

"You're right. I'm sorry." I picked up my glass and tapped it gently against his. "You're here and that's wonderful." I sipped the champagne, the bubbles tickling my nose. "It's frustrating. He's so handsome. I don't trust handsome men."

Henry ahem-ed.

"Present company excluded, of course."

"Of course." He looked at the piano. The man playing it was in his mid-twenties. His complexion was a deep tan, his eyes and hair were dark, his jawline strong and chiseled, and he wore a tuxedo that molded to his brawny shoulders so well it could've been a second skin. "You think he's handsome?"

Colin Sharpe was easily the best-looking man I'd ever seen, and I was sitting next to a movie star. In Henry's defense, at least he was taller than Colin. "A bit, yes."

Henry sighed. "I suppose. He doesn't look much like his father, however, who I would argue is a better-looking gentleman."

Colin's father, Silas Sharpe, was the Pinnacle Hotel's manager and, by extension, my primary babysitter growing up. He was in his forties, his salt-and-pepper hair more salt now, with a mustache he kept waxed and combed, and a light Scottish accent that his two decades spent in the States had shaken, but not completely erased. He and Henry were, one could say, good friends. Very good.

I laughed.

Henry drummed his fingers on the tabletop, gave me a most unsmiling look. He was not joking.

I raised a hand to my mouth and coughed. "Oh dear," I said. "I . . . um. You understand. I was thinking about something else. A joke."

"What joke?"

I glanced about the room for help. Something—*anything*—a spark of a joke I could tell. It was busy in the Gold Room, but not crowded. A group of four women were a few tables away from us, drinking champagne and stabbing at their salads. Well, three of the women were. The one at the head of the table seemed to be doing a lot of talking and pointing.

There were no jokes to be had anywhere. Instead, with a big sigh of relief, I said, "Here comes Poppy!" and rose from my seat.

Henry muttered something unhelpful.

Poppy was my newest assistant. She used to work as a maid at the hotel before I scooped her up for my own purposes. She got my mail, took care of my dog, and—as I am the Pinnacle Hotel's own party planner—assisted in getting the parties planned.

The job used to belong to her brother. But we don't speak of him if we can help it.

Poppy arrived carrying my mail and the Sunday edition of the *Times*. I gave her my seat and moved over, one away from Henry.

"Hello," she greeted, looking between the two of us. She put the package, the newspaper, and a postcard on the table. "For you."

"Wonderful!" The postcard had a picture of a sunset, or perhaps a sunrise, over green hills speckled with horses. The words "Texas Welcomes You" were stamped on the bottom right. "My cousin Martha," I said, flipping over and reading the back. "She's back home in Texas after graduating from university in Arizona. And she's accepted the invitation to visit for Christmas. How delightful! She's *definitely* not a communist, you know."

My assistant bit her tongue between her teeth. "Does she know that's how you describe her?"

Henry cleared his throat. "Poppy, settle a debate for us."

I rolled my eyes and reached for the package.

"Who is more handsome? Mr. Sharpe? Or Mr. Sharpe?"

She shook her head. "Oh no. No, thank you. I will not be taking sides in this debate."

"Surely you must have an opinion," Henry insisted.

She mimed zipping her lips and throwing away the key.

I peeled the brown paper wrapping back to reveal a small white box. I lifted the lid and gasped. A beautiful diamond tiara shone up at me. "It's just like Lorelei Lee's!" I pulled it out reverently and let it glimmer in the light of the Gold Room.

Henry whistled. "Look at the rocks on that!"

"Oh my goodness," I said, "it's real too! Can you believe it? How positively ginchy! Poppy, who sent it?"

She dug around in the package while I fiddled with the hairpins holding my hat in place.

"DeBeers," Poppy said with a note in hand.

I snorted, working the last pin free and freeing my hair from my hat. "I can see that, Poppy. Who sent it?"

She grinned. "Mister."

I hesitated a moment, the tiara hovering inches above my head. Having been to the salon only yesterday, my platinum curls were perfectly coiffed. I set the tiara instead back in the box. "Is that so?" I don't know what I was expecting. Maybe that Daddy had sent me a present. Ugh, *Daddy*. "It seems my father has been telling all his contemporaries and their progeny that I am single and ready to be married."

Henry reached out and put a reassuring hand on top of mine. "It's pretty, at least."

"Well, so am I," I said. "Just because I wanted to marry one particular person doesn't mean I'm looking to be married to any old body."

"I don't think a *DeBeers* is an *any old body*," Henry replied. "But I see what you mean."

Poppy put the note back in the box and closed it up, the tiara hidden from view. "My brother is an idiot," she said. "He'll come crawling back, Evelyn. I know he will."

"Let's hope he doesn't wait too long." Henry gave the piano player a significant look.

I looked over at him too. He was still dreadfully handsome, but it didn't fill me with any sort of thrill. It was like looking at a piece of art that somebody else picked. Yes, it looks nice, and it adds a bit of class to the space, but it doesn't *move me*.

Maybe nothing would ever again. What a terrifying thought.

"I'll have to hire him for the gala," I said. "We need entertainment anyway, and it will give me a chance to snoop on him for you and *your* Mr. Sharpe."

From what I knew of the history between father and son, I gathered that the son did not know about the father's relationship with Henry, and we were all keeping that close to our vests until we knew what kind of man he was. I'd volunteered to get to the bottom of his character, and I meant to keep my word, no matter how much I'd rather be alone in my room. With my dog and my cat. And probably a Christie novel too.

"What is the gala for again, Ev?" Henry asked.

I waved a hand. My analyst had suggested I organize a charity gala to help me through the grieving process. That doing something productive and helpful might make me feel better. So far, it was turning out to be hogwash. "Starving mothers or hungry orphans or something. Poppy knows the details."

Poppy laughed. "It's a good cause, Ev. Really."

"Excuse me? Miss?"

I blinked away from my friends and looked up into the wide eyes of a woman I didn't know. But I did recognize her. She'd been dining at the nearby table with three other women.

"Yes?" I forced a smile. I was at lunch with my friends, of course, but I was also The Owner's Daughter and knew how to play hostess. "How may I help you?"

"It's only"—she blushed fiercely—"my friends and I saw your tiara and realized you were a woman of taste. We happen to . . . well." She visibly shook herself, rolled back her shoulders. "We represent a company called Ladies Love to Sparkle and have quite a collection of affordable costume jewelry for sale. I would love to invite you to have a drink with us and show you some of our pieces."

Affordable and *costume* were not words that I, for one, had ever put before *jewelry*. But, as a rule, I didn't say no to a drink when offered by a guest.

"You two will be all right without me for a moment?" I asked Henry and Poppy out of politeness rather than actual concern. They had gotten close since I'd hired Poppy as my personal assistant to replace her brother. A welcome friendship, honestly, as it kept Poppy from turning into a stammering fool every time Henry smiled at her and meant I didn't have to keep secrets any longer. At least not between the two people I cared about the most.

Who currently lived in New York, anyway. And not somewhere else. They hadn't *boarded a ship* and left me behind. Not yet. There was always tomorrow, I supposed.

I followed the woman over to the other table, bringing my glass of champagne with me.

"I'm Prudence, by the way," the woman said, offering me her hand. "Prudence Cartwright."

I had to shift my glass to my other hand to shake hers. "Evelyn Murphy. Nice to meet you."

"Ladies," Prudence said to her group, interrupting a one-sided conversation, "this is Evelyn Murphy, and she is interested in seeing what we offer."

The woman at the head of the table—the one who'd been carrying on the conversation—looked at me with twinkling eyes. "I know exactly who this is. Evelyn Murphy, as I live and breathe. Well, Prudence, you have done exceptionally well today. I'm so proud of you. Ladies, you can learn from Prudence." She turned her twinkling eyes to the other two women at the table, except the twinkling went out like someone had pulled a string. "It's worth putting yourself out there and making introductions, even when you feel uncomfortable. You might end up inviting *the* Evelyn Murphy to your table. Come." She patted the seat closest to her. "Sit next to me, Evelyn. Prudence, go ask a waiter for another chair."

Prudence left without a word. This was surprising to me, as getting a waiter's attention here in the Pinnacle Hotel was as easy as raising a hand, but the poor woman had marched off before I had a chance to help.

"I'm Lois," the head woman said. "Lois Mitchell. I'm sure my reputation proceeds me."

I smiled blankly. I had absolutely no idea who she was nor any inkling about her reputation.

"This is my team of successful saleswomen. You've met Prudence, but that's Ruth"—she motioned at the woman to her left, and Ruth waved—"and Veronica." Veronica sat at the very end of the table. She nodded her head.

Prudence arrived with two waiters trailing behind. One was carrying a chair, and one a tray of freshly poured champagne. He apologized when he was one short because of my arrival, but I held up my glass to show him I still had plenty.

"Veronica, why don't you share a catalogue with Miss Murphy? We have our own catalogue," she said. "Like Sears. It's quite the business."

I took the catalogue from a smiling Veronica. "Sears?"

"What? No." Lois laughed, but it didn't sound genuine. "Ladies Love to Sparkle, of course. It's a wonderful business with an incredible product. Costume jewelry so good it'll fool a jewel thief! But that isn't the best part."

"No?"

"No, the best part is that it is a foolproof way for a housewife to bring in a little extra money. Mostly, all we must do is hold parties, which, I understand, is something you're good at, Miss Murphy?"

"I do try." I sipped my champagne and flipped through the pages of the catalogue in my lap. The pieces sparkled in the photographs, and from the way the pictures were taken, it was hard to tell that they weren't real gems.

"Pass the strawberries, Prudence," Lois said. "I'm running low. Don't bother Miss Murphy with it—she's busy shopping." Prudence handed the tray of fruit to Veronica, who passed it to Ruth, who passed it to Lois.

"I just love strawberries," Lois said. She put a few in her salad and one in her drink. "Do you love strawberries, Miss Murphy? Ladies, please, put a strawberry in your drink for me. I'd like to make a toast to my sales team."

The tray was passed back around, and they all followed orders. Lois picked up her glass and raised it. "I just know you three will improve. This time next year, I expect all of you to have tripled your sales and doubled your own teams."

All four of them took a sip. I watched, more interested in the group dynamics than in the products they were selling. She sounded more threatening than positive, but none of the women looked bothered.

Lois covered her mouth with her hand to clear her throat. "You know, Miss Murphy, I have a friend." She swallowed hard, picked up her fork. "He's a very wise man, a successful businessman. And when I was first thinking of joining this opportunity, well, I brought all the details to him for his opinion, and you know what he said?" She paused to take a bite of her salad and another sip of champagne. "He said if anyone fails in this line of work, it's because they're lazy, stupid, greedy, or dead."

The words hung in the air. It would've been silent, except the piano never stopped playing.

Ruth coughed and the spell was broken.

Lois chewed on a crunchy piece of lettuce. She wiped her mouth with a cloth napkin and drank her champagne. "Delicious," she said. "I love to eat here. It's a beautiful hotel."

I smiled. "Thank you ever so. And thank you for asking me over. I do think it's time for me to head back to my table, but—"

Lois's cheeks went red. I stopped talking, thinking she was angry at me for excusing myself, wondering how someone could get that angry that fast. But then Lois grabbed at her neck with both hands. She opened her mouth, closed it, opened it again, her eyes wide with terror.

"Are you choking?" I asked. "Lois, are you choking?"

She shook her head, but she wasn't breathing.

"Lois?" I was frozen in my seat. My eyes could move though, and they darted over to the other women, who were all as frozen and helpless as I was. "Help?" The idea came to me the moment I said the word out loud. "Help! We need help! *Help!*"

The music stopped.

Lois fell into my lap, the catalogue fluttering to the floor.

Chapter 2

Help arrived in a blur. Lois was in my lap until Colin Sharpe and Henry Fox pulled her off me and laid her down on the ground. Every eye in the Gold Room was trained on her, lying there, purpling up something fierce. Her friends didn't move to her side. I swallowed hard and took a deep breath before kneeling next to her head. Her skin was warm, and the pulse in her wrist lightly buzzed under my fingers.

I did my best to look reassuringly at her tablemates. "She's alive. Poppy? Where did Poppy go?"

"She went to go get Mr. Sharpe," Henry said, looking at me funny. "Colin went with her."

I nodded, swallowed again, another click in my throat. Lois's breath was shallow, and it rattled in her chest. I brushed her dark hair off her forehead, said a quick prayer, and made the sign of the cross. Henry, bless him, did the same, still looking at me like I was the one whose skin was rapidly morphing from beige to magenta.

The police arrived not much longer after that, trailing behind a frantic Mr. Sharpe, his son, and my assistant. I didn't recognize the officers. This was both a good and bad thing, as I've had both good and bad experiences with our local police department. A still-breathing Lois Mitchell was removed from the Gold Room. I watched the doors close behind the young men tasked with transporting Lois to the hospital. Colin began playing the piano again.

Mr. Sharpe stood in front of him and raised his arms, a false smile underneath his mustache. "Guests, on behalf of the Pinnacle, I'd like to apologize for the unfortunate event that you witnessed. Let me encourage you not to worry. I am assured by the medical professionals that Mrs. Mitchell will be given all needed attention at the nearest hospital. Please, raise a fresh glass, on the house, and let us toast to Mrs. Mitchell's health and speedy recovery."

While I'd been frozen, Mr. Sharpe had been busy, because the moment he said those words a bevy of waiters appeared, carrying silver trays of champagne. I shook my head. My legs had gone numb underneath me, the pins and needles feeling attacking my calves with gusto.

"Evelyn?" Henry offered me his hand and helped me stand, though I was shaking. "What happened?"

"I haven't the foggiest idea, darling. One moment she was talking business, and the next . . ." I shrugged. "What could it have been? A heart attack?"

He pushed his palm against his forehead. "I don't know, darling. Do heart attacks make you go all swollen and purple like that?"

One of the women at the table whimpered. I turned around to take their measure. It was Prudence, the one who'd walked me to the table, who held a napkin folded in the shape of a triangle under her watering left eye. "Do you think? I mean, we were so careful about what we ordered." She dabbed at her right eye. "Lois is allergic to shellfish. But the salad? That couldn't have had any shellfish, could it, Miss Murphy?"

I stared at the table. Five glasses of champagne, including my own. Four bowls of half-eaten salad. Garden salad, with tomatoes and croutons and lettuce. Slice strawberries on a silver tray. No shrimp or crab or lobster to be seen. "Maybe in the dressing? In Caesar dressing, there's anchovies. Maybe Marco did something similar today? I'll speak with our chef." Marco would be in *knots* over this. He was such a sensitive creature when it came to his food. A sweet, dear soul.

"Anchovies?" Henry's handsome face twisted into disgust. "I'd never have guessed."

I ignored his thrust-out tongue. "They're salty and delicious, darling. Eat whatever Marco makes you and you'll be happy." Unless you ended up like poor Lois Mitchell, of course. "Ladies." With a deep frown, I met all their eyes. Everyone looked scared, surprised. Only Prudence had mustered tears, and there were few. Strange, that. "Ladies, is there anything I can do for you right now?"

Prudence shook her head. "No, thank you, Miss Murphy. I'll need a phone, though. I should ring her husband, let him know what has happened. What hospital she is in. Do you know which hospital she has been taken to?"

"Manhattan General." I spoke from experience on that matter. "And the front desk will give you use of their phones for as long as you need."

Prudence dabbed her eyes with her triangle cloth once more before rising to her feet. "Otherwise, then, it's just the check."

"Please, let me cover that."

"Even the tip?" Veronica asked, standing as well. "I'd hate for the waiter to suffer because of this." She shrugged, arms wide.

"You're a doll for thinking of the waiters in your time of need. I'll take care of them, I promise."

The three women looked at one another, sniffling profusely and then nodding in sync. They left the Gold Room as a group, without another look back. I wrinkled my nose as busboys descended on the table to clean it for the next guests. "Boys," I said, "would you do me a favor? Would you save Mrs. Mitchell's salad bowl and champagne glass exactly as they are, please? Do any of you have a pair of gloves?"

"Evelyn, darling." Henry wrapped his arm around my shoulders and pulled me into a side hug. "Surely, you don't think this was done on purpose, do you? Something nefarious afoot? You were sitting right next to her. She was having lunch with her friends."

"She was having lunch with her subordinates," I said. "I don't know what I think."

Pinpricks of sweat appeared on the youngest busboy's forehead. "Marco won't like it."

"Don't you worry." I reached over and placed my hand on the young man's arm. "I'll handle Marco. Put on some gloves and put Mrs. Mitchell's dishes in my fridge, please. Better put a note on it so M—" I forced a smile. It felt wobbly on my mouth. Mac wasn't around. I didn't need to worry about him poking into my fridge and accidentally eating evidence. "Better put a note on it so the maids don't toss it."

He ducked his head in a nod. "Yes, miss."

★ ★ ★

The Pinnacle's kitchen was a hive of activity as cooks in white uniforms chopped vegetables on gleaming surfaces; puffs of steam that smelled like garlic and onion and everything good in the universe swirled out of cast-iron pans. Marco was in the middle of the hubbub, his white hat by far the tallest in the room, and his eyebrows the bushiest in the city.

Spotting me as I walked into the room, he frowned, and said, "No."

"No?" I repeated. "But, Marco, I need to speak with you. It's important."

"I have no time to discuss your *gala menu*. Have your girl arrange a meeting for later. Much later."

I planted a fist on my hip. "The girl's name is Poppy, and I will have her arrange a meeting, but not for too much later. It's only a week away, Marco—don't we need to order the food?"

He waved a knife in the air as if to slice my words away. "Galas, galas, galas. Every day, a gala. I order, I cook, you eat. My menu, not yours."

With a sigh, I said, "Fine. Your menu. Poppy will let you know the number of RSVPs. But that's not the reason I came in here right now. I need to talk to you, Marco. Please? Privately?"

He rolled his eyes heavenward, though how he saw heaven underneath those impressive brows was a mystery to me, before setting his knife down and swaggering toward me. As he cleaned his hands on his stained apron, he pointed his chin at me, and I knew I had his full attention for the next five, maybe ten seconds.

"A woman was taken out of the Gold Room and to Manhattan General by ambulance after having what appears to be an allergic reaction to her lunch."

He dropped his apron but continued wiping his hands together. "This is not my fault. We list the ingredients of every dish on the menu."

"Of course it's not your fault." I took his moving hands in mine, steadying them. "Her friends said she was allergic to shellfish. Is it possible the salad got contaminated with shellfish in some way? Or was it in the dressing?"

He shook his head. "No shellfish in salad. No shellfish in the kitchen, actually."

I reached for the pendant of Saint Anthony I kept around my neck. It was the last gift my mother ever gave me. She said it was because I was so good at finding things, and Tony is the patron saint of lost people and things. It's become such a source of comfort for me that I often don't realize I've grabbed it until the metal is between my fingers. "What do you mean?"

"Last night, we ran out. No shrimp, no lobster. New order should be here by dinner." With a deep frown, he pulled away from me. "I must work now. Busy. We are very busy."

"All right. Go back to work. You will talk to Poppy when she stops by, yes?"

He didn't reply by way of words. No, he picked up his knife and with a big whack took the green part off a bunch of carrots.

I would not be intimidated. "Marco? You'll talk to Poppy. Won't you?"

"Fine, yes." He tossed the greens behind him. They smacked a cook with a much smaller hat in the back, who then spun around, confused. "Numbers only! Only numbers."

I giggled. "Numbers only, Marco. Toodle-oo!" Just a peach, that one. I left the buzzing of the kitchen behind me, choosing to take the "Employees Only" route to the lifts in the lobby. People passed me by, several waving hello. I waved back, not focused on who they were or where they were going. My brain felt positively befuddled.

She'd been eating right next to me. I would've seen if anything nefarious had happened. And yet she went from talking about her jewelry to fainting in my lap, her skin swollen and purple. An allergic reaction made the most sense. But Chef Marco had basically removed that from being a possibility.

Maybe she was allergic to something else? Something she didn't know about?

It was strange, though. The way her friends didn't cry. Not really. A few tears from one of them, but nothing dramatic. No panic. No terror. When I had found my father, hurt, sick, convulsing, I'd been *wrecked*. And we aren't even close! What did it say about Lois Mitchell's friends and employees that they'd barely reacted to her medical emergency?

"Miss Murphy?"

I blinked. The lift boy smiled at me. He was Poppy's newest beau, a young man named Russell Castillo. He had a friendly smile that lit up his dark eyes; short, dark hair; deeply tanned skin; and the hint of what might be a tattoo on his arm, visible when his green uniform sleeve moved up his wrist. "Going up?"

"Yes. Thank you ever so." It was only the two of us in the elevator. We stood there, near each other, and my thoughts were so focused on Lois Mitchell that I almost didn't notice how tense the atmosphere in the elevator was between us. Almost. It must be strange for him, going steady with my assistant, unsure how exactly that affected our relationship. After all, he worked for the hotel and I was the owner's daughter. I smiled at him as best I could. "Are you well, Mr. Castillo?"

His posture slumped visibly in his relief. "Very, thank you. And you?"

"I've been worse," I said, because that was true. A few weeks ago, I'd been torn apart, but I was putting myself back together again. Slowly. A tortoise might be quicker, actually, but at least I was trying. I was trying to help whatever charity I'd selected as the beneficiary for the gala I'd been coerced into throwing for my own good. Starving single mothers indeed. "We had an incident in the Gold Room."

"Oh no!" The lift came to a stop. Russell opened the doors. "Another murder?"

"No," I said, waving a hand. "Oh. Well. Maybe."

Chapter 3

Poppy was in my kitchen. I knew this because she called out, "I'm in the kitchen!" the moment I stepped inside my penthouse suite. Presley hopped off the white couch and trotted over the pink carpet until he was at my ankles, twirling in delight. Presley is my little dog, a Pomeranian who looks like a five-pound black bear cub. I cooed and scooped him up, dropping kisses on his little head.

"How are you, my perfect boy?" I asked between kisses. "Have you had fun with your sister?"

The "sister" in question—my cat—was lounging in a large patch of sun behind the living room furniture. The doors to my private patio were glass, the gauzy curtains pulled back, letting in light and a view of the park. She was long and sleek, her black fur mixed with spots of dark orange and white, and she looked at me for a long while before licking her paw.

"Good to see you too, Monroe."

Presley and I had just sat down on the couch when Poppy came out of the kitchen. "Mrs. Mitchell's half-eaten salad is in your fridge, with a note that says 'Do Not Eat,' as requested. Same as her half-drunk glass of champagne. Both are on the middle shelf, in the back. I like your fridge, Ev. The shelves roll all the way out and everything."

"Thank you, Poppy. You really are the best assistant I've ever had."

She grinned but shook her head. "I know your only other assistant. That isn't much of a compliment."

Presley settled himself on my legs. I stroked his soft fur and tried not to think about my only other assistant.

"Evelyn?" Poppy sat next to us. "You all right?"

Presley's breathing was slow and even under my hand. "I think so. It was all so sudden. She was talking to me, and the next moment she was in my lap. I wish I knew what happened."

"It looked like she was simply allergic to something in her salad." Poppy placed her hand on top of mine, stilling it over Presley's fur. "You always look for trouble, when sometimes the most obvious answer is the correct one."

I nodded, even though I didn't agree with her. "Thank you again, Poppy. I don't know what I'd do without you. Why don't you take off early?"

"Really?" Poppy smiled. "Thanks, Ev. I appreciate it. With the gala and my art school projects, I've been feeling like a wet rag lately. I'm going to ask Russell to take me to the pictures. *Anna Lucasta*. Have you heard of it? With Eartha Kitt?"

"No, I can't say I have. But you two have a wonderful time. Tomorrow you'll have to give Marco the gala RSVP numbers, so be sure to drink something stiff before bed."

Poppy rolled her eyes and stood up. "He's all bark and very little bite. You relax this afternoon, Ev. You deserve it. Room service. Elvis tunes. The whole deal."

She gave Presley a rub between the ears and left with a happy wave that made me smile. Her happiness was contagious.

"The most obvious answer is the correct one," I told Presley. My gaze drifted to the living room phone. "Of course, it wouldn't hurt to poke around a little bit. Why, it's practically my duty as the owner's daughter. To double-check."

With an apologetic kiss, I took Presley off my lap and walked to the phone. The rotary dial spun easily. I asked the operator to connect me to the twenty-third precinct and there left a message for Chief Harvey. Ever since Detective Hodgson lost his job, the chief of police was my closest police connection, something I believe all hotel heiresses should have in their repertoire.

I hadn't eaten anything during my lunch with Henry, unfortunately, so I made a call to room service and ordered steak. I was not in the mood for salad. Presley followed me into the bathroom, where I began my evening routine—washing my face with cold cream and soap, applying moisturizer, wetting my hair and wrapping it in curlers—when the phone rang. Dashing out of the bathroom, curlers only on the right side of my head, I snatched the receiver off the phone in the living room before the third ring completed. Presley followed after me, hopping excitedly but confusedly.

Monroe was missing. Probably in the bedroom. She loved to claim my pillow whenever she knew I was about to lie down.

"Evelyn Murphy speaking!"

"Hello, Miss Murphy. It's me. Uh . . . Chief Harvey?"

"Why, of course—hello, Chief! Thank you ever so for returning my call. And so promptly too!"

The chief of police cleared his throat. I could picture his cheeks reddening and his fingers pulling at the collar of his uniform. He was a bit sweet on me, a fact I was careful not to abuse.

"You left a message inquiring about the state of Lois Mitchell, who I understand suffered some sort of medical emergency in your hotel today?"

I already knew what I'd left a message about, as I was the one who had left the message. I shared a look with Presley. "That's right."

"Yes. Miss Murphy, I'm sorry to be the one to tell you, but I have been in contact with the hospital. Lois Mitchell died about an hour and a half ago."

My stomach lurched. I grabbed onto the back of the couch to steady myself. I didn't know this woman, didn't care for her first impression either, but she'd been in my hotel, in my lap, for goodness sakes. "What did the doctor say?"

"Looks like a case of anaphylactic shock," Chief Harvey quoted. "But we won't know for sure until the coroner has finished their report."

Anaphylactic shock for a woman allergic to shellfish, eating in a hotel restaurant that was completely out of all things shellfish. Something was missing. A piece of the puzzle that had gotten lost somewhere, swept up in a hurry and tossed in the dustbin. I needed to sort through the trash to find it again.

"Chief Harvey?" He couldn't see me, but I still twirled a piece of my unfinished hair around my finger. "When the report comes in, would you mind . . . telling me about the contents of her stomach? It's only, her friends told me she was allergic to shellfish, but I spoke to our chef personally, and he assured me there was no shellfish in his kitchen today."

He hummed.

I pressed harder. "Oh, please, will you, Chief? I feel like she's my responsibility. She was eating at my hotel. I was at her table, did you know? I was sitting right there with her when she fell over and I—" I'm not proud of myself. I closed my eyes and forced a warble into my throat. "I only want to be able to handle it properly. You understand, don't you, Chief Harvey?"

He sighed. "I do. I'm sure you'll be tracking inventory and reprimanding chefs depending on the results. Fine. I will give you a call when the report comes in."

"Oh, Chief! You are just the ginchiest!"

We said our goodbyes, and I hung up, smiling widely at my dog. "Works every time."

There was a knock on the door. I opened it up to room service, forgetting what state I was in until the busboy kept glancing at my head with wide eyes.

I only tipped him a single dollar.

Chapter 4

Monroe woke me up, as she is wont to do, by pawing at my chest and sniffling my chin until I gave up. I yawned and scratched the top of her head. "Is it breakfast already?"

She hopped off the bed as if to say, *"Yes, it is. Please meet me in the kitchen."*

I tied a silk robe over my nightgown and followed her. Presley was in the kitchen too, like they'd hatched the scheme together. I patted him on the head and set out feeding both of them—Monroe on the counter, and Presley on the floor. I checked the time and found it barely seven thirty.

It took all of forty minutes to get ready for the day. Getting my makeup just right is ever so time consuming, but worth it. One never knows who one will meet at the hotel. By the time I was removing the curlers from my hair, my arms ached. I stretched them out above my head, yawning, and walked around my closet. It used to be the second bedroom in my suite, but nearly every available wall and surface was dedicated to my first love: fashion. I chose a rose-pink sheath dress and matching peplum jacket. Black pumps went on next, and then I grabbed Presley's black bag. Giving Monroe a quick kiss goodbye, I scooped Presley up and put him in his purse.

"Don't want to be late for our appointment, do we, darling?" I asked him.

The lift boy who took us to the lobby was none other than Poppy's Russell. "Mr. Castillo," I greeted. "How was the picture last night?"

"Ah, gee." He shook his head, his half smile giving him a single dimple in his left cheek. "I couldn't make it. Wanted to, but I was busy."

"Oh," I said. "I didn't realize you work Sunday evenings."

He cleared his throat. The elevator stopped, and we picked up more guests. Mr. Castillo didn't so much as look at me again until I walked out of his elevator and into the lobby, and when he did, it was with a quick glance and a jerky nod of his head.

I opened Presley's purse and stared down at my panting dog. "Strange."

"Miss Murphy?" One of the Pinnacle front-desk employees greeted me. His name was Mullins, and he'd been around for *ages*. He was the employee who'd trained Mac when he started two years ago.

My heart hollowed out at the memory. Darn Mac, that traitor. When would thinking about him not cause my chest to burn?

"Is Mr. Presley ready for his walk?"

I handed the gentleman the entire purse. "I'll be at my appointment in the café when you're done."

He held the bag in his outstretched arm, a fine sheen of sweat popping up on his upper lip. Presley wiggled and growled, and the bag twitched in Mr. Mullins's hands. "Ha ha," he said. "Always so spirited, this one. I'll be, um . . . back. Soon. Ha ha."

I sat in my usual seat at the café, traded my order of a cappuccino and blueberry pastry for a newspaper with the waiter who materialized immediately, and started to read the front page.

Above the fold was a salacious headline: *"The Gentleman Thief Strikes Again."* I rolled my eyes. This so-called gentleman thief seemed to be nothing more than a regular cat burglar who broke into rich people's homes in the middle of the night, stealing one or two items and leaving behind a bright red pocket square. Dottie Stewart was the name of the journalist in the byline, and she thought more of him than I did. I considered him to be someone with a desperate, pitiful need for attention, and she considered him to be a pressing danger, hellbent on harm. To the side was yet another piece on Sputnik, this one a brief warning that Sputnik III's rocket carrier would enter Earth's atmosphere in a few days and disappear, but as far as I was concerned, space was none of my business.

The article below the fold was also written by this Dottie Stewart.

Tragedy at the Pinnacle, Take Three

by Dottie Stewart

Another month, another death at the Pinnacle Hotel.
Mrs. Lois Mitchell was dining yesterday afternoon in the Pinnacle's famed Gold Room when tragedy struck, a common occurrence for the Manhattan landmark as of late. While not quite as incendiary as a knife to the back or a heroin needle in the arm, Lois's lunch, consumed on Pinnacle property, caused her to die a few hours later at Manhattan General. So far, her death has been ruled an accident, so-called anaphylactic shock, but this reporter has to wonder what is going on inside the world-famous hotel for so many people to be meeting their Maker before they

check out. Mr. Mitchell, a retired NFL player, expressed deep sadness over the loss of his wife. "We've been together for two decades, but I always thought there'd be decades more. I pictured forever with Lois. Now I don't know what tomorrow will bring."

"Murphy?"

I jumped in my seat, the paper crinkling in my hands. Mr. Laurence Hodgson, formally Detective Hodgson, was my newest employee. I'd hired him as a private investigator to crack the case in my mother's unsolved murder. My mother had been killed when I was a child, days before Christmas, while taking me to a toy store because I wanted to make sure I had the most current list for Santa. And though the police had tried to find her murderer, they'd yet to make any progress in fifteen years. Hodgson slid into the empty chair next to me and waved over a waiter. My cappuccino and pastry were already on the table, steam rising from the drink, frosting flaking on the blueberries. I'd been so preoccupied by the blasted paper, I hadn't noticed when they'd been delivered.

With a deep breath to still my racing heart, I set the newspaper down and fixed a wayward platinum lock. "You're late."

"Working," he grunted. And then, with a grin, he put a folder on the table. I stared at it for a long while, the name written in black ink on the side tattooing itself inside of me: *Gwendolyn Murphy.*

The waiter brought Hodgson a black coffee and an omelet. He waved his fork at me. "Go ahead. Open it up."

My hand shook, but I flipped the folder open. The typed document stared back at me, the letterhead of the lawyer royal blue and faded. "Her will."

Hodgson nodded. "Lot of clothing items went out to a Tiffany Boone."

"My aunt," I said. "Her daughter, my cousin, is visiting this Christmas. But she's my father's sister, not Mom's."

He took a big bite of eggs. "Tell your cousin to buy a big suitcase and fill it up with all of it."

"You think my mother's old dresses will help solve her murder?"

"Can't hurt. She also left a stipend and some personal effects to the local nunnery."

I glared at him over the porcelain cup. "It isn't called a nunnery, Hodgson."

"The place with the nuns. How should I know? And she left a sizable amount of money to a horse stable, and what's interesting there, is that two horses are listed in the will, and she left them both to you."

"To me?" I sipped my drink. It wasn't as hot as I'd like it to be, but it was warm. I savored the bitter flavor on my tongue. "I don't know anything about horses. Why didn't Daddy tell me she left me horses?"

His way of answering was scraping his fork over his plate to get another large bite of breakfast.

The horse conundrum wouldn't leave me alone. "They're my horses, but I've never heard of them! Hodgson, she died a long time ago. Are the horses still alive?"

He shrugged.

"How long do horses live?"

He set down his fork and, omelet complete, picked up his coffee. "I'd wager . . . not as long as a human but longer than a dog?"

"Huh." We sipped our morning drinks together in silence. Mom had horses and I'd never known, and now they were technically my horses—if they were still alive, that was. Mullins returned, holding Presley's purse in a stiff arm, the bag wiggling and vibrating to and fro. The growling stopped once I peeked in and removed the little ball of fluff from his confines, settling him on my lap, though he did snip at Mullins when I handed the poor man his tip.

Hodgson put his empty mug on the table and clapped his hands. "Good. Now that the gang's all here, I'd like to visit the nuns and ask them about the effects your mother left them."

"Have a wonderful time."

Hodgson raised his eyebrows. He scratched Presley between the ears, and the little dog happily licked his wrist. Presley was picky about the people he adopted as friends. Mr. Mullins got snips and growls and assault, whereas Mr. Hodgson got pats and licks and spins. "You two are coming with me."

I smiled wide. "No, thank you."

"Murphy." He sighed. "The nuns will give your mom's things to you. Probably. If you ask nice enough, like I know you can, sometimes, when the mood strikes. They don't have to give me anything."

"You'll have my mother's will with you, and you'll introduce yourself as working for me. I'm sure they'll be happy to help."

He closed the folder but left his hand on top, his index finger tapping a slow beat. "Kid," he said, "when was the last time you left the hotel? Huh? Even to walk your dog?"

My skin heated, flames flaring on my cheeks and running down my neck and chest. "Are you and my analyst exchanging notes, Hodgson? Honestly. I fail to see how that is any business of yours."

"You were out and about, doing so well, and then Cooper hightails it-"

"Thank you ever so, *Mr. Hodgson*, for the summary of my life up until now, but that is quite enough."

"Fine." He sat back in his seat. "I'll see the nuns alone."

"Thank you. Now, I do have a question for you."

He glared at the fish tanks and did not look my way.

"Oh, don't be cross with me. I want your opinion about something, and I know how much you love to give your opinion."

With a huff, he looked my way, the glare as intense for me as it was for the fish. "Did you see the paper this morning?" I handed it to him. "I was at Lois's table when she choked and fainted. It was dreadful. She landed right in my lap! She was taken to the hospital, where she later died. Chief Harvey told me it looked to be anaphylactic shock."

"So? What?" His dark eyes skimmed the article. "What do you want from me?"

"Well, what do you think? She was allergic to shellfish, but not only was there no shellfish in her salad, there was none in the kitchen. Had she been murdered?"

He shook his head. "Murphy, if you hear hoofbeats, think horses, not zebras. She ate something she shouldn't have. You don't know if shellfish was the only thing she was allergic to. It's an accident. Unfortunate, to be sure, but simple. Now, if that's it"—he set the paper on the table a little too roughly and picked up my mother's will—"I'm off to go interrogate nuns. Alone."

So much attitude from someone I was paying to do exactly what he was doing. "Fine!" My voice was louder than I meant it to be, and several nearby guests stared at us.

Hodgson noticed and pulled his hat low over his head.

"Fine," I said again at a normal volume, and smiled at the starers. "Thank you. I appreciate you."

"Yeah, yeah." He gave Presley one more pat, and then both he and my mother's will were gone, off to the nunnery.

I left a tip for our waiter and carried Presley to the lift. "It isn't called a nunnery," I told him, "though I can't remember what it's called right now. Rectory? Parish?"

Presley licked my chin in response. The lift boy was not Mr. Castillo, and I was still so distracted by the fact that my mother had owned horses and left them to me, and I hadn't known, that I didn't make conversation anyway.

The phone was ringing inside my suite, the harsh noise audible in the hallway. I rushed to unlock the door and picked up the receiver with a breathless "Evelyn Murphy!"

"Miss Murphy, hello. Glad I could reach you," Chief Harvey said. "It's, uh, Chief Harvey."

"Good morning, Chief! How are you today?"

"I'm well, thank you. I have the results back from the Mitchell woman's autopsy. Um. How are you this morning?"

My palm slapped my forehead. *Men.* "I'm much better now that you've called, Chief. What were the results of Mrs. Mitchell's autopsy?"

"Yes." He cleared his throat. "Her death has been officially ruled as anaphylactic shock, and just like you thought, there was shellfish in her stomach contents. Liquified shrimp, to be exact. Probably a shrimp stock."

My hand slid off my forehead and hit my leg. "Shrimp stock," I repeated. "I see. Thank you ever so, Chief Harvey. I'll be following up with my kitchen staff today."

We said our goodbyes. I clucked my tongue as I hung the receiver back on the phone. *Zebras, indeed.*

CHAPTER 5

Poppy let herself in not long after I finished my call with the chief. "Hi," she said, "How are—what's happening?"

I was sitting on the couch with Monroe on my lap. I had no idea how to answer her obvious question without giving an obvious answer. "I'm sitting on the couch with my cat. Why?"

"You've got that *look* on your face, Ev."

"What are you talking about?"

"A gleam in your eye. I can see it from here!" She set her hands on her hips. "What? What happened?"

"Well, I did just get off the phone with Chief Harvey."

Poppy made a rude noise with her lips. "There we have it."

"Don't be ridiculous. It's only that there was shellfish in Mrs. Mitchel's stomach contents—shrimp, specifically—but Marco insisted there was no shellfish of any kind in our kitchen last night. So, I am wondering if perhaps, maybe, she was . . . a little bit murdered?"

"A little bit murdered," Poppy repeated. "Righto. Fantastic. I'll let you focus on that while I finish preparations for the gala. I did tell Chef Marco the current RSVP numbers. Actually. I sort of shouted it at him multiple times while he ran around the kitchen waving a large knife in the air, but that's essentially the same thing. Have you decided on what you're wearing?"

Monroe stood up and stretched, her front claws digging into my dress, before she hopped off the couch and away. "Not yet, but there's loads of time to pick an outfit."

"It's in six days."

"Really? I had no idea."

Poppy flopped down next to me. "Ev," she said, patting my knee, "you picked the day."

"My thoughts have been preoccupied as of late." I scooted closer to her, bending down to rest my head on her shoulder. "Now Hodgson is cross with me, and the newspaper lady was ever so mean."

Poppy pressed her cheek to the crown of my head. "Why?"

"Because people keep getting murdered in the hotel I won't leave."

I could feel her nod.

"I spoke with Mr. Castillo. You didn't go to the pictures last night?"

"No." She sighed. "He said he was busy, but he doesn't work Sunday evenings."

"That's what I thought." I pushed my cheek against her shoulder in a pathetic attempt at a hug. *"Men."*

"Men," Poppy agreed.

There was a knock on the door. "Come in!" Poppy and I yelled simultaneously.

Henry strolled in, whistling far too cheerfully for the early hour. "Good morning! Oh, what's with all the frowns?" He made himself comfortable in the space next to Poppy, spreading his arm on the back of the couch. "Frowns lead to wrinkles, darlings."

I sat up. "I think Mrs. Mitchell was murdered."

"You think *everyone* who dies in the hotel is murdered."

"And usually I'm right!"

Poppy held up a hand. "The chief of police called and told Evelyn they found evidence of shrimp in Mrs. Mitchell's stomach contents—which is a terrible sentence, and I hate having said it, much less having thought it. Chef Marco told Evelyn yesterday that they were completely out of shellfish in the kitchen."

"Beyond that," I said, "Mrs. Mitchell only had salad. A garden salad, no shrimp, and certainly no shrimp stock."

Henry's handsome brow furrowed. "Are you sure that's all she had?"

"I was sitting right there," I said. "She collapsed into my *lap*, Henry."

"Yes, but how exactly did it go down? What did she do right before she fell into your lap?"

It was my turn to furrow my brow. "I don't remember. She ate a bite of salad or had a drink of champagne? She was talking and . . ." I shook my head.

Henry nodded like he expected my answer. "I know what we have to do."

Poppy and I looked at each other before turning out attention to him. "What?"

"We have to return to the scene of the crime." He stood up, his smiling lips threatening to whistle at any moment. "So to speak. Besides, it'll give us a chance to see Colin again."

My nose wrinkled. "Who?"

Henry's smile fell.

I gasped as realization slammed into my memory. "Mr. Sharpe's son! My goodness. I'd forgotten all about him. I'm so sorry, Henry. You must think me a terrible friend."

He offered me his hand and pulled me to my feet. "You've had a lot on your mind lately. I could never think ill of you, Evelyn—not for long anyway." He kissed my cheek. "Poppy? Will you join us?"

"No. It's like we talked about, Evelyn. You can focus on the murder. I've still got gala stuff to deal with, besides art school stuff to do."

"Uh-uh," Henry said, shaking his finger, "we do not know if it was a murder. Not yet."

She rolled her eyes. "Are you taking Presley, or are you leaving him here with me?"

"I'll take him." I picked his purse off the coffee table and called for him. "Would you schedule an afternoon appointment for the two of us at the salon? I have had a rough morning."

Henry offered me his arm and smiled. "That's so sweet of you to include me, Ev."

"Oh, do you want to join me and Presley at the salon? Poppy, better make the appointment for the three of us. Toodles!"

★ ★ ★

"Speak of the devil," Henry whispered in my ear. We were in the lobby, and when I looked up at him in confusion, he pointed across the marble floor.

Colin Sharpe, Mr. Sharpe's son, was walking around the Pinnacle's fountain. As he was wearing neither a suit nor Pinnacle green, I almost didn't recognize him. He looked like the picture of James Dean, in blue jeans and a leather jacket. If he noticed the two of us staring at him, he gave no indication, instead walking out of the lobby and toward the employees-only area, his large bag carrying his bespoke tuxedo swinging at his side.

"We'll catch him later," Henry said, pulling both my thoughts and my body toward the Gold Room. "We've got work to do."

"I still don't understand what it is we're even doing." I adjusted Presley's bag on my arm. He poked his head out of the purse, his tongue lolling out of his perfect little snout.

"You don't have to understand." Henry smiled at me over his shoulder. It was that grin, that twinkle in his blue eyes, paired with his obnoxiously perfect jaw and thick head of hair that made it no wonder that the silver screen loved him as much as it did. "You just have to do exactly what I say."

I smiled back. "Don't I always, darling? I'm perfectly agreeable every single day."

He laughed. Happily and heartily and without a hint of mockery. The Gold Room wasn't open to guests yet, but there were staff members sweeping the floors and setting tables. They looked up at us when we entered and then went back to work, used to me intruding on important tasks without explanation.

"All right, let's start. This is the table where it happened, yes?"

"Yes."

"Good. Give me the dog, and you sit exactly as you were before."

I handed the purse over. Presley didn't wiggle or growl at the handoff and instead lolled his tongue even harder. Following Henry's orders, I sat in the same spot as I had before, next to the head of the table.

"Wonderful. Now. Close your eyes."

"Honestly, Henry."

"Evelyn, trust me. I use this exercise when I'm trying to memorize a script. It will help you. Close your eyes."

With a loud sigh, I did what he asked and closed my eyes.

"Good. Tell me where Lois is sitting."

"She's at the head of the table, of course."

"And what is she doing?"

I glared at him as best I could without opening my eyes.

"Pretend you're back there, Evelyn. Pretend you're in the moment again. You've just sat down with these ladies. What are they doing? What is Lois doing?"

"When I first sit down." I wrinkled my nose. What had she been doing? Prudence left to go fetch a chair, and that had been silly, because waiters weren't difficult to come by. Lois Mitchell had known who I was and expected me to know who she was. "She introduced her friends. No, I'm sorry—her team. Successful saleswomen, she'd called them. Ruth sat at her left. Veronica was on the end. Prudence came back with a chair, and a waiter passed out champagne. Everyone took a glass. And then Lois . . . wanted strawberries. Everyone at the table put a strawberry in their champagne."

"How gauche," Henry said.

I snorted. "Right? And then, let's see. She was vaguely threatening. She wanted them all to get better at their jobs. Then they ate their salads again, and she told me about a businessman who said if a person couldn't succeed at selling the Ladies Love to Sparkle jewelry, she was lazy, stupid, greedy, or dead."

"Ain't that a bite," mumbled Henry.

I clenched my eyes as tight as I could, desperately trying to recall what had happened. "She was eating her salad, drinking her champagne, but they all were. Wouldn't you taste shrimp stock in your champagne?"

"I suppose so. But how allergic to it was she? Maybe only a drop would do it, and good champagne would cover the taste of a single drop of shrimp."

If it was a single drop, I thought, *then how did they find it in her stomach?* But I ignored that line of reasoning and focused on recalling the events of the evening. "They all passed the fruit tray. Could they have poured it on the strawberries? Lois was the only one who put the strawberries in her salad."

"Did you see any of them shake something onto the fruit?"

"No. I—I was looking at the magazine. But no one besides the waiters with the chair and the champagne approached the table, and he offered the tray to the women to pick from. He didn't specifically give one champagne to Lois."

"So, you don't think the waiter added shrimp stock to Lois's glass?"

I shook my head. "No. It had to be the strawberries, Henry, because she'd been eating her salad before I moved over, and had no reaction. It wasn't until the strawberries were added that she stopped breathing."

I opened my eyes to find Henry smiling at me. "You know what that means then, don't you?" he asked.

"Yes. Someone at that table killed her."

Chapter 6

"There's some good news here, at least," Henry said with that movie star smile of his. "It wasn't the fault of a Pinnacle employee, and so, it's not your problem."

I blinked at him. "Henry Fox, I cannot believe what I'm hearing. She fell into *my* lap!"

"Yes, but she did not die in your lap, Evelyn." He sat down in Lois's seat, Presley and Presley's purse in his arms. "Tell that detective of yours and focus instead on the gala."

"But I hate the gala." I stuck out my bottom lip as far as it would go. "I hate it, and I hate the hungry mothers or whoever they are, and I hate the people who are going to come here and eat Marco's food." I gasped. "Marco! He's so sensitive, Henry. I have to solve the murder so he will feed the children."

"I thought it was the mothers who were hungry."

Waving a hand, I said, "It doesn't matter. Marco's feeding my guests anyway, not the recipients of the charity. This was Dr. Sanders's ridiculous idea, and it has done *nothing* for me. Absolutely nothing."

"Why did she suggest it anyway?"

"Thinking about the problems of others and using my skills to help them was supposed to, I don't know, help me not focus so much inwardly on my own suffering."

"And you do love to suffer."

I poked him in the cheek with my index finger. "Watch it, or next time I'll use a nail. No, the gala will continue as planned. Poppy is doing an excellent job of it. I will be there with bells on—figuratively, of course. And I'll solve the murder in time for Marco to shine, unworried about rumors that he poisoned a guest to death."

"Was he very worried, then? Marco, I mean?"

I bit my lip. Marco was complicated. It was hard to read any emotions from him that weren't blind rage. "He's a sweet soul, Henry. I must do whatever I can to clear his name and his conscience."

"That was a terrible lie, Evelyn. Your eyes."

I raised a hand to my eyes. "What about them?"

"They get all glassy and unfocused." He sighed. "Honestly. It's a good thing you're not in my line of work."

Music began playing. I jumped in my seat, the sudden noise like a shock of cold water down the back of my neck. Henry laughed. Colin Sharpe had taken his place at the piano, his fingers gliding over the ivory keys. He was looking at us as if we were invading a sacred space.

"Now's your chance," Henry said. "Would you like me to talk to him with you or are you going to handle it on your own?"

"I'll go," I said, smoothing out my jacket, wondering if I should take it off before I approached the piano. "Would you take Presley to the salon? I'll join you both in a minute."

Henry did so with a wink, and then I was alone in the Gold Room with the biggest dreamboat in possibly the entire world playing piano just for me. And a handful of waiters and bus boys who were setting up the room. I cleared my throat, longed for my compact and a lipstick, and approached Colin Sharpe with my chin raised; one high-heeled foot in front of the other, step by step, a sway in my hips that my body knew from memory, even if my brain recoiled from the action. What I wanted to do was hide. What I wanted to do was go get my nails done with my dog and then eat something cheesy and go to sleep for a day or two, and if I couldn't do that, then what I wanted to do was solve a murder. Someone had murdered Lois Mitchell. One of her friends had slipped shrimp stock over the strawberries without anyone else noticing.

But I'd made a promise. I *would* find out what sort of man Colin was and report my findings back to Henry. I would *not* forget again that Colin Sharpe existed. And if that meant making myself as noticeably feminine as possible, then darn it, that's what I was going to do.

Also, he had been here, in this room, when Lois fell over. Maybe he had seen something.

With a skip in my step, I cleared the rest of the room and stood before him with a smile. "Hello," I said. "I don't believe we've met yet. I'm Evelyn. Evelyn Murphy. We're having a gala in this room next week, and I'd be ever so honored if you'd consider performing for us. You'll be fairly compensated, of course."

He didn't stop playing. He looked at me as the music swirled around us, his dark brown eyes mesmerizing and intense. "Your boss lets you pick the music acts? Nice boss." His voice was that deep, throaty Scottish accent that Mr. Sharpe only fell into when he was particularly stressed. Mr. Sharpe—*my* Mr. Sharpe I mean—had very little hand in raising his son, seeing as how they had been on separate continents during the majority of the younger Sharpe's life. Colin had moved to Chicago a little while ago, and then made his way to New York City. He'd begged his father for a job. The two did not know each other very well, and with throwing Henry in the mix—well, that's where I came in. I suggested Mr. Sharpe offer his son a job on a trial basis, and I'd keep my eyes open, so to speak.

I smiled. At least, my mouth was open. "Um," I said, "I don't know what you mean."

He shrugged a shoulder, the simple tune changing tempo. "Your boss? You know, the pretty brunette? Her father owns the hotel."

I barked out a laugh, though it didn't feel like laughter when it left my chest. It felt like a punch. "That's Poppy," I said. "She's my assistant. I'm the owner's daughter. Evelyn . . . Murphy? I think I gave you my name a second ago, didn't I?"

Colin's intense gaze swept me up and down before he shrugged again. "If you say so. They talk about you in the newspapers, but there hasn't been a picture, so I just assumed you'd be the prettiest girl in the room."

I'd been in hiding for the last few weeks, though I wasn't about to tell him that. And it was fine that he thought Poppy was prettier than me. That didn't bother me at all. She was beautiful, and we are all beautiful in our own ways. I had certainly told Henry to his face that I thought Colin was better-looking than his father, so what right did I have to be upset? None. Which was a good thing, because I wasn't upset. At all.

"If I take this job, will I be working closely with Poppy?" Colin asked. "Is she single?"

My mouth closed and puckered. *Fine.* First he thought I wasn't the owner's daughter, and now he's interested in my assistant. That's fine. I didn't care. I hadn't even remembered he existed twenty minutes ago! He could be interested in whomever he wanted to be interested in, and I didn't care at all. "Yesterday, there was an incident over there." I pointed at the table where Lois had eaten her last meal. "You were here, weren't you?"

He nodded, his attention on the piano now, having obviously found me wanting.

I was an absolute delight to look upon, especially in this shade of pink, but he was allowed his own wrong opinions.

"Did you see anything?"

"Saw lots of things," Colin said. "Can you be a little more specific?"

I smiled again, showing all of my teeth. "The woman who fell over? At her table? Did you see anyone suspicious approach it before she collapsed? Or one of her tablemates pull anything out of her purse?"

"I wasn't looking that closely," Colin said. "Not at that table. I did see Poppy sitting next to that familiar-looking man. Are they dating?"

"You mean Henry? Henry Fox? Is Poppy dating the movie star Henry Fox?" My skin was hot from the top of my head to the middle of my stomach. "No, no, they are not going steady. Friends only. Through me. They're friends through me."

His intense gaze swept me up and down again before refocusing on his own hands. Guests were beginning to come into the Gold Room, well-dressed businesspeople who looked like they had rented out the room for a company meeting. I nodded at them politely. "Do let me know when you've decided whether to perform at our gala, will you, Mr. Sharpe? Have a wonderful day."

I marched out of the room, my hands fisted at my sides. What an insufferable man! He thought I was the assistant. Honestly. Honestly! *Men!* I was sick of them. Sick of them leaving me, sick of them asking me to go visit nuns, sick of them dismissing me like I was unimportant! I could have him fired, if I wanted! *How's that for unimportant?*

By the time I made it to the salon, I was positively stewing. I plopped down in a chair, took off my shoes, and held out my hands. Four women approached with files and polish, and I relaxed into the chair as a fifth began massaging my shoulders.

"You're the only man I can stand," I said to Presley. He was in a smaller chair next to me, a woman carefully trimming his nails while another combed through his fur.

Henry sighed from underneath the hot, wet towel placed over his face. "That means a lot to me, Evelyn, but I take it things with the piano player didn't go well."

"Oh. I was talking to Presley. But no. We'll have to enlist Poppy in our plans."

"Needs must, I suppose."

Chapter 7

Freshly pampered, Presley and I returned to our suite. Poppy greeted us and then took Presley to the park to do his business and collect his daily cheese sample from a pretzel vendor. I picked up the phone and asked the operator for Lois Mitchell, Manhattan. I didn't know how fast names got taken off the operator's list once a person died, but I doubted it was next day. Sure enough, after a few minutes, I was connected to the Mitchell household in Manhattan. A woman answered, and after I introduced myself and asked to speak to Mr. Mitchell, she said she was their housekeeper and that Mr. Mitchell wasn't available at the moment.

Obviously. His wife had just died. Of course he'd be out.

I massaged my fingers into my forehead. "Would you please take a message for me? Would you tell Mr. Mitchell that Evelyn Murphy from the Pinnacle Hotel called to offer her sympathy and condolences, and to please not hesitate to contact me for anything?"

"Yes, miss."

"Thank you. I know this is difficult. But Mrs. Mitchell was dining with friends here at the hotel yesterday, and I'd like to ring them up and offer my condolences as well." And invite them over for individual questioning, but the less the housekeeper knew, the better. "I believe their names were Prudence, Ruth, and Veronica. Do you happen to have their numbers?"

"No, miss. But if you'd hold for a moment, I could check Mrs. Mitchell's address book."

Oh, an address book. It would be lovely, to get my hands on that. Every person that she knew and spoke to regularly in one little checklist. "Yes. Please do."

It took several moments, but the housekeeper found all three phone numbers and gave them to me. I wasn't sure how to feel about that. If one of my maids answered my phone and then gave out Daddy's number to whoever asked, I'd be a wee bit peeved. But I wasn't about to point that out to the woman who was doing her best after her boss died. "You're a peach. Thanks again. Ta!"

Presley and Poppy returned, both full of cheese and looking ready for naps.

"You've still got that look in your eyes, Ev." Poppy shook her head. "It makes me nervous."

"No need to be nervous, darling. I'm simply inviting friends over for a chat."

She rolled her eyes. "Uh-huh. Shall I make myself scarce, then?"

I tapped my lips with my index finger. Normally, I'd ask her to stay. The more the merrier, and maybe if there were other people around, the women would relax. But also, Mrs. Mitchell's acquaintances might not be so keen to speak as freely as I'd like if there were another person present. But I also didn't want them to know that I suspected them of murder. "Stay," I said with finality. "Please. Play the part of my assistant."

"I am your assistant."

"Exactly."

"It's a good thing you're pretty, Ev."

★ ★ ★

One by one, I called and invited over Lois's friends. I decided the best way to talk to them was not as a group, but as individuals, and so I staggered their arrival times by one hour. Poppy was tasked with collecting the new arrival from the lobby and bringing her up to my suite, and once the guest was comfortable, serving any beverages or snacks she might require.

"Terribly sorry about this," I told Poppy.

"This is my actual job, Ev."

My brow furrowed, but I didn't argue. Was it her job to cater to my every whim? I thought I was paying her to be my friend. I mean, walk my dog, schedule my appointments, address envelopes, and send out invitations. She was paid to dot my *i*'s and cross my *t*'s. The friendship was free. Hodgson tells me I shouldn't have to pay people to be friends with me, but what did he know? I had to pay him to investigate my mother's murder. And then he had the nerve to get mad at me for having to do his own job! *Men*.

The first invited and the first to arrive was Ruth. Ruth was a curvaceous blonde, with ice blue eyes and a delicate nose. Her dress was simple, a soft blue the color of her eyes, and her hat, belt, shoes, and purse were all a black patent leather. She smiled and shook my hand and jitteringly accepted Poppy's offer of something to drink.

"Water is fine, thank you so much," she said, and had the softest Southern drawl. Not something I'd expected to hear up here in Manhattan.

"My cousin Martha, she's from Arizona—well, originally Texas. She moved to Arizona a while ago, but she just moved back to Texas. She sounds a bit like you."

"Oh, really? I've never been as far as Texas. I'm from Georgia originally. My husband and I were married in Atlanta, but his work brought him here about a year ago. Thank you." She took the glass of water from Poppy and had a sip.

I watched closely, wondering if I was in the presence of a cold-blooded murderer.

She coughed in the middle of her drink and water dribbled down her chin.

I handed her a Kleenex. I was doubtful of her murdering capabilities, no matter the temperature of her blood. "That must be difficult for you, moving to a different state after being in one place all your life. Do you have any family up here?"

"Not really. It's just my husband and me and our twin boys. But they're freshman in high school now, so they don't need their mom so much anymore."

"Teenagers," I said, being not much older than a teenager myself—and Poppy still nineteen. Ruth didn't need to know that. "How about friends? Have you made any friends here in Manhattan?"

She smiled, nodded. "Oh yes. The Ladies Love to Sparkle have become my dearest friends. Veronica and Prudence and, well, Mrs. Mitchell." She looked down at her half full glass of water, smile falling. "That was awful, what happened yesterday."

I reached out and set a comforting hand on her forearm. It was not lost on me that she used the given names of only two of her associates. "It really was. I am so sorry you lost such a good friend in such a terrible way. Is there anything I can do for you?"

"Oh, thank you, Miss Murphy. I'm just fine." She swallowed hard, her tongue making a soft clicking noise, before she swiveled on the couch and pulled out her purse. "I did bring a Ladies Love to Sparkle order form. In case you were at all interested in ordering anything? But there's no obligation, of course."

The magazine cover was smooth in my hand. "Of course," I said, and flipped open the pages. "I do love to sparkle."

We both laughed, but it sounded like neither of us found my joke funny.

"The order form is in the back," Ruth said, fishing a pen out of her purse as well. "Fill it out for me, and I'll get you whatever you want lickety-split."

Wonderful. I was going to have to order costume jewelry from all three of Lois Mitchell's saleswomen, one of whom was possibly a murderer. Where was that tiara I had gotten from Mr. DeBeers? What would a tiara look like with one of these giant, fake emerald necklaces? A tiara could jazz up any item.

I jotted down the number for the necklace. "Do you like working for Ladies Love to Sparkle?"

"It's nice because I set my own hours. I don't have to go to an office. I can stay home and get dinner ready and host a party here or there." She took a deep breath. "The more parties you can have, the better you do at sales. And you know lots of people, don't you, Miss Murphy?"

I made a differential gesture with my full hands.

Ruth continued, "I don't know too many people yet. But once I start making connections, I think my sales will grow too. I can't wait until I can use my own money to buy groceries for my family one day."

Veronica's answers were similar. She arrived ten minutes after Ruth left, and when Poppy offered her a beverage, she requested coffee. "With cream and sugar, please." Veronica had straight red hair that frizzed on the ends; large, almost doe-like brown eyes; and a splattering of freckles across a thin nose. She wore a green tea dress that suited her coloring, but the vibrant color was visibly fading.

When asked about her involvement in the Ladies Love to Sparkle group, she also referred to Lois only as "Mrs. Mitchell," while referring by Christian name to Ruth and Prudence.

"Would you like to take a look at our catalog, Miss Murphy?" Veronica asked, already pulling said catalog from her purse.

"I'd like nothing more." I skimmed through the same material I'd looked at now twice before. Once with Ruth, and once at the table before Lois Mitchell met her untimely end. "I am ever so sorry for what happened at lunch yesterday. I understand that Mrs. Mitchell was a mentor in this business?"

Veronica sipped her coffee. "She was definitely my mentor," she said. "I met her at a party for the jewelry and she took me under her wing. With her guidance, I started my own business selling this jewelry."

"And it's doing well?"

Veronica cleared her throat. "It will. It has the potential to do well, Miss Murphy. That's why Mrs. Mitchell had meetings with us every so often, so she could guide us in our choices, help us become excellent saleswomen. Already, I've got my mother and my mother-in-law starting their own Ladies Love to Sparkle businesses. We all find it very fulfilling."

I flipped to the order form in the back and filled in a few more pieces. "Do you? How wonderful."

"Yes. The parties are great fun, and it's a fantastic way for women to bring in some money of their own. My husband and I found ourselves in a bit of a tight spot when he lost his job, and us with three young kids still at home. This opportunity felt like a gift from God."

I smiled. "I understand. Has your husband found work?"

She nodded, returning my smile. "Yes. He's got a job on a boat, actually. A fisherman's mate. It's quite exciting. Hard work, but he does it without complaint. One day I'll earn enough money that he won't have to work so hard or be gone so long from our kids."

Ten minutes after Veronica left, Prudence arrived. Prudence was by far the oldest member of the group of friends. Her dark brown hair was graying and curly, her skin a deep tan with heavy-set wrinkles around her smiling mouth, her eyes bright green. She wore red toreador pants, a white turtleneck, and a black shirt jacket. When asked what she wanted to drink, she requested herbal tea.

"A bit damp out," she explained. "Tea is good for the throat and the sinuses."

I hadn't been outside all day. Truly, I hadn't been outside in days. Weeks. Ever since Mac had left. Ever since I'd visited Yonkers for the first time. I'd never be going back there, not for as long as I lived. But both my analyst and my private investigator were gung-ho about me venturing outside the Pinnacle again, insisting it was *good for me*, or some other drivel. Doing things that were good for me was such a drag.

"Prudence, thank you ever so for coming back here, especially after what happened yesterday. Please, let me extend my condolences. I am so sorry for the loss of your friend."

She nodded gratefully. "She was more than a friend. Mrs. Mitchell was a good deal younger than me, but she was razor-sharp, and she could sell ice to a snowman. I admired her a lot."

How quickly could admiration turn into disdain? In my experience, one afternoon was all it took.

"I, uh . . . I did bring my catalogue, Miss Murphy. If you're interested in looking at it again? I know your time was cut short yesterday."

"Indeed. I'd love to." By now I had the item numbers practically memorized, but I feigned looking the pages over yet again in order to keep the conversation going. "Do you enjoy this line of work, Prudence?"

"Yes. It gives me something to do. Purpose."

That made me pause. At my look, she continued, "My kids are grown, and my husband died about a year ago. I don't need the money—Richard made sure of that. But the parties are lots of great fun. I've made real friendships selling this jewelry, and if you don't mind me saying, they're pretty pieces too. Affordable and lovely. I own quite a bit of it myself for my own personal use. I've even purchased some to give out as Christmas presents."

"How very thoughtful." I filled out the order form and handed it over. "If there's anything either the Pinnacle or I could do for you, please don't hesitate to let me know."

Once Prudence left, I collapsed back in my chair, exhausted.

Poppy wandered out from the kitchen. "Did you learn anything?"

"Yes," I said to the ceiling. Was that dust in the light up there? I'd have to speak to the new maid. "All three of them are lonely. And none of them have earned any money."

Chapter 8

I didn't bother going downstairs for my usual breakfast the following morning. I hadn't scheduled an appointment with Hodgson, and it was raining outside. It was nice to sit in my robe on the couch, with a cup of hot coffee and a room-service omelet, and watch the rain fall, a sleepy dog by my feet and a purring cat on my lap.

None of the women I'd spoken with yesterday seemed to dislike Lois in any way. Certainly, all of them spoke about her respectfully, almost reverently. But all three of them shared one common thread: they'd joined Lois's sales team during a period of change and hardship. For one, it was moving away from family. For another, a massive loss of income, followed by a husband who was hardly home. And for the last one, being a widow with fully grown children. All of them were lonely; some of them were anxious for money; and none of them gave me even the slightest inclination they were capable of poisoning someone in the middle of a crowded room.

The knock on the door made me jump. Mr. Castillo had already come and gone, as it was his turn to take Presley for his morning walk. I wasn't expecting any more room service. And

Poppy wasn't scheduled to meet with me until lunchtime, after her art school classes let out for the day.

Walking to the door, I tightened my chenille pink robe across my stomach and checked the peephole. Hodgson stood in the hallway, wetly.

"Good morning." I welcomed him into my suite. "I wasn't aware we had a meeting today. Did your visit with the nuns go well, then?"

"No, it did not." He hung up his dripping hat and pulled something out of his wet jacket. Another folder, this one much thicker and well used. He handed it to me before shrugging out of his jacket. "They wouldn't even meet with me, Murphy. You have to come."

"I do not have to do anything," I replied. The folder was heavy in my hands. "What is this?"

"Your mother's case file. Chief Harvey is easier to work with than those damn nuns, let me tell you." He wandered over to the room-service cart and grabbed an uneaten pastry, then poured himself what was left of my carafe of coffee.

"I don't think you should say 'damn nuns,' Hodgson. And you have an open tab in the café. You don't need to eat my scraps." He did not pause in his eating and drinking. I set my free hand on my hip. "Shall I order you something from room service?"

Hodgson took no notice of my annoyed tone. "No. Go put on some clothes. We're going to visit the nuns today. Together."

"I can't go out today. It's raining!" To put a line under it, I moved to the curtains and waved them about. Monroe thought this was a marvelous game and began swatting at the ends.

Hodgson licked his teeth. "So, bring an umbrella."

"I simply cannot leave the hotel today. Thank you for your understanding. I will write a letter to the nuns on your behalf. Then they'll have to talk to you, won't they?"

"A letter."

"Yes. A letter. It'll only take a minute, and then you can be on your way."

He finished off the pastry. "You gonna look at her file, or what?"

I'd forgotten I was holding it. When I remembered, my palm burned. I set it down on the end table and cleared my throat. "I'll be back in a minute with your letter."

Hodgson looked at me over the rim of his borrowed coffee cup. "You might see something useful, Murphy. Ain't that what you're good at? Finding things?"

"Not when it comes to her," I said. "I'll be right back."

Presley followed me into the bedroom, and I shut the door, leaning against it for support. My mother's file was sitting in my living room. The heat from my palm traveled up my arm, left it tingling. My breathing got shallow, my heartbeat erratic. I sat down on my bed and put my head between my knees, breathing deep. In and out. In and out. Giving the feeling a name. *Anxiety.* Experiencing the panic. Letting it happen. Not fighting it. I was okay. I was in my room, and my dog was licking my ankles, and my robe was soft. *Breathe in. Breathe out.*

Gradually, my heart rate slowed enough that the dizziness subsided. I grabbed the notepad with the Pinnacle Hotel logo at the top, from beside the phone in my bedroom, and jotted a quick note naming Hodgson as my employee and asking that the nuns please treat him as they would treat me directly. I signed my name after doodling a little heart.

"There." I smiled brightly as I left my bedroom and handed the paper over. "Now you should have no trouble."

He glanced at it, sighed, and stuck it in his trouser pocket. "You're paying for the gas in my car, Murphy."

"Of course. Before you go? I spoke with Chief Harvey yesterday, after we had our meeting. And do you know what he said? He said that shrimp stock had been found in Mrs. Mitchell's stomach contents. Hmm? What do you think about that?"

"What did she eat again?"

"A salad. Some strawberries. And champagne."

"Not something you'd season with shrimp, then." He nodded a few times. "Looks like you were right. She was murdered."

My bright smile was real this time. "Do you have any advice on how to move forward?"

"Have you talked to the husband yet?"

"Not yet."

"It's always the husband," Hodgson said. He pointed at my mother's case file with his chin. "Your dad was overseas, though. Already checked."

I flopped down on my couch. "That is of no help to me whatsoever. I was sitting *right there*. No one approached the table."

He clicked his tongue. "Who says it happened at the table?"

Getting ready for the day is always quite the process, but an important one. I find it helps me tremendously to look my best. To put care into my outfit, my makeup, my hair. Things that are all within my control. So many things are not in my control, which is ridiculous, especially inside the Pinnacle. But I can't control who lives and who dies and who writes the newspaper articles about it. All I can do is line my lips in cherry red, swipe some Vaseline on my cheek bones for a highlight, and lengthen my lashes with mascara. I donned a navy-blue, long-line princess dress, and paired it with a matching brief jacket that had the most adorable little bow at the bottom of the throat, a pair of Christian Dior gloves, silk stockings, and black kitten heels. Presley's large black tote bag matched my shoes, and so it was no trouble to bring him with me back to the Gold Room.

Once more, employees were getting the room ready for whatever activity was scheduled that day. The table and chair I had sat in when Lois Mitchell choked were no longer available, replaced instead by tall, standing-room-only tables, fit to hold nothing more than champagne glasses and hors d'oeuvres. I set Presley's bag down on the table and scratched behind his ears.

"This is pointless. Everything is all moved around. I can't do Henry's exercise again."

He licked my wrist in commiseration.

Janitorial staff was in the room, mopping the floor, shifting decorative plants and other furniture around to get everything clean. A large table was moved, and from under the legs an umbrella spun out. I bent down to scoop it up, my attention catching on a wayward potted plant, moved over to make way for a mop. Something strange and plastic was lying on the mulch. I picked up the almost empty bottle, no bigger than the palm of my hand, with Erno Laszlo's label on the front. Another man was sweeping the corners, and his pile contained not only crumbs but a room key, a scarf, and a man's wallet. "Excuse me," I said. "Shall I take those to the Lost and Found for you?"

"Oh, that's all right, Miss Murphy," he said. "Once we're done cleaning the room, I suspect we will have lots of items to bring to the front desk. One time I even found a banana. A *banana*! We do not serve whole bananas for dinner. Or even lunch."

"All right. I'll let you all get back to work." With a sigh, I hoisted Presley's bag onto my shoulder, tucked the umbrella under my arm, and the bottle of Phelityl Oil in my jacket pocket. "It seems we are in the way. Let's take our goodies to the Lost and Found and grab lunch in the diner. I need a cheeseburger, or I'm afraid I'll simply fall over in defeat."

Presley yipped.

Chapter 9

I twirled the umbrella in my hands. It was a nice one, dainty, made more as a fashion accessory than an actual tool against the rain, with a tortoise-shell handle. Not made of real tortoise, I'm sure, but that pretty light brown and dark brown mix that people call tortoise, which is strange, because I've seen turtles in books before, and they are all sort of greenish.

I'd seen horses before too, in real life, but not for years and years. And now I owned some. What other surprises would Hodgson's investigation into my mother's life bring to the surface? I'd have to go see the horses eventually, if they were still alive. Who did I know that knew about horses? How long did they live for? Did they live long enough to meet their grandchil— grand horses? What were baby horses called?

I was so focused on twirling the umbrella and thinking about horse grandparents that I didn't see Mr. Sharpe until I was practically on top of him.

He said, "Ow, my toes!" in his light Scottish accent, worn down by years in the States, and pushed me away.

"Gracious! Are you all right? So sorry about that—I didn't see you. Or your feet."

His mustache twitched as he glared at me. "You have a visitor. I left him at the bar."

My heart rate spiked. A male visitor? Who was important enough for Mr. Sharpe to search me out himself? "Henry?" I guessed him to be the most likely suspect while also the least painful one. If it were Mac . . .

Well, in that case, I hoped Mr. Sharpe cared for me enough to warn me ahead of time. I'd run the other way and lock myself in a hidden room somewhere. I happen to know of a very good little spot down by the boiler room that almost no one else uses.

"No. Mr. Mitchell. The husband of the woman who—well . . . you know." He spread his hands wide. "It's best if you could offer your condolences on behalf of the hotel and perhaps give him a night's stay or a free meal?"

I blinked. "Of course I'll offer him anything the Pinnacle can provide. I'm surprised you think you need to ask me to be a good hostess, Mr. Sharpe. You know me better than that."

"It's only. With the bad press and all." His outstretched arms closed in tight around his lithe frame. "We don't need the attention a wrongful death suit would bring."

Presley poked his head out of his purse and licked my arm. "Ah. I see. You've spoken with Daddy already this morning."

Mr. Sharpe nodded, a twinge of guilt crossing his face.

"I'll put my best foot forward with Mr. Mitchell, I promise. I can be quite charming when I want to be, you know."

"I do know. How are things going with my son, by the way?"

I grimaced, tried to hide it with a cough, but Mr. Sharpe caught it. "Not well?"

"He thought Poppy was the owner's daughter, and I was the assistant. Not sure how he managed that, since she does all the work. But never fear, Mr. Sharpe. I haven't forgotten what we talked about when you offered him this job. I will feel him out for you, I promise."

"Good." He pulled on the hem of his vest, wiped off imaginary wrinkles. "Good. Thank you. Shall I introduce you to Mr. Mitchell?"

"That would be lovely." I looped my free arm through his. "Lead the way."

★ ★ ★

Mr. Sharpe introduced me to a man sitting at the back of the U-shaped bar with his head in his hands and a half-drunk glass of scotch on the rocks in front of him. He looked up when we approached and shook my hand. The soft skin around his brown eyes was swollen and purple. His dark hair looked unwashed. His facial hair was unshaven to the point of being late for its five o'clock appointment. His white shirt and navy trousers were wrinkled.

He looked every bit the husband in mourning. Without fail, Hodgson's voice floated up to the surface of my memory: *"It's always the husband."*

Mr. Mitchell certainly didn't look guilty, but then again, a guilty person would be doing everything in their power not to look guilty. At least, if they had half a brain. Most criminals weren't very bright, as a general rule.

"May I join you, Mr. Mitchell?"

He nodded and moved his drink out of the way, the heavy glass sliding against the highly polished dark wood of the bar. The entire room was done up in dark wood and velvet upholstery, making the entire place feel more masculine than any other room in the hotel. Even the crystal chandelier hanging above us seemed less delicate in this room than in any others.

Mr. Sharpe excused himself.

The bartender approached, and I grinned. "Mr. Peters! They've moved you downstairs, I see."

Mr. Peters normally worked at the rooftop pool bar. But, with the rain and changing of the seasons, the pool was closed.

"Hello, Miss Murphy. Good to see you. Sorry to hear what happened with Mac." There was a pause. "What's that noise?"

I cleared my throat, and the mysterious, low hum Mr. Peters was referencing disappeared. "Please, may I have a chocolate shake, a cheeseburger, and French fries?"

"That's at the diner. Across the lobby."

"Yes." I agreed. "Please and thank you. I am ever so hungry."

Mr. Peters's shoulders sagged.

"Would you like a cheeseburger as well, Mr. Mitchell? They are delicious, if I do say so myself."

"I . . . um . . ." He wiped his large hand over his mouth. He was a big man, Mr. Mitchell. Even sitting on the stool, he towered over me, and I am a tall woman. "Yes. I haven't eaten in— yes. Thank you."

"So, two of my order, Mr. Peters. Thank you."

When Mr. Peters left, I placed Presley's purse on the bar top. He didn't hop out, but looked around, his ears and nose twitching from all the new sounds and smells.

"Cute dog," Mr. Mitchell said, stretching out his hand.

Presley sniffed his fingers, and then he sneezed and ducked back in the purse.

Mr. Mitchell stared at his hand.

"He doesn't like a lot of people," I said. "Please forgive his terrible manners."

"It's all right." He sipped his drink. "He probably smelled my dogs. I have big ones. Great Danes. At home. They keep waiting at the door. All night they waited. Lois, she's never gone all night. They didn't understand where she was."

My brow furrowed. I held on to his arm. "Mr. Mitchell, I am so, so sorry for your loss. I didn't know Lois very well, but I could tell just by talking to her that she was a singular woman."

"No one else in the whole world like her," Mr. Mitchell agreed, a far-off look in his eyes. "I don't know what I'm going to do without her."

I stared at his face, trying to take the measure of him. Was this man a killer? He looked tired and sad, and it seemed real enough. What motive did he have to kill his wife? With a deep sigh, I squeezed his arm before letting go. "Nobody knows. It's an awful thing. Truly. The most important person in your entire life dies, and time doesn't skip a second."

His attention snapped back to me. "It's like the world hasn't realized it's changed yet."

"Exactly. And the worst part is, it never will. It's only you who realizes it. Who just gets used to it. To the big, gaping hole in your life. You get used to living with it. Taking it with you everywhere you go. Eventually, the gap becomes a part of you." I shook my head. "I'm sorry. That's not very helpful, is it?"

"No. No, it's nice to hear someone speak honestly with me about grief. So far, everyone's treating me like a child. Or worse, ignoring me completely."

"It's good you have your dogs," I said. "Mine gets me through every day. Do you have family nearby?"

Mr. Mitchell shook his head. "I lost my parents a while ago, and Lois never was able to carry a baby to term, though we tried a few times. Those dogs are the closest things I have to children." I couldn't tell whether the note in his voice was sadness or bitterness. Perhaps it was both. Death did that sort of thing to the living left behind.

We sat in silence for a few moments before he shifted in his seat and tossed back the rest of his drink. "I'm sorry I missed your call. Thank you for reaching out to me."

"Of course. Your housekeeper was exceedingly professional." That was an outright lie. I told it by keeping my eyes on Presley's twitching ears.

Mr. Mitchell huffed. "No one has ever called my housekeeper professional. No one. But she does a good job keeping things clean, and really, what more can you ask for?"

I thought of my long-time maid, Florence, who'd kept my suite clean and never spread a single piece of gossip about me, even though she'd be the first to see my misdeeds. I had her cat now, inherited after her murder. Monroe, like her previous owner, minded her own business most efficiently.

"How long were you and Mrs. Mitchell married?"

"A long time," Mr. Mitchell said. "We met in high school. She was with me throughout my football career. I played for the Rams out in Los Angeles for a while, then got traded to Philadelphia. Got too old to keep playing and inherited a bit of money when my old man passed, so when I retired, I let Lois pick where she wanted to live. Only seemed fair since she'd never had a say in it before. She picked Manhattan, and let me tell you, Miss Murphy, Manhattan picked her. She *flourished* here."

"Yes, I was introduced to her business last night."

Mr. Peters arrived, carrying a large tray full of food. Presley almost knocked his purse over in his glee at the arrival. I settled him in my lap and picked off small bites of hamburger for him to eat out of my hand.

"Another scotch, when you get the chance," Mr. Mitchell ordered. "On the rocks like the last one."

I sipped my shake, let him get a few good bites of food in before I broached the subject. "Speaking of Mrs. Mitchell's business, what do you think of the ladies who love to sparkle?"

He shook his head, swallowed a mouthful of French fries. "It kept her busy. Gee, Miss Murphy, you should see our guest room. Stuffed to the brim with jewelry. Not even room for guests."

"Really? I was under the impression that she sold quite a lot of it."

"Nah. Most of the money comes from recruiting people to sell the product. She took building a sales team very seriously, and she was seriously good at it."

"I met some of her team. Quite a collection of characters."

He agreed with a small huff.

I picked up my burger and ignored the way Presley tried to lick it out of my hands. It was delicious and warm, the bread soft, the meat juicy, the cheese American. The lettuce and bacon crunched between my teeth. I closed my eyes and forced down a moan.

Mr. Mitchell finished off the last of his burger and downed the rest of his scotch. I winced in sympathy for the burning he apparently did not feel.

"I should be heading out," he said. He stood on his feet and swayed only a little. "Lots of stuff to arrange."

"Well." I set my burger back on the plate and then held Presley to my chest before he could jump up after it. "Please. If there's anything we can do here at the Pinnacle. If you need some rooms for visitors? Or a meal catered? Please, don't hesitate to call. Ask for me when you do, and someone will connect you to me directly."

"Thank you, Miss Murphy. I'll keep that in mind." He reached into his back pocket, but I stopped him.

"This was on me," I said. "It was my idea, after all. The drinks too. You go home and give your dogs a hug for me, will you?"

He knocked on the bar. "Sure thing. See you around, Miss Murphy."

I watched him walk away, still unsure of what to make of him. In his fifties now, but still athletic, with a broad build. *"It's always the husband."* If he had approached the table and poisoned the drinks or the salad or the strawberries, I would've seen him.

I would've.

Wouldn't I?

Chapter 10

After dropping both the umbrella and Presley at the front desk with Mr. Mullins, I crossed the bustling lobby to the lift bay. Russell Castillo was working, chatting amicably with a couple when the elevator's door slid open.

"Oh, Miss Murphy!" the woman called in greeting. She pulled me into a hug and kissed me on one cheek. "We were hoping to see you before we checked out."

I returned her embrace, offered her husband a hand. "Mr. and Mrs. Taylor. Happy anniversary! How many years is it now? Thirteen, isn't it?"

Mr. and Mrs. Taylor were locals who had gotten married in the Pinnacle Hotel and spent every subsequent anniversary as guests.

"Lucky number thirteen, that's right," Mr. Taylor said as he shook my hand. "You've got a fantastic memory."

Mrs. Taylor held up her wrist to eye level. A diamond tennis bracelet sparkled in the light of the lobby. At least five karats, total weight.

I whistled. "And you have fantastic taste!"

"As he should." Mrs. Taylor winked. "I picked it."

We all laughed before I bid the couple farewell, leaving me and Mr. Castillo alone in the lift.

"Back home?" he asked me.

I nodded and once the doors were closed and the elevator was ascending, I turned to him. "I know you were busy the other night when Poppy asked you to the cinema, but I've been thinking. She's working so hard on this upcoming gala. Perhaps you could help alleviate some of her stress by taking her out tonight? If money is a problem, I could pay for it."

He winced. "Thank you, Miss Murphy. I, uh . . . I wish I could. Trust me, I do. But I have plans."

"Plans that you can't get out of?"

"Yes, ma'am. I promise, I'll make it up to Poppy. Soon."

With my toes curled in my shoes, I forced a smile. "Wonderful. I'm happy to hear that, Mr. Castillo." The lift stopped on the top floor, and I flounced out with a wave.

He was hiding something. I didn't know what, but I didn't like it. Not one bit.

★ ★ ★

"Hey, Murphy," Hodgson greeted me when I opened the door to my suite. At least, that's what I think he said. After the initial 'Hey,' I screamed so loud I couldn't hear the rest.

He sipped his coffee while he waited for me to stop screaming. Then he said, "Jeez, you're jumpy."

"Of course I'm jumpy! Goodness gracious, Hodgson. Someone was murdered!"

"So. What? Like any other Tuesday at the Pinnacle?"

I glared at him, ran my fingers through my hair, half expecting to find it standing straight up after that fright. "What are you doing here?"

"Waiting on the rain to let up before I try the nuns again." He motioned to my coffee table, littered with papers and empty plates. "Need the space to work, and there's free food and coffee here."

"It isn't free," I said. "I pay for it. But this won't do. You can't work in my suite. What you need is an office."

"If all I wanted was office space, Murphy, I'd work at my apartment."

I moved around him, picked the phone up off the receiver. "Yes, yes. You want my food and my coffee. I've got just the thing." Then: "Hello? It's Evelyn. Connect me to Mr. Sharpe, please."

★ ★ ★

When Mr. Sharpe met us outside the thirteenth room on the thirteenth floor, he was moist.

"Take the key," he said to me, dripping. Unfortunately, it was not rain that pooled in his palms.

I recoiled. "Hodgson. Would you mind?"

He fished a handkerchief out of his pocket and took the key from the manager. Mr. Sharpe exhaled loudly, as if giving up a heavy burden. "You're a brave man, Detective. I do hope you know what you're getting yourself into."

Hodgson examined the key. His dark, narrowed eyes flicked up to Mr. Sharpe and then to me. "Are you talking about Miss Murphy or . . . what? Are you okay, Mr. Sharpe? You look . . . not okay."

"I can feel the presence, even out here." Mr. Sharpe shuddered. "Miss Murphy, if that's all? I need to leave before I'm sick."

"Of course," I said, trying desperately to keep from laughing. "Thank you ever so, Mr. Sharpe. Toodle-oo."

Mr. Sharpe tripped over himself in his haste to get to the elevators. He straightened his jacket, ran his hand over his hair, and managed a quick wave before disappearing in the lift.

Hodgson still held the key inside his handkerchief. "Murphy?"

"Yes?"

"What the hell was that about?"

"Oh, Mr. Sharpe's nervous because he believes the rumors."

"What rumors?"

"That room 1313 is haunted. It's never let out to guests because of it."

Hodgson tapped the wrapped key against his forehead. "You're giving me an office filled with ghosts?"

I rolled my eyes. "Don't tell me you're superstitious, Hodgson."

"A fully grown, fully terrified man just handed me a key covered in his own sweat. Don't matter if I believe in ghosts or not. Something's wrong with that room."

"Nothing's wrong with it anymore," I said. "A few years ago, sure. But not now."

"What happened a few years ago, Murphy?"

I shrugged. "I haunted it. Are you going to unlock the door?"

His mouth opened. He stepped forward, finger in the air. Stepped back. Closed his mouth. "You haunted it?"

With a grin, I said, "I was a troubled youth."

"Make no mistake. You're still troubled." Hodgson put the key in the lock and the door swung open. That was a trick I'd forgotten about. A loosening of the hinges is all, but it slammed against the wall like the owner of the room was mad you had intruded on her private space.

"A few things might still be wrong with it," I admitted.

Hodgson stepped inside with his arms outstretched. There was furniture, and plenty of it, completely outfitted like the rest of our standard hotel rooms with a couch and a king-sized bed and a wooden table with two chairs. Every single inch was covered in white blankets, sure, but it was all still solid, still usable.

He pulled the chain on the overhead light. The light flickered rapidly before extinguishing. The chain fell into his hands.

"Murphy?"

"Yes?"

"If I open the curtains, will a bat hit me in the face?"

"Of course not," I laughed. "It's spiderwebs."

Chapter 11

Monroe woke me up the next morning by lying down on top of me, her paw gently resting on my chin. Her soft purr on my chest had me drifting off again, but it wasn't long before the paw became clawed.

"Fine, fine." I yawned and started to move. She obligingly jumped off me and headed toward the kitchen. "Good morning to you too."

Walking out of my bedroom was like walking into a wall. Something smelled *terrible*. Torn between covering my nose and smelling that terrible smell again, I hesitatingly sniffed. Monroe meowed at me. "Sorry, sorry."

I ducked into the kitchen, surprising Presley, who was directly between my ankles. "Sorry," I told him. I was on a roll apologizing this morning. I fed both of the animals and then began walking around my suite, nose first.

"What *is* that?"

The animals were too busy eating to answer me. I sniffed every pillow on the couch, the curtains, then opened the fridge and smelled inside there. Underneath the bathroom counters was fine, and the shower was clean. But when I opened the door to my closet, the smell was overwhelming. I covered my nose and breathed only through my mouth. My vanity wasn't the source, the shoe rack wasn't bad, considering what it held, and the hanging clothes were fresh.

I unpinched my nose over the clothes I wore yesterday and instantly regretted it. Gagging, I pulled the almost empty bottle of Erno Laszlo's Phelityl Oil out of a pocket. The same oil that Marilyn Monroe uses. Or at least, it should've been, but someone had replaced it with something that smelled an awful lot like old shrimp.

I sat back on my heels and swore up at the ceiling. Yet another murder weapon that I'd put my fingerprints all over.

"I am never going to hear the end of this, am I?"

It was still too early in the day for Hodgson to be in, so I left the murder weapon in my closet, washed my hands, and ordered breakfast. Two days in a row without me making my usual morning appearance in the lobby was bound to cause some tongue wagging, but there was nothing for it. My world lately was getting smaller and smaller. I wondered if it would get so small I'd never leave my suite.

I don't need to leave my suite, of course. Even for the salon downstairs. With a phone call, I could have it brought up to me.

That did have some benefits. Staying in my suite meant not having to feel uncomfortable around other people. But how could I solve a murder by only talking to people who would come into my suite?

Easily, I expected. All my current suspects had come to me with barely an inconvenience on my part.

Which one of them had poured the shrimp stock out of a skin-care bottle and into the meal? Prudence, Ruth, or Veronica? Perhaps it was as easy as finding out who used Erno Laszlo products and who did not. Unfortunately, I couldn't simply ask that question, though, because the killer must've realized she'd lost the murder weapon. Would she throw out any other Erno Laszlo products back at home after realizing she'd lost the Phelityl Oil? Any good criminal would, I was sure, but these women didn't seem like good criminals.

Mr. Mullins delivered my breakfast with a dramatic sniff at the door followed by an even more dramatic dry heaving.

"Are you quite finished?"

He coughed, nodded. "Is Mr. Presley ready for his walk?"

Hearing his name and being of above average intelligence—some might say bordering on genius—my fluffy little Pomeranian growled menacingly by my feet. Mr. Mullins stepped back.

"Oh, do calm down," I said, and clipped Presley into his leash myself. "He's harmless. His teeth are so small."

"And yet," Mr. Mullins said with a wide smile, taking the leash between his fingertips, "so sharp. Thank you, Miss Murphy. We will be back shortly."

I left my suite door open in an attempt to air it out a bit. That didn't work, so I opened the doors to the patio as well. Monroe made herself comfortable on the outdoor dining set, licking her hind legs in the cloudy sunlight. I brought a coffee, a croissant, and a newspaper and joined her, minus the hind leg licks.

"You're right, Monroe. It is better out here." The patio led to the fire escape, something that had been used once not too long ago. Mac had still been here. He'd barred the door and kept me from stepping into a dangerous situation, and it had both angered me and made me feel all soft inside. Rarely in my life had anyone sought to protect me.

But now he was gone. And I was alone on the patio. And no one was threatening to toss my pet anywhere.

The front page of the paper, blessedly, did not mention the Pinnacle Hotel. No, that was saved for page three.

Gentleman Thief and the Pinnacle Hotel Team Up for a Double Feature

by Dottie Stewart

Mr. and Mrs. Bradley Taylor, staples in the New York charity scene, have been spending their anniversaries at the Pinnacle Hotel since getting married there thirteen years ago. Their anniversary yesterday is the first one that ended with a rude awakening when the gentleman thief burgled their home and stole Mrs. Taylor's diamonds—including a new bracelet just purchased by her husband—mere hours after they returned home. Is the curse of the Pinnacle stretching its wings, putting guests now in danger of not only dying on the premises but possibly being robbed of their hard-earned possessions when not even in its shadow? This reporter thinks something smells fishy.

★ ★ ★

"Yes, my apartment!" I slammed the newspaper down on the table. Monroe gave me a displeased look. "Sorry," I said. I growled and stood up, marching to the phone. "Something smells fishy? The Taylors! Robbed? Well, how is that our fault? The thief targets rich people, and rich people stay here. It's not that hard to understand, is it? I'll get this Dottie person straightened out, you can bet your bottom dollar. Fishy! The nerve! How did she know?"

I picked up my phone and dialed the operator. "I want to speak to the *Times*. Now!"

Chapter 12

Hodgson pulled the door to room 1313 open a crack, one eye peeking out at me.

I stopped knocking but kept fuming. "Good morning!"

He opened the door the rest of the way and stepped back. I marched past him and took a turn about his new room. The furniture was no longer covered with sheets, and the curtains were open, the window framing the treetops of the park glittering in golden-brown hues like a picture.

"It's nice in here." I was still stomping. "I found the murder weapon!" I thrust the mostly empty bottle into his hands.

Hodgson recoiled. "What the . . . ?"

"Mrs. Mitchell's murderer—talk about alliteration—put shrimp stock in a skin-care bottle, and I put my fingerprints all over it. And don't worry about reprimanding me! I have reprimanded myself enough. Did you see the paper?"

He blinked. "What? The newspaper?"

"No, Hodgson, just any old paper—I feel like jotting down some notes. Of course the newspaper—the *Times*! This Dottie character is *mmpphhh*. She's driving me mad—positively mad!"

"You are red," Hodgson agreed. "Did you take the steps down here, or . . . ?"

"I am turning the murder weapon over to you, and I am going to have a chat with Marco about the bloody menu that he won't talk to me about because, darn it, someone *will* talk to me today. Dottie wasn't available. I had to leave a message and hope that Dottie will get back to me. But Marco works for me. He works for *me!*"

"He works for the hotel that your father owns, but sure."

I glared at him. "Have a lovely day!"

"I also work for you," Hodgson called as I stormed out of his new office. "And I have to visit some nuns. You could yell at them? Maybe?"

Without slowing down I shouted, "Yeah, maybe!" and continued my march to the kitchens. I was not going to be visiting any nuns. Not today, not ever.

★ ★ ★

Perhaps it was the red color my face was turning or the steam that was evaporating out of my ears, but no one interrupted me or even spoke to me as I made my way to the kitchen. In fact, a substantial number of employees jumped out of the way or hurried to open doors, much like they do when my father is in town.

That realization slowed me down.

It wasn't their fault that people were dying in the hotel. Or maybe it was. Maybe one of them had done it. Maybe one of them had poisoned Lois Mitchell because they knew she wouldn't tip well. I added waiters on my list of things to talk to Marco about.

I hesitated outside the kitchen door. With a deep breath, I closed my eyes and reached for the pendant of Saint Anthony around my neck. The silver felt cold on the pad of my thumb, the etching familiar to my skin. I could not approach Marco angrily as he would simply match my anger and throw it back at me.

Help me find some patience, I prayed. *Please, for the love of God.*

The kitchen was a hive of activity, chefs and waiters buzzing about the massive room, one of the largest in the building. "Good morning!" I called out, waving a hand at no one in particular. "Good morning! Good to see you all! Is Marco available?"

Marco, from behind a towering pot of boiling water, said, "No."

With a great big smile that I absolutely did not mean, I approached the pot and the chef that hid behind it. His hat and his eyebrows gave him away, no matter how much he squatted out of sight. "Marco. The gala is this Sunday. I'm not asking to change things, only to be told what is happening. That's all. That's not so terrible, is it?"

He glared at me from his near-kneeling position. "Have you eaten?"

"Today?" I blinked. "Or in my lifetime? Yes. Both. Yes."

He stood up, still glaring. "What did you eat? Today."

"I had a croissant."

"A croissant isn't food. It's dessert."

"Technically, I had it for breakfast."

He pointed at the end of the nearest counter. "Sit. Jim! Get Miss Murphy a stool! Now!"

A waiter—the aforementioned Jim—set a stool down at the end of the counter, and I hopped on it obediently. "Why am I sitting?"

"You will eat. Then you may talk to me."

Always lovely, being told what I was to do inside my own hotel. But Marco was a doll, and so I obliged him whenever I could. It cost me nothing but a little bit of pride, and I have a lot of that to go around. Marco plated my meal himself, a generous portion of chicken à la king that was so delicious I cleared my rather large plate. Full to the brim, I tried to refuse the slice of chocolate cream pie that came next, but Marco was not to be deterred. I thought to only have a bite of appeasement.

I ate the entire slice.

"And?" Chef Marco prompted.

I wiped my mouth with a napkin. "It was delicious, Marco."

"Everything I make is delicious. You stop worrying about me. I will cook for your rich friends, and you will eat the food. It is called delegation. You will learn that word."

Marco and I stared at each other for several long moments before I gave up with a heaving sigh. "Fine."

He grinned. "Jim! Come clear Miss Murphy's plates! Why are they still here?"

A waiter came over and did just that. I told him thank you and handed him a dollar. "Marco, before I leave?"

"What is it now?"

"On Sunday afternoon, the day Mrs. Mitchell died?"

Marco's nostrils flared. "This again? I had nothing to do with that. She died, and that is bad. Yes. But she ordered the food, and I made the food, and there was no shrimp *anywhere*."

"I know. I know there was no shrimp in the kitchen, Marco. I know this wasn't your fault."

"Of course it wasn't! What do you mean? Does somebody think it is? Not that I care what they think—*bah*. What do they know? Who is saying this?"

Answering him was difficult considering the fact that it would involve lying. Instead, I asked the question I'd been trying to ask. "Were there any new cooks or waiters around? Did you notice?"

Marco tossed a rag on his shoulder and looked at me as though I had suggested his mother was haunting Hodgson's new office. "Am I supposed to know every waiter? Every cook? I call them *all* Jim. All of them are Jim to me!"

"Perfect. That's perfect. Thank you for your time, Marco. As always."

I saw myself out of the kitchen, too full to be furious. Annoyed, sure, but there was always room for that. I decided to head to the front desk and check on my messages. Dottie had had plenty of time to get back to me by now. More than enough time—I'd eaten a giant meal from start to finish, minus a salad course.

Salad made me think of Lois Mitchell falling into my lap. Thinking of Lois Mitchell falling into my lap made me stop noticing things around me until I walked straight into a man.

The man in question went "Oof!" in a Scottish accent.

"Mr. Sharpe!" I rubbed my throbbing nose. "Oh. It's you, Mr. Sharpe."

The younger Mr. Sharpe. The exceptionally handsome musician. The dreamboatiest of dreamboats. He was in dungarees and a white T-shirt, the sleeves rolled up and bulging, hiding a pack of cigarettes on each arm. In his hand was his case where his tailored tuxedo resided. I'd run into two Sharpes in as many days. *What are the odds?*

"It's me," he said. "And you. Again."

"I do live here." I was in flats, so our height difference wasn't extra noticeable, but it was always nice to smile *down* at men who confused me with my assistant. "Are you all set for Sunday?"

He nodded once, dismissively. "If you're still open by Sunday."

"I beg your pardon?"

"Oh, do you not read the newspapers?"

I could feel my mouth making a strange, downward, twisting motion, but I was powerless to stop it. "I read newspapers," I said, instead of what I wanted to say, which was incredibly rude and unnecessary when I was still obligated to learn more about him for Henry's sake.

"Then I'm surprised you don't already know. Everyone's talking about the murders. And now the thefts too?" He shook his head. "My dad worries."

Everyone seemed a bit of a stretch since today's article, written by Dottie, who had written all the articles so far, was on page three. But I was simply too full to scream in rage. Instead, I reached out and patted his arm. "I am quite aware of the articles in the *Times*, and I assure you, I will be speaking to the reporter personally."

Eventually. I didn't have a meeting planned yet, as such, but perhaps a message asking me to sit down to tea was waiting at the front desk, and Colin Sharpe was blocking my way with his broad, manly chest and his perfect hair and his dark eyes framed by incredible lashes.

I cleared my throat. "I will see you on Sunday?"

"As I said. If you're still open Sunday." His smile was crooked. Why do all handsome men have crooked smiles? Did they get together, have some sort of a meeting, and decided that, universally, they would only smile crooked smiles from that point forward?

I patted his arm again—my goodness his forearm was firm—and moved around him. I was so full, it took every ounce of restraint not to pop open the button of my jeans then and there, but that would be terrible manners and I was nothing if not a good hostess.

"Hello," I said to the man behind the front desk. "Are there any messages for me?"

He looked for a moment and handed me a piece of paper. "Just one, miss."

I breathed a sigh of relief. Good. Dottie had gotten back to me in a timely manner, and I'd be able to straighten out all this gentleman-thief nonsense before the end of the day.

I opened the paper. It said: *Please call me back at your earliest convenience. Wallace Ferretti.*

"Mr. Ferretti? Mac's lawyer? Why, whatever would he want with me?"

The man behind the front desk shrugged.

I shrugged back and decided to return Mr. Ferretti's call as soon as I'd changed into more forgiving pants.

Chapter 13

Back in the very same robe I'd worn that morning, I phoned Mr. Ferretti's office and was quickly connected to him.

"Hello, Miss Murphy. Thank you for returning my call."

Presley jumped onto the couch and settled himself on my lap. I winced when his nails pressed against my thighs. "Of course, Mr. Ferretti. Your message was rather vague, though. Is something the matter?"

"That's what I was calling about. To see if there was anything the matter? With you?"

I furrowed my brow, stared at the phone in my hand like it had sprouted a mouth and asked me a riddle. "I'm not sure I understand, Mr. Ferretti?"

"Your hotel has made several appearances this week in the paper, and I wanted to make sure you were doing all right. I understand a woman you were eating lunch with died from a food allergy."

"Oh! Oh, that's so sweet of you, Mr. Ferretti. Yes, it was quite distressing. I'd only met her moments before, and she was fine one minute and in my lap the next."

"I'm sorry to hear that, Miss Murphy. Did she have children?"

"No. I spoke with her husband. He's distraught, of course."

"He wasn't there?"

"No, it was a girls-only lunch, it seemed. With Mrs. Mitchell and a few of her friends." I didn't bother telling the lawyer about the Ladies Love to Sparkle portion of the meeting because I was still trying to wrap my head around it.

"I suppose the good news here is that it wasn't a murder this time."

I chuckled quietly by means of response. I didn't want to tell him I thought it was a murder, in case he got it in his head to talk me out of it.

"Listen, Miss Murphy, I was wondering." He paused, cleared his throat, paused some more.

"Yes?"

"Would you ever—what I mean is, I'd like to take you out to dinner sometime."

My mouth fell open. Of all the things I thought Mac's old lawyer might ask me, out to dinner wasn't one of them. I buried my hand in Presley's luxurious Pomeranian coat and tried to push my surprise down. "I see. Well." Why not? Daddy was obviously telling people I was single. Mr. Ferretti's family was well connected in the Manhattan social scene. Daddy wouldn't be able to complain about Mr. Ferretti's wallet or his work ethic. And he had been sweet enough to ask me how I was after Mrs. Mitchell's death. Sure, I was still hung up on Mac, and probably would be for the rest of my life. But why should I waste my twenties mourning the loss of a boy who had left me?

Besides, Mr. Ferretti was a defense attorney, and it is always a good idea, when solving murders, to have a defense attorney sweet on you.

"It would have to be at the Pinnacle. Does that work for you?"

"Oh." He sounded surprised, by either the yes or the location request, I wasn't sure. "Yes. Yes, that works for me. How about tonight?"

"Tonight?" I checked the clock. It was barely noon. I'd have enough time to digest my expansive early lunch. And if not, there were always loose-fitting dresses. "Tonight sounds marvelous. Seven? Just tell the front desk you're here, and they'll send for me."

"Seven works for me." He cleared his throat. "See you. See you then."

"Toodles!"

I hung up the phone and, with a giant sigh, picked up Presley and held him under my chin. "I should ring Dr. Sanders! She'll be so proud of me, the evil witch. Oh, Evelyn, have you talked to your father about your feelings? Oh, Evelyn, perhaps focusing on charity work will soothe your heartache. Oh, Evelyn, don't drink so much coffee. Caffeine isn't good for you." I sighed again, held Presley tighter as he licked my chin. "She is usually right. Unfortunately. The know-it-all."

A knock on the door interrupted my loathing.

I let in Mr. Mullins, carrying three boxes in his arms. Only his eyes were visible above the brown cardboard. "They're all from different people," he huffed as he set them on the coffee table.

I checked the label of the topmost box: from Ruth. Ah, the sparkles were here. Affordable costume jewels.

Presley growled.

Mr. Mullins jumped back. "Do you need anything else, Miss Murphy?"

"No." I went to my purse and pulled out a dollar. "Thank you, Mr. Mullins."

He left with his dollar, nervously glancing over his shoulder at my still-growling dog. I opened up the boxes and put the jewelry on the table, tossing the boxes away.

The jewelry was pretty and shiny. At a glance, it looked real enough. Only when you held the pieces in your hands could you tell that they were not the real deal. Real gold and diamonds and emeralds are heavy in your palm.

I put a diamond bracelet on my wrist and held it up to the light. The fake gems were multifaceted, so they caught the sun and threw it back into the room as dappled rays.

There was yet another knock on the door, but it swung open before I had a chance to stand. Poppy entered, looking flushed.

"The reporter is downstairs! Russell is stalling long enough so I can warn you. What are you wearing?!"

I sprang to my feet, taking off my robe and tossing it at Poppy as I ran into the second bedroom. "Stall her with coffee, please!" I yelled from inside the closet. "And make one for me too."

"I thought you're supposed to be cutting back on caffeine?"

"What does Dr. Sanders know about caffeine anyway? She's an analyst, for Pete's sake!"

Chapter 14

Brewed coffee covered up what remained of the horrible shrimp smell. Or at least the coffee made it less horrible. Poppy served both me and Dottie and then excused herself, hiding away in the kitchen. I did hope she was listening to the conversation so that I wouldn't have to fill her in with every detail when we dissected what happened later.

Dottie could not have been much older than me. Mid-twenties, well dressed in a woman's tweed suit from Sears, with a silver watch on her wrist and pearl earrings that matched the buttons on her jacket. Her skin tone was dark, and her hair was a deep, shining black, with the bangs curled and the rest pinned up at the base of her head. She wore no makeup, but her nails were well manicured and painted a soft pink. Her brown eyes looked me up and down as she sipped her coffee, no doubt mirroring my own assessment of her. I wonder what she saw when she looked at me. Did she know how frantically I had redressed before her arrival? Could she tell I was out of sorts?

I felt out of sorts sitting next to her. She was well put together and naturally pretty. She had a high-profile job writing for a prestigious paper. She had made her own way in the world. And I was living in my father's hotel.

"Isn't it strange to keep your jewelry in the living room?" Dottie asked me, opening her purse.

I'd completely forgotten about the Ladies Love to Sparkle collection sprawled across my coffee table. I smiled, gave a small shrug, and hoped I was coming across as aloof but lovable. "I wasn't expecting company."

She took a small notebook and a pencil out of her purse and placed them in her lap. "You did call my place of work and ask to see me as soon as possible."

I nodded once, still smiling. "Yes," I agreed, "but I assumed you'd schedule an appointment first."

"You didn't ask to schedule an appointment, Miss Murphy. You demanded that I see you as soon as possible. The poor secretary was shaking when she handed me your message. What did you say to frighten her so?"

"Excuse me, but that isn't fair. I would never be mean to a poor secretary trying to do her job."

She scribbled something in her notebook. "What makes you think she's poor?"

"I beg your pardon?"

"You said, and I quote, 'I would never be mean to a poor secretary.' How could you possibly know what her finances are? Are you saying if she was richer, you'd be meaner?"

I held up a hand. "Hold on one moment, please. I did not invite you into my home to fight. I invited you here to have a calm, civil discussion about the articles you've been writing about my hotel in the papers. You are wrong about the Pinnacle."

"I see." She tapped her pencil against the paper. "Is there something you'd like to say, on the record, to the concerned public about the recent rash of violent crime in your hotel?"

"A *rash*? I'd hardly call it a rash. A blemish, really."

She was writing furiously, and I had the sinking realization she wasn't missing a single word out of my mouth.

"What do you have to say to people who think it's strange that you're the one who keeps solving all the crimes in the hotel?"

I patted my hair, even though every strand was in place. "I've solved a few, but that's only because I'm good at finding things."

"So, you admit there's been a lot of crime happening at the Pinnacle lately."

"Not a lot." I smiled and tried to hide the way I was panting. "There's been a slight uptick but—"

"You call three murders on Pinnacle property in a matter of weeks a slight uptick?"

"No, no, of course not. Obviously, those deaths are tragedies."

"And Mrs. Mitchell, who ate her last meal at your hotel? Is that not a tragedy?"

Was I sweating? I felt like I was sweating. My upper lip was definitely moist. "I was dining with Mrs. Mitchell when she had her medical emergency. I can assure you, that was an unsettling experience, and my heart goes out to her friends and family."

"So, you admit you were there?"

"Yes. I've never pretended otherwise."

"A woman having lunch experiences a life-threatening allergy, and Evelyn Murphy is there. A judge with a heroin needle in his arm dies in the parking garage, and you are there. A maid is found strangled and stuffed in a closet, and you are there. An artist is stabbed to death in a hallway, and you are the first one on the scene."

The back of my neck and knees were sweating. The moisture beaded on my skin. I licked my lips, and they tasted like salt. "As I said, I'm good at finding things. I was also the person who found my father after he'd been attacked by the judge's murderer."

"You must have the worst luck of anyone I've ever known."

"I wouldn't say that." I swallowed. "I've also brought their killers to justice."

Dottie's scribbling never stopped, not even when she was looking me straight in the face. How was that humanly possible? "The Taylors stayed at the Pinnacle for their anniversary, and on the night they return home, they are burgled by none other than the Gentleman Thief. It seems that even guests who check out from your hotel get robbed."

There! That's what I had wanted to talk about. What was I saying to Monroe that morning? Fishy and rich? "My understanding is that the Gentleman Thief targets rich people. Rich people stay at our hotel. There's bound to be some crossover."

"Are you saying the Pinnacle is only for the elite? For the wealthy?"

"No, of course not. Anyone is welcome to stay at the Pinnacle. We have a variety of dining options as well, if an overnight stay is out of the budget."

"Do you know how much it costs to rent a room for the night, Miss Murphy?"

"Um." I had absolutely no idea. I'd never had to pay to stay at the Pinnacle. How was I to know how much it cost? "It varies from room to room and season to season."

She smirked like I'd said something noteworthy. As she had presumably written down everything I'd said, it was a wonder she hadn't been smirking the whole time.

"If the Gentleman Thief targets your customers, so they aren't even safe in their own homes when they leave here, and murderers stalk your halls, killing maids and guests alike, how can anyone feel safe at the Pinnacle anymore?"

"I live here," I said, stretching out my arms to include the entirety of my suite. "I assure you, I always feel safe. I *am* safe. We are all safe at the Pinnacle. What happened to Mrs. Mitchell and my good friends the Taylors was unfortunate, of course, but there was nothing malicious done by the Pinnacle or its staff or its guests."

"The Taylors are your good friends?"

"I've known them for years. I went to their wedding."

She smirked again but didn't speak until her pencil stopped moving. "It's strange, Miss Murphy, how you're never the victim, and yet you're the one guest who lives here full time, isn't it?"

I scoffed. "That's hardly fair. My room was ransacked, my boyfriend was arrested, and my father was injured, almost fatally."

Her smirk widened into a full grin. "Thank you so much for clearing up this matter, Miss Murphy." She put her supplies away in her purse and rose. "Have a wonderful day."

Dottie excused herself, and all I could do was stare after her, my mouth open and my heart pounding. Poppy appeared like an apparition, holding a glass of water and a damp hand towel.

"What do you think?" I asked, wiping the back of my neck with the cool towel before gladly taking the water. "Did it go as badly as I think it did?"

"Oh no. No." She plopped down next to me and patted my shoulder. "Much worse."

Groaning, I collapsed against the sofa and draped the washcloth over my face. "Maybe I should postpone my date tonight."

Poppy gasped. "You have a date tonight? With who?"

"Your brother's lawyer. He called when he read in the paper about Mrs. Mitchell's death and wanted to see if I was doing okay. Then he asked me to dinner." I sighed dramatically, the washcloth moving with my breath. "A girl who gets in as much trouble as I do could use a defense attorney who is sweet on her."

"That's wonderful, Ev! Where are you going?"

"Nowhere. The bar here." I sat up and the washcloth fell in my lap. "I know it's pathetic, Poppy. But I haven't left the hotel since the day your brother left me."

She wrapped her arm around my shoulders. "It's not pathetic." At my look she said. "Well, it's a little pathetic. But you'll get better, Evelyn. You've done it before. You'll do it again. Right now, you're healing, and dinner and dancing with a well-respected lawyer will be good for you."

I pouted, my bottom lip protruding as far as it would go. "I hate doing things that are good for me."

Chapter 15

I wasn't interested in Mr. Ferretti romantically. How could I be when half my heart was overseas? But I wanted to be a good date for him because he was a good man who had called to see how I was doing, and by all accounts, a fantastic defense attorney. I needed one of those on retainer at all times. I soaked and sulked for a while in a hot bubble bath. Mac was gone, and the reporter was difficult, and Mrs. Mitchell had fallen into my lap while I had somehow missed the fatal action that led to her death.

Monroe leaped onto the edge of the bathtub. She swished her tail back and forth and stared at me with her unblinking green eyes.

"I'm fine," I told her. "I promise. I'm only confused and heartbroken. That's all. Same as always."

She carefully dipped a paw into the nearest bubble.

"Someone poisoned her in front of me. I was sitting right *there*, and I didn't notice. And what am I supposed to do with all that costume jewelry?"

Monroe lifted her paw out of the tub. The bubble stayed on her fur. She sniffed it lightly and it popped on her nose. She jumped straight into the air and then landed on all fours on the ground, galloping out of the bathroom.

I shook my head. "Thank you for your help."

The three women, my main suspects, were somehow all very similar to one another and yet different. Prudence, the one who had taken charge and introduced herself to me, who had brought me into the lunch, was a widow not in need of financial gain, but looking for social connection. The fact that she had invited me over should be proof enough that she hadn't done the poisoning. Unless she had absolutely no idea who I was. And why would she? Sure, I'd been in the papers, but not everyone reads the papers. *Not everyone should! The dribble that gets passed off as news these days.*

Ruth was lonely too, like Prudence, and away from family. But she had joined the business to help earn money, make no mistake. She wasn't as desperate for money as Veronica, whose husband had lost his job. But they had both signed up to sell costume jewelry with the hopes of making money.

If they hadn't yet earned enough, was that reason to kill Lois? In public?

Every single one of them had touched that tray of strawberries, which had happened when I was at their table. Maybe someone had been able to pour some of her homemade concoction into Lois's glass when she was busy with me. But wouldn't Lois taste it?

Her husband looked every bit the man in mourning, from his unshaved face to his wrinkled clothes. And, he was a dog lover, which had to mean something. I hadn't seen him approach the table. I hadn't seen anyone approach the table. But Hodgson had said it's always the husband. *How?* And why? What motive could he have had to kill his wife?

The rain had brought with it a chill in the air, but inside the Pinnacle was toasty as ever, our terrifying boiler working all hours. There was a small room next to the boiler where prohibition gangsters used to hide alcohol, and then later, where a young Evelyn used to hide from her nanny. It was large and loud and scary to behold, but it worked well enough that I could wear a sleeveless dress to dinner, which was really the most important thing.

After donning a merry widow corset with a plunging neckline, I decided on a pink linen, halter-style wiggle dress. It closed with seven pink buttons running from my sternum to just below my belly button. Marilyn Monroe wore this same style dress in the movie *Niagara*. It was a little revealing with my arms and shoulders exposed, and it enhanced my cleavage. I decided not to wear gloves, and instead paired the dress with some strappy pink heels, that tied around my ankles for security. We might dance during the course of the evening, and I wanted to be prepared.

I took off my pendant of Saint Anthony and hung it up in my jewelry box before taking out a pair of gold hoops and a gold bracelet. Otherwise, I had no accessories.

For make up, I went with my signature red lip and a full set of false lashes. Admiring myself in the mirror, I gave a nod. My heart might not be in the date, but at least Mr. Ferretti would have something pleasant to look at.

Evelyn Ferretti. The thought did nothing. It didn't inspire dread or excitement. I ran my hands down my stomach to smooth out my dress. Its being linen made that a losing battle.

Evelyn Cooper. I took a deep breath and held it. That would never be my name. Mac had seen to that when he'd left me all alone in Yonkers. I exhaled and smiled at my reflection.

"Evelyn Murphy it is, then. For better or worse."

The phone rang, and I turned off the light in my closet before I answered. It was the front desk. Mr. Ferretti had arrived.

★ ★ ★

I saw my date before he saw me. He was standing in the middle of the lobby, his hands in his pockets, his eyes on our crystal chandelier. Mr. Ferretti wasn't a tall man, and he didn't give the impression of an athletic one either, but his steel-blue suit was perfectly tailored. His white shirt was crisp. His tie was a perfect match to his jacket. His dark hair was slicked back. And when he caught sight of me walking toward him, his eyes lit up.

That made my heart dance a bit. The truth is: I like men. I've always been a bit of a flirt. It was fun, being wined and dined. Being twirled around on a dance floor.

"Miss Murphy," he greeted me, and held out his hand.

His cufflinks were silver and engraved with the letters *WF*.

I put my hand in his. His grip was firm, but not overly so, the way some men feel the need to crush your fingers to prove a point. "Call me Evelyn, Mr. Ferretti."

He smiled. "Wallace, then."

"Wallace," I repeated, matching his smile. "Does anyone call you Wally?"

He put his hand back in his pocket, and when he looked me up and down, I got the feeling he was taking my measure and not admiring my dress. "Would you like to be the first?"

I giggled and threaded my arm through his. "Let's see how tonight goes. Have you been to our bar?"

"No, I can't say I have."

"You'll love it. It's got a speakeasy feel to it and its own special menu."

We started walking out of the lobby. "It's interesting that you'd describe your bar as a speakeasy. My grandfather used to hide liquor here in the Pinnacle."

I gasped. "I've seen the hidden rooms! And the—"

"Hidden corridors," Wallace finished. "Technically, he didn't do the hiding. He served in more of an advisor role and represented the owners in court cases."

"Wow." I rested my free hand on his arm, pulling myself even closer to him. "Did he know Meyer Lansky?"

Wallace nodded. "They're still friends. Mr. Lansky is in Cuba most of the time now, but Grandad will fly out to Florida and play golf with him in the spring."

We entered the same bar where I'd eaten lunch with Mr. Mitchell, but instead of sitting at the bar itself, I led us to one of the booths tucked in the back corner. The seats were cushioned in dark green velvet and we had a fantastic view of the rest of the room. The U-shaped bar was underneath another crystal chandelier—we have plenty of them at the Pinnacle—and a single bartender was taking care of about a dozen guests. The bar itself could seat two dozen. There were a few tables big enough for two or three people, between the bar and us, in one of the two alcoves in the room. And off to my right was a piano, currently sitting all by its lonesome. I frowned at it. I'd been hoping to dance.

A waiter dropped off two menus and two glasses of water. The options here were limited but delicious. Chef Marco's kitchen handled all the meals in the bar and most of the meals in the entire hotel. Only the diner by the entrance and the café in the lobby had their own, smaller kitchens.

Wallace put his menu down on the table and reached for his glass of water. "What do you recommend?"

"Champagne," I said. "And the steak and potatoes."

He lifted a hand to signal the waiter and ordered each of us a glass of champagne and the steak and potatoes. I positively beamed at him afterward. He listened to me. He asked my advice, and he followed it. Maybe, just maybe, this could turn into a second date, after all.

Chapter 16

We clinked our glasses together when the champagne was delivered. I took a sip and enjoyed the bubbles on my tongue for all of one second, until I remembered the last time I'd had champagne.

Lois Mitchell had fallen into my lap not long after. Shrimp stock in the drink or the salad or on the strawberries. However it got delivered, it ended up in her stomach, a deadly weapon, all the same.

"So." I set my glass down carefully. "Did you ever meet Meyer Lansky?"

Wallace swallowed a mouthful of champagne before nodding. "Yes. I recently visited him in Cuba, actually."

I held my chin in my hand, leaned in close. As I said, I like flirting. "What was Cuba like?"

"Hot." Wallace grinned. His grin wasn't crooked; it was perfectly even. "Humid. The humidity was unlike anything I've ever experienced. I am not in a hurry to go back."

Piano music began to play softly in the background. I glanced over and found Colin Sharpe at work, his eyes on his hands. He didn't notice me. But then, he only noticed me when I bodily ran into him.

"Have you met many gangsters, Wallace? Lucky Luciano? Did your grandfather know Arnold Rothstein?"

He chuckled. "I don't think Mr. Rothstein considered himself a gangster."

I sat up, delighted. "He did know him, then?"

Wallace nodded, took another sip of his drink.

"You must've heard lots of stories growing up. Did he really," I began, and Wallace made a face. "You already know what I'm going to ask."

"Did he rig the World Series."

I giggled, covered my open mouth with my hand.

Wallace's smile lit up his face. He wasn't traditionally handsome, not like Colin Sharpe or Henry Fox, and there was nothing boyishly charming about him, like Mac. But there was something about him, some hidden spark, something in his eyes. I play up the ingenue thing often with men—and murder suspects—but I've rarely met men who are actually smarter than me.

I had absolutely no doubt that Wallace Ferretti was an incredibly intelligent man doing his best not to show it off.

Our steak and potatoes arrived, cooked to perfection. The steak was tender and flavorful, the potatoes soft and buttery. I was surprised by how hungry I was, considering the massive lunch Marco had forced me to consume only hours before.

Two couples had left their barstools and were slow dancing on the marble floor beside Colin's piano. His tune was melancholy and lovely and unfamiliar. I watched the couples sway back and forth and made up my mind.

"Wally." I set my knife and fork down and wiped my mouth with my napkin.

He looked at me with surprise in his eyes, still chewing.

"I'd like your advice on a murder I'm investigating."

His swallow was harsh. He sat back, looked at me in that appraising way again. "All right. I'm happy to be of assistance."

I fortified myself with another sip of champagne before launching into the death of Mrs. Mitchell. I regaled him with the conversations I'd had with her saleswomen in my suite, with her husband at this very bar. About halfway through, he picked up his knife and fork and continued eating, but his attention was wholly on me. I ended my story, just as he ended his steak, with my conversation with Marco that afternoon.

"I was right there, Wally. Why didn't I see anyone slip something in her glass or in her food?"

"You were looking at their magazine," he answered. His gaze had moved to the middle distance. "You need to narrow down how the shrimp was administered. If it was in, say, the salad dressing, perhaps that was a kitchen mistake. But if it was in the drink or the strawberries? That's murder."

I nodded. "Good thing I saved her plate and glass. I'll ask Chief Harvey to send them to the lab for me. Do you really think, if someone slipped it into her drink, I wouldn't have noticed?"

"If you were distracted enough, yes. The women at her table were busy eating. A waiter approaching the table isn't anything out of the ordinary."

I sighed. "You think it's the husband, don't you?"

"In my experience," he said, his voice taking an apologetic tone, "it's almost always the person closest to the victim. That's the easiest story a prosecutor has to tell."

"What do you mean?"

Wally tapped his the handle of his fork against his plate. "As attorneys, there is nothing more important than 'the story,'" he said, making air quotes with his fingers. "Not the evidence, not the witnesses, not even the crime itself. Both sides are doing everything they can, using the aforementioned evidence, witness, and details, to weave the most convincing story. 'Husband Kills Wife' is a tale as old as time."

"But isn't poison a woman's weapon? And it was hidden in a bottle of a product used almost exclusively by women."

He leaned back against the booth, stretching his arm along the top of the seat, his fingers coming close to my shoulder. "Not too long ago, we represented a man who, during his free time, foraged for mushrooms. His wife was an expert cook, I'm told. One day she made dinner with the mushrooms he brought home, and the next day, she was dead. Doctors said her symptoms indicated she'd eaten death cap mushrooms. Now, the husband, he swore they'd eaten the same food, and he was fine. He also said he'd know what death cap mushrooms looked like, and he would never bring them home. The police arrested him all the same."

As if to prove Wally's point, a waiter materialized before our booth without me noticing his approach. "I am terribly sorry to interrupt, but Mr. Ferretti has an urgent message."

Wally took the paper from the waiter, and I could tell by the expression on his face that he was going to end our date early. I had my pout ready and waiting before he looked my way again.

"I am sorry, Evelyn," he said.

"But we haven't danced. And I need to know about your mushroom case!"

He folded up his message and put it in his jacket pocket. "Next time." He reached for my hand to press a chaste kiss to my knuckles, and then he was gone.

★ ★ ★

I hadn't noticed the absence of music until Colin Sharpe slid into Wally's recently vacated seat. He looked over-dressed next to me, in his jet-black tuxedo.

"Hello?"

"Hi." He had a much thicker accent than Mr. Sharpe. I wondered how long he'd lived in the States. "You gonna eat that?"

"My steak?" I blinked. He reminded me of Presley, begging for scraps. "No. Are you hungry, Mr. Sharpe? I can order you your own."

"Break's too short for that."

He reached across the table and pulled my plate toward him. I stared, mouth agape, as he picked up my knife and my fork and finished off my steak.

"Golly," I said. "Remind me to tell your dad you need longer breaks."

"I figured too," he said with a shrug, "you didn't want to be seen in here alone. You know. After just being ditched publicly like that."

"Oh, you eating my food is a favor to me, is that right?" I huffed. "I was not ditched, by the way."

"Your date left you here."

"Fine. Yes. He left early, but only because he was called away on an urgent matter."

"What?"

My brow furrowed. "What what?"

"What was the urgent matter? Or did he not tell you?"

Under the table, I crossed my legs, my right foot tapping frantically in the air. "He did not share that with me, no."

"Right, so he ditched you. Did he even pay the bill?"

My mouth snapped open as I prepared to defend Wally's honor, but then Colin's question sunk in. He hadn't settled the bill. I hadn't even thought of it. It was my hotel. I was used to paying for everything.

Well, actually, I was used to getting whatever I wanted, and the bill being sent Daddy's way.

"Men like you," I said instead, narrowing my eyes and crossing my arms, "are all the same. Your good looks make you arrogant. But your looks won't last forever. And then what will you have?"

He shrugged a shoulder and polished off the last of my potatoes. "My talent."

"Ugh!" The nearest bar patrons glanced at us. I smiled at them and then scooted closer to Colin, dropping my voice to whisper level. "You only got this job because of me. Not your talent. Mr. Sharpe wasn't even going to hire you. I told him, I said, 'What's a bit of nepotism?' And that's how you got your job. Not your looks. Not your talents. Not even through your familial connections. Me. The owner's daughter."

Colin's dark gaze never left my eyes as he stuck his thumbnail between his teeth as a makeshift floss. When he finished, he grinned his crooked grin and rose. "Wanna dance?"

Chapter 17

At least the hand he offered me wasn't the one that had been in his mouth.

I stared at it in disbelief. I *did* want to dance, but Colin Sharpe was not the man I'd had in mind when I'd put on my strappy shoes.

"There's no music. And you might be talented, but even you can't play and dance at the same time."

He winked at me and then turned to the room at large. "Good evening, everybody. I'm your piano player, Colin Sharpe. Having a ball?"

The group in the lounge wasn't large, less than two dozen altogether. Most people nodded, some clapped.

I couldn't see his face, but I just knew he was flashing them his crooked grin. "Do you know Miss Murphy? Miss Murphy over here in this pretty pink dress? Well now, she's the owner's daughter. And she hasn't had a chance to dance all night. It'd be a shame to let that getup go to waste, wouldn't it?" He looked at me over his shoulder, and sure enough, half of his mouth was curved. "Stand up and show off your dress, love."

I rolled my eyes. But guests were watching, so I stood up and gave a little twirl.

"Miss Murphy is being generous and letting me dance with her, so I need to steal your bartender away for a song. That all right with you lot?"

Now the guests were smiling as they nodded.

"Feel free to dance with us. We can turn this night into a proper bash." Colin said, as the bartender ambled his way over to the piano. "Eddy's not as good as me, but you don't need excellence to cha-cha, eh?"

He spun around and took my hand in such a fluid movement I was swept off my feet and would've fallen if he hadn't been there to catch me. Colin squeezed my hip, his face so close to mine I could feel his breath on my cheek.

With a swallow to steady my racing heart, I stood up straight and set my free hand on his shoulder. In my pink shoes, our height difference was more pronounced.

"Take it easy," I said. "This isn't *American Bandstand*."

"I'm just trying to make it look good enough to print." He winked. "Help fix your image, right?"

My nose wrinkled. "My image is quite fine without your help, I'm sure."

The bartender started playing an upbeat tune, and sure enough, a couple people joined us in the space reserved for dancing.

Colin quirked a brow, his dark eyes twinkling. "I assume even a lass like you can handle the cha-cha."

I huffed. *A lass like me?* The other couples had already started moving to the rhythm while the two of us stood still, holding each other. "Are you able to lead? Or do you need me to do that?"

He pulled me even closer, close enough to kiss, and then pushed me away, his hold on my hand sending my body into a spin. When he brought me back into his arms, he was moving with such grace it caught me off guard. He winked again.

I did my best to mirror his steps as he skillfully led me across the dance floor, and when I failed to keep up, I shimmied instead.

Colin laughed. He grabbed me around the waist and lifted me up off my feet, spun us around so fast the other dancers were nothing but blurs on the peripheral of my vision. He set me down just as Eddy finished playing. Everyone applauded. I was giggling as I tried to catch my breath and clapped along for the bartender-turned-musician.

"Not bad," Colin said in my ear. "Come sit with me while I play."

"It's late," I said, but allowed myself to be led by the hand to the piano. It was an upright model, unlike like the grand piano in the Gold Room. But in the Gold Room, space wasn't a consideration.

Colin picked me up by the waist again and set me on top of it. I squealed a laugh, grabbing on to his shoulders for balance. "A little warning next time," I reprimanded without any heat.

He pulled a Zippo lighter and a pack of smokes out of his tux jacket and held it out to me, but I shook my head.

"I don't like how they taste." Mac was a smoker, but he had given up the habit for me. I wondered if he'd picked it back up again now that he was gone. Wherever he had landed.

"That's too bad." He stuck a cigarette in his mouth and lit it. "Everybody's allowed a vice or two, Miss Murphy." Colin blew out a big puff and sat down in front of the keys. "What's yours?"

I crossed my legs and smiled down at him. "I don't give out that information to just anybody."

"As it happens"—with his cigarette burning between his teeth, he played out an enchanting melody on the keys—"I'm not just anybody."

I recognized the song but didn't place it for a few measures. This close to Colin, I could see his strong fingers moving with effortless precision. The way his dark eyes crinkled at the corners as he focused. The slight tick in his square jawline. The way his dark hair had been tousled during our dance.

"I'll Be Seeing You." It was a beautiful song that I knew best by Etta James. Every time I played it on my record player, I thought of my mother. That I'd be seeing her in the moon and in the park and in the familiar places of my life. I closed my eyes so his handsome face wouldn't distract me any longer. And when Colin played the last note, I squeezed them tighter, begging the tears not to gather and show him how moved I'd been by his talent.

He snuffed out his cigarette. "Miss Murphy?"

I sniffled and smiled at him. "That was wonderful, Mr. Sharpe. But it's late. I think I need to be heading home."

"Of course." He rose and helped me down. "I had a lovely time with you, Miss Murphy." He kissed my hand, in the same spot that Wally had as he bid his goodbye. But unlike Wally's chaste parting, I felt Colin's kiss all over.

Uh-oh.

Chapter 18

Princess in the Tower

by Dottie Stewart

Evelyn Murphy, the only child of American businessman Mark Murphy, the owner of Manhattan's own Pinnacle Hotel, is completely out of touch with the rest of us. Some might say it's because she never leaves her ivory tower. Some might say it's because she is showered with the finer things. This reporter saw an entire table filled with diamond and emerald jewelry in the middle of Miss Murphy's suite. When asked how much it costs to stay for a single night at her hotel, the one in which she lives, Miss Murphy was unable to give even an estimate. "Rich people stay at our hotel," she said.

"A blemish" of crime has moored the face of the Pinnacle as of late, she admits, with no less than three murders taking place on the property since only September of this year. Miss Murphy has been present for each and every one. An unfortunate coincidence? Perhaps, but this reporter is doubtful. Wherever Miss Murphy goes, trouble follows. Isn't it odd that at a party Miss Murphy is attending, a painting goes missing? Isn't it odd that at a lunch where Miss Murphy is eating, a guest has an allergic

reaction and dies? Isn't it odd that her friends spend the night at the hotel and find, upon returning to their home, that they have been robbed by the Gentleman Thief? Her father is attacked, and her boyfriend is arrested for it, but Miss Murphy sits in her room, surrounded by diamonds. One starts to wonder if perhaps Miss Murphy isn't finding trouble, but bringing it with her. But Miss Murphy is not worried. "I am safe," she said, locked in her ivory tower. And in this reporter's opinion, that seems to be the only thing she cares about.

I tossed the newspaper onto the table, positively steaming. At least this incredibly rude opinion piece was on the third page, not the first, but still! It hadn't even included a picture of me! Diamonds? Goodness, all those jewels sparkling on my table were paste crystals from Ladies Love to Sparkle. I bet those women were thrilled with this diatribe today. If their stuff could fool the *Times,* who else wouldn't notice?

"Unbelievable!"

Guests from the nearby café tables stopped talking to look at me, and then started whispering to one another. The fish tank bubbled, and a little blue fish swam headfirst into the corner over and over. I kept on stewing, bitter. Mad. Stupid fish. *Stupid me!*

"Miss Murphy?" Mr. Sharpe approached the table, wringing his hands and with a worried expression on his face, the way I'd only seen Mullins approach a yipping Presley. "Is something the matter?"

I gestured at the paper before crossing my arms and my legs, my foot tapping in the air. "Dottie is out to ruin me, Mr. Sharpe!"

He read over the article, his frown deepening with every second. When he put the newspaper down, his drooping mustache hid his lips. "This is dreadful. She ambushed you, did she? Here, on Pinnacle property? This is private property, and I have a very strict no-press rule. If one of the bellhops—"

"No, no." I held up a hand to stop him. "I invited her into my suite."

"I see. Well. She still showed up here unannounced, looking for an opportunity—"

"No, again. I called the newspaper's office and asked to set up a meeting at Dottie's earliest convenience."

Mr. Sharpe ran his thumb and forefinger over his salt-and-pepper mustache. "I see. But surely she misquoted you?"

"No!" I hit the table. "I said all those things!"

He nodded and sighed loudly. "That is unfortunate, then. There is nothing we can do. Except perhaps follow the rules and not allow the press onto the property ever again? Hmm? Could we do that?" His right eyebrow twitched.

I glared at him. "Are you joking? They didn't even take my picture!"

"Does that mean you're going to risk another article painting both you and the hotel in a horrible light so you can have your picture beside it?"

With a huff, I stood up. "Not now. Not anytime soon. But I am going to fix this *and* get my picture in the paper. No, I don't know how yet. You know, Mr. Sharpe, it isn't my fault people keep getting murdered at the Pinnacle."

"I know."

I picked up the paper, fully intending to line Monroe's box with it, when my attention fell on my hand. Looking at it now, I could almost feel the kiss that Colin had left behind. "By the way, I spent the evening in the company of your son. He is very charming."

"I know."

"I do not trust him at all."

He nodded, sighed loudly yet again, but didn't say anything and didn't stop me from storming off. No, that honor belonged to Hodgson, who called out my last name as he entered the lobby.

I sat back down at the table and waved over a waiter. Mr. Sharpe and Hodgson said good morning to each other before the manager went off to attend to things elsewhere. Hodgson sat across from me and ordered a cup of a coffee and an omelet with extra veggies. He then held out his hand for my paper. I pursed my lips and clutched it tighter.

"What, you're not done reading it?"

"What about, instead of you burying your nose in the paper first thing in the morning, we have a civilized chat?"

"Civilized. Yeah, okay. You're looking to bash my ear about murder."

"Not about committing it."

He rolled his eyes. The waiter dropped off the coffee, and Hodgson blew on the steaming liquid a few times before having a sip. "Fine. What do you want now?"

"I've hit a dead end in the death of Lois Mitchell. What should I do?"

He sipped his coffee again. "You've interviewed them already?" When I answered in the affirmative, he said, "Tell me about them."

"First, you have Ruth. She is a mother of twin boys who are in high school. They moved to Manhattan a year ago for her husband's work, so she is away from family for the first time in her entire life. She's hopeful one day she will sell enough costume jewelry to help buy groceries for her boys. Second, there's

Veronica. She has three young children and recently suffered a financial loss when her husband was without work. He's now employed on a boat and gone a lot. She hopes she'll earn enough money so he will be able to be home more. Finally, we have Prudence. Prudence is older, and her children have all moved out of the house, and though her husband did pass away about a year ago, he left her well off financially. She has yet to earn any money selling for Ladies Love to Sparkle, but is more interested in the social aspects of being a member of the team. None of them have found any success in their new career, but none of them seem particularly heartbroken over it."

During our one-sided conversation, the waiter had delivered Hodgson's breakfast, and Hodgson had sprinkled it liberally with salt and pepper before digging in.

"Why would they show you they were upset about lack of profits?" Hodgson ate a big bite of egg and bell pepper. "That's the main motive for murder, after all."

"Lack of profits?"

"Money," he said. "You know that. Money, revenge, jealousy. Those are your three main motives."

"I thought love was one?"

"Love and lust both fall under jealousy most of the time. But sure, I've seen cases where a man falls in love with a woman who is not his wife, and so he kills his wife and thinks things will work out from there. Money, revenge, jealousy, and love. Hiding evidence, sometimes. That can be one. Like killing a witness before they can rat on you. Beyond those motives, you get the occasional religious fanatic who thinks they're doing something for a higher power."

"That is six motives, Hodgson. Six."

He ignored me to say, "But all those women, each one of them, is connected to Mrs. Mitchell by money, which means if one of them is your killer, money is the motive."

"None of them have earned any money yet."

"Right." He pointed at me with his fork. "But which one of them has lost the most? Start there. And then work your way back to the husband, because it's always the husband. *If* it even was murder. The police are still treating it as an accidental death."

"Oh, and the police are always correct." I stuck my tongue out at him before rising. "I'm going to my room. Enjoy your breakfast. Once you are finished, I need you to collect the champagne glass and salad I have in my fridge and give them to the lab. They were both Mrs. Mitchell's, and I want to know which one contains the shrimp stock. Don't forget to test a strawberry too."

Hodgson covered his eyes with his hand, his fork pointing toward the ceiling, a bite of egg slipping off and landing on the tablecloth. "You kept evidence back from the police?"

"The police never took it!" I pushed my hair out of my eyes and lowered my voice, lest I disturb guests further. "A detective was never even sent around, Hodgson. I preserved what I thought was important because I think it was a murder while the police still think it's an accident, remember?"

He rolled his eyes but nodded. "Fine. I'll go up to your room when I'm done. Can I have the paper before you go?" He held out a hand. I glared down at it. He wiggled his fingers. "Please?"

I opened up the paper, removed the section containing my article, and handed him the rest of it.

"What the . . . ?"

I did not offer any explanation. I simply folded up the offending page and stuck it in my purse. "Have a good day, Hodgson."

"I can just get another paper, Murphy," he called after me. "I got plenty of nickels in my pocket."

"Congratulations on jingling when you walk!" A fair number of new guests and employees glanced our way but went back to whatever they were doing shortly thereafter. It wasn't as if public outbursts were the weirdest thing to happen in the Pinnacle, after all. The elevator doors slid open, and I hurried inside. "Good morning, Mr. Castillo. Top floor, please."

"Yes, ma'am. Right away, ma'am."

Chapter 19

Poppy made a few phone calls for me while I dressed for tea. This meant I actually needed to wear a tea dress, but which one? I wanted to look approachable—"of the people," so to speak—regardless of what Dottie and the *Times* thought of me. *Golly. Out of touch.* The fact that she was right didn't stop it from hurting either. I had absolutely no idea how much it cost to stay the night at the hotel. To be fair, I didn't know the cost of most things. When you have more money than could possibly be spent in a single lifetime, you don't tend to focus on price tags. It simply doesn't matter.

Mac had lived like it mattered. That's why he'd left. My father had threatened to cut me off financially should I keep dating Mac. Mac didn't believe me when I said Daddy was all bluster, that he didn't mean it. Daddy was trying to exert control over me, but I said he'd tire himself soon enough, give up, and accept the inevitable. Not unlike the way that Presley chases Mullins with every fiber of his five-pound body, yipping with rage until he is too tired to run anymore, then accepts the leash on his collar and goes to the park for his business and cheese. Well. I wasn't going to waste my time thinking about Mac. Or about Daddy. I wasn't even going to waste my time thinking about Dottie and the *Times*.

I was going to solve a murder!

Chief Harvey and his officers had decided that this was an accidental death. That Chef Marco had somehow slipped some shrimp stock into the salad dressing and then forgotten about it or else was too embarrassed to admit it. Hardly murder in the first degree, in their opinion. And without the chef knowing of her allergy and without her clearly stating it to the kitchen staff—well, it's not like you could take that before a jury, with any lasting consequences.

Could you?

Huh. I'd have to call Wally.

Oh, Wally. What a wonderful man. Intelligent and attentive. However, he hadn't swept me off my feet at all. No, I'd found myself quite swept up by that boorish oaf Colin Sharpe instead. I didn't want to talk to either of them any time soon, and I wouldn't waste my time thinking of them either.

Murder only. *Focus*. Lois Mitchell. Shrimp. Erno Laszlo. What would the bottle of skin care filled with shrimp stock turn up? I doubted the police were in a hurry to check it for fingerprints since they didn't believe Mrs. Mitchell's death was a murder anyway. But Chief Harvey was my close, personal friend, so he might put my stuff on the top of the pile.

Hodgson said it was always the husband, but this afternoon, I was focusing on Lois's sales team. Ruth, Veronica, and Prudence were joining me for tea in my suite. I planned on plying them with champagne as well, because alcohol does wonders when it comes to getting people to talk. Which one of them had been impacted the most by their work for Ladies Love to Sparkle? She would be my lead suspect. I'd deal with the husband another day. Something was strange about him, but I couldn't put my finger on what, exactly.

It could've just been grief. Grief does strange things to people, and no one experiences it the same way.

The phone in my suite rang. I heard Poppy answer it, ask who was calling, and then place the caller on hold. "Evelyn?" She knocked on the door of my closet. "Dr. Sanders is wondering if you would like to speak with her? Except it wasn't a question. She actually said, 'Evelyn needs to speak with me.' Like that. Did you call her earlier or something?"

Dr. Sanders is my analyst. She is constantly insisting that I speak about my *feelings*. She also says ridiculous things, like I should drink less coffee and get out of the hotel more often. The nerve of some people.

"Oh, I am definitely not wasting time on that!"

Poppy blinked. "What?"

"Please tell her I am not in and will call back. Eventually."

"Do I say the 'eventually' part?"

"Best not, I think."

"Okay. I'll lie to your analyst for you. The champagne is on ice, but I've told the kitchen not to bring the tea until I ring. Don't want to serve cold tea! The women should be here in less than ten minutes."

I still hadn't picked out a tea dress. "Thank you, Poppy." With a sigh, I grabbed the closest one, a soft blue dress, and paired it with white heels. The gloves, I decided, would be too much of a hassle while eating finger sandwiches. I wore pearl jewelry, tucking the pendant of Saint Anthony in my jewelry box for safekeeping, and applied a fresh coat of pink lipstick. By the time I was done, there was a knock on the door, and Poppy was letting in my guests.

"Murder," I told my reflection. "Only murder. Don't get distracted. Especially not by *men*, of all things."

★ ★ ★

I had never been good at talking to people about money, mainly because everyone else had such a different opinion of money than I do. I had so much of it—why couldn't I tip as much as I wanted without my father reprimanding me? Why did people balk at twenty dollars? I had twenty-dollar bills stuffed into every pocket of every purse I owned. Sometimes the maids fished them out between the cushions of the couch. There was no lack of twenty-dollar bills. Why did my friends insist I pay them *fairly*, and not allow me to simply buy their buildings and let them live in their apartments for free? I would be so happy if only Poppy would let me do everything for her the way she does everything for me! She says she wants to be independent, and yet she moved in with Jennifer fast enough when Florence died.

That was probably due to the fact that when her brother left me, he left her too. She couldn't afford the apartment they were sharing on her own. And Jennifer couldn't afford hers without Florence. Oh, poor Florence. I still thought about her all the time, though I suppose that was natural. She had been my day maid for years and years, and she had only passed away a few weeks ago. Jennifer had been her roommate, and the reason that Monroe was in my care was because Monroe had been Florence's cat, and Jennifer was not a cat person. Monroe brought me so much joy, but even if I didn't like animals, it was the least I could do to honor Florence's memory.

Back to the murder at hand. If one of these women had murdered Lois, money was the most likely motive. Maybe vengeance, for costing them money, or jealously, that she had more money than they did.

It was most likely not love or lust, as all three women were either currently married or had been previously. However, sometimes circumstances changed in surprising ways. The heart is a fickle muscle, after all. Mine was currently on the other side of the Atlantic, although a rather wrong sort of man was trying his best to wrangle it back to the States.

"So," I said, and sipped my tea, "I cannot thank you all enough for how quickly my purchases arrived."

The three of them grinned like cats who had feasted on canaries; they were actually nibbling instead on cucumber sandwiches.

"It's important always to have stock ready for customers," Prudence said.

"That's why my garage is so full of goodies," Ruth agreed, giggling. "You should hear how my husband complains! But I love going in there now and playing dress-up like I did when I was a child."

"Besides," said Veronica, "you need to display as much as you can for parties. Women attending a party want to go home with a full set most of the time. Otherwise, what's the point?"

I nodded. "You are so right. I've never enjoyed window shopping. I want to be awarded with something lovely for my efforts."

"Exactly." Prudence leaned toward me and lowered her voice like she was sharing a secret. "That's why we throw the parties in the first place. Everyone wants to buy something then."

"Everyone wins," Ruth said, barging in on the conversation. "The buyers get a shiny treat, and my husband gets space in his garage."

"Do you make a lot of"—I swallowed, begged my mouth to form the words—"money from the parties?"

Veronica tilted her head from side to side. "It costs money to buy the jewelry, although we do get it at a discount!" She said the last part in a rush, like she was in a hurry to get impart that information. "It *is* profitable to do nothing but host parties. But the way you make the most money is by building a team and helping other women."

Prudence asked, "Have you heard of Brownie Wise?"

I shook my head.

"You've heard of Tupperware, though, right, Miss Murphy?" Ruth asked.

"Please, call me Evelyn. I think I've seen ads for Tupperware in the newspaper and magazines, but I've never used it myself."

"Of course, why would you?" Ruth giggled a bit too maniacally for our physical closeness. "You're so glamorous, Evelyn."

"Anyway," Prudence said, flashing Ruth a look that went completely unnoticed, "Brownie Wise started her own Tupperware sales business. She's the brains behind the product parties. She says, 'If we build the people, they'll build the business.' You see? It's all about allowing women the opportunity to make money for themselves from the comfort of their own homes, like Brownie did, in a relaxed social environment. It's good for everybody."

I was being sold.

I was used to this, as people often wanted me to exchange my money for whatever product they were offering. Typically, this was done in my room when a salesgirl from a brand would bring a sampling over at my request. I hadn't realized I'd arranged one of those meetings with the Ladies Love to Sparkle team, but I wasn't about to shut them down, at least not until I'd asked my questions.

"Please," I said, signaling Poppy to start serving champagne, "tell me more."

Chapter 20

"Oh, champagne," Ruth sighed. "How lovely. I'd never had any before that lunch in the Gold Room, Evelyn."

"You might turn us all into proper ladies if you keep serving us like this," Prudence agreed, raising her glass high.

Veronica giggled and had a sip. "Yum! This is very sweet, Evelyn. I like it."

I lightly tapped my glass against theirs, one at a time, and we got back to business. Poppy kept their glasses full as the three of them chatted away about how much fun they have throwing parties. When Veronica asked, "Would you ever consider throwing a party, Evelyn?" I took the opening.

"What is the budget for throwing one of these parties? They certainly sound . . . elaborate."

"Everybody's different," Ruth said. "Prudence hires a caterer! But me? I ask everybody to bring a covered dish. And Veronica is in the middle. She sets out a spread herself but asks for wine donations."

"The best kind of donations," I teased, raising my glass. We all had a sip of champagne. Poppy, from the kitchen doorway, rolled her eyes. "Does it cost anything to join?"

"There's a small fee, of course," Prudence said. "But it buys you your first box of product. You do have to keep your own stock, but as a Sparkling Lady, you get a discount."

I ran my tongue over my teeth. "A Sparkling Lady. How charming. This endeavor sounds quite remarkable."

The three of them nodded in unison.

"How did Mrs. Mitchell throw parties?"

Veronica's red brows drew together in a thin line, her lips pursing. "Not like we do. She would host events where she would teach us how to throw parties. You know, how to talk about the jewelry, how to tell women about the business opportunity. Even how to approach people in public and invite them, once you run out of friends and family, I mean. She was the best at explaining the benefits to people."

"What do you mean? 'Run out of friends and family'?"

"Oh, you know." Ruth shrugged a shoulder. "You can only invite the same church ladies over for a party so many times before you've either recruited the whole bunch or they've started declining invitations. I mean"—she grinned—"why would anyone decline one of your invitations, Miss Murphy? They'd decline mine, because, well. They're busy. With their families."

"Which is silly, of course," Prudence added. "Because joining this business opportunity would actually give them *more* time with their families."

I signaled Poppy over for another round of champagne and tried to convey with my eyes that I wanted these women's glasses topped off at all times. Getting a suspect drunk is not something a police officer could do, I was pretty sure, but I could do it easily. Was it ethical? That was a question for my analyst. I'd say a priest or a nun too, but I hadn't stepped inside a cathedral in a decade or more, and I was *not* visiting those nuns with Hodgson, no matter how hard he might pester.

"Would you say you enjoyed yourselves at Mrs. Mitchell's parties?"

"Oh no, they were work," Veronica said. Her speech was a hair slurred. "She was all about business all the time."

Ruth nodded, her crystal-blue eyes glassy. "She didn't like jokes, and if you didn't recruit anybody for over a month, you definitely didn't joke about it."

"I don't really understand," I said. "What is the purpose of recruiting? Why would she be upset with you if you didn't recruit anyone? Surely it wouldn't impact her in anyway."

"No, that's the beauty of this business model," Prudence explained. "If you recruit somebody, you get a percentage of not only what they pay to enter the business, but any sales they make in the future, and a percentage of what they earn when *they* recruit somebody. If you recruit enough people into the business, the way Mrs. Mitchell did, you never have to throw a party again."

I sipped my champagne, taking a longer time than necessary with my glass to my lips while maintaining eye contact with the group, who then also had long sips of champagne. When I lowered my glass, I asked, "And all of you have recruited women to join Ladies Love to Sparkle?"

Ruth bobbed her head from side to side. "A few church ladies, but our church is so small, you run out of ladies quickly and . . . well, you have to buy product every month, you know, to stay in the business, and if you're having trouble selling it . . . because your circle is too small. The business opportunity is great for people who are well connected, Evelyn, really—great for anybody who is extroverted or just anybody, ha ha ha . . . hmm." She cleared her throat. Prudence was glaring at her. "They've all left. Is what I mean."

Veronica patted her shoulder. "My mother and sister have both joined," she said. "They're so happy to wear their jewelry out and about, like I know you will be too, Evelyn. A picture of you in the paper wearing some of our pieces? Oh gosh, just think about all the sales! All the women hoping to help contribute to their families' finances while also longing to be a homemaker! It'll be wonderful, Evelyn, simply wonderful."

"The point is," Prudence said, her voice full of authority, "this business is the perfect fit for a woman who is a lot like you, Miss Murphy. Friendly, well connected, fashionable, and excellent at throwing parties. What do you think? Would you be willing to join?"

And there it was. I smiled like I meant it. "I'd like to have a few days wearing the pieces before I make that decision. I'm sure you all understand."

"Of course," Veronica said. "And if you happen to go outside with, um, Henry Fox?" She whispered, "And there's press? And they ask what you're wearing?"

"I will mention Ladies Love to Sparkle," I promised, offering her my pinkie. She stared at it for a moment before hiccupping and wrapping her pinkie around mine. I had absolutely no intention of going anywhere, with or without Henry, so it was a very easy promise to make.

There was a knock on the door. Poppy answered it, revealing a bouquet of flowers with legs. Upon further investigation, it was Mullins, carrying a rather large assortment of yellow pansies wrapped in a beautiful green bow.

"Oh," Ruth cooed. "Yellow pansies are some of my favorites. You know what they mean? *Thinking of you.* Isn't that sweet?"

Somehow Presley knew it was Mullins at the door. He came out of my room, growling, but his tail wagging his entire little body. Mullins sighed. "Shall I take Mr. Presley on a walk, then?"

"Would you be so kind, Mr. Mullins?"

Poppy took the flowers from him. She pulled a card from the ribbon and handed it to me on her way to the kitchen, most likely to find a vase. Mr. Mullins snatched Presley's leash from the entryway table, put it on my perfect dog with the least amount of physical contact possible, and gently began pulling him to the elevators.

Once he left, all three of my guests turned to me. "So, who is it from?"

There was no way to get out of this without reading the card in front of them. My heart was in my throat. Was this from Mac? Was he coming back? Did he think about me as often as I thought of him?

My heart dropped out of my throat and into my stomach when I read the card:

Sorry for the abrupt exit last night. Let me make it up to you? Wally

"It's from my attorney, actually," I told the women, blinking away the burning in my eyes. I stood. "Poppy?"

She poked her head out of the kitchen, the flowers in her hands. Her brown hair and her gray eyes were so much like her brother's I had to look away. "Would you please make sure all our lovely guests have a ride home? I'll cover the cost, of course." I winked at them. "Thank you all ever so much for visiting me. We will do it again—soon?"

"Yes, please." Veronica stood and shook my hand. "Whenever you want, Miss Murphy. I mean, Evelyn."

"Yes, goodbye, Evelyn." Prudence also shook my hand.

Ruth was the last one to do so. She hovered in my personal space. "Are you all right, Evelyn?"

"Of course." I squeezed her fingers. "It's kind of you to ask. I'll invite you all over again very soon. Safe travels home!"

Chapter 21

When Poppy returned, I was face down on the couch, Monroe making herself quite comfortable on the small of my back. Poppy shook her head and tsk-tsked at me. "More champagne?"

I sighed. "I don't know."

"You want to talk about the murder?"

My cheek pressed into the cushion when I nodded.

"Okay." She sat on the armchair. "Let's discuss. What did you think of the women?"

"They're all lovely but getting nowhere in this jewelry-selling business. They want me to join because they think I'll do better, and then they will get a percentage of everything I do. Lois got a percent of what they sell, but they don't sound like they ever sell much."

"Right. I was listening." She tapped her finger against her lips. "I heard one of them say that she had to buy new product every month or she'd lose her business opportunity. Do you think Lois got a cut of those purchases as well?"

I furrowed my brow. Monroe dug her claws into my back and began kneading my dress. "That's a good question. If she did, she makes money from them every month by simply keeping them invested in the possibility of one day being successful like her. None of them had made any money yet, not really."

"No. But which one struck you as a murderer?"

"Ruth was the most thoughtful, the most in tune with my feelings. So. Probably her."

Poppy laughed. "That's not a good reason to suspect someone of murder."

"One time I suspected someone of murder because they mispronounced the name of a French designer."

"I remember." There was a knock on the door, and Mullins delivered Presley. My dog trotted over to the couch, looked at the cat on my back, and chose Poppy's lap instead.

I closed my eyes because I didn't want to look at her when I admitted what was bothering me. "I thought the flowers were from your brother."

"My brother is an idiot," she said. "He wouldn't think to send flowers. He did, however, send me a letter."

I sat up quickly, sending Monroe scurrying off my back. "What did it say?"

"Let's talk about the murder first." She set Presley down and went into the kitchen, then came back with a bottle of champagne and two glasses. "I'll let you read it when we're done."

"It's here? In my apartment?"

Poppy poured each of us a glass. "You'll have to earn that information, Evelyn. Go on. What else do we know about Lois's death?"

"Not much. The police are treating it as an accidental death. I don't know if the Erno Laszlo bottle will change that or not. It must, right? If it contains shrimp stock and has someone's fingerprints on it, isn't that enough?"

She shrugged. "Why would one of them drop it?"

"They wouldn't have done it on purpose." I sat comfortably on the couch and sipped at more champagne. In for a penny, and all that. "She'd be in a hurry to pocket it, it would miss her pocket, and out it would fall. She might not have even noticed. Or maybe it made it mostly into her pocket, but when she stood? It fell out. Same goes for a purse. She didn't even notice. At least, not until she got home."

"You think whoever murdered Lois realized she lost the murder weapon?"

"Definitely." I watched the bubbles pop in the amber liquid. "She noticed and she panicked. Did she lose it in her house? In the cab? In the subway? What are the odds she dropped it in the dining room and not the bathroom? She'd be retracing her steps."

"Have any of the women tried to go back into the Gold Room?"

"I don't know, and honestly, Poppy. I don't know how to find out. All the women and Lois's husband have been back in the hotel. I suppose it's worth bringing up to Mr. Sharpe, but I wouldn't hold my breath. The older Mr. Sharpe, I mean. If I ever talk to the younger one again, it'll be too soon."

"What? You don't like him?"

"On the contrary. I am fascinated by him, and that makes me hate him, and that is a very dangerous position to be in because hate is only a few steps away from dating."

She laughed and downed her drink. "You have the most peculiar way of looking at relationships. Speaking of which, the flowers from Mr. Ferretti *are* lovely. Will you call him today?"

Presley hopped up into my lap. He licked my chin before settling down on my thighs. I stroked between his ears and took my glass from mostly full to mostly empty. "I suppose that's only polite. It isn't his fault I don't find him interesting romantically. But I don't like to be a tease. I'd much rather be friends with him."

"So, tell him that."

I nodded because she was right. But I hated talking about my feelings, and I hated conflict, and worse, hurting someone because my feelings were different from theirs.

"Let's discuss our suspects. Prudence, an older woman, was left well off when her husband died."

"Or so she said."

"Right. We only have her word to go on, but based on her clothes and the way she presents herself, I'd wager she's not lying. She was lonely, so she joined Ladies Love to Sparkle. Ruth, similarly, left her hometown and her family behind. Her husband works full-time, and her sons are older. She joined because she was lonely. Veronica, however, joined for money."

Poppy nodded and refilled our glasses. "Let's call her number one."

"Hodgson says Mr. Mitchell is number one."

"But what would his reason for killing his wife be?"

I closed my eyes, raised a hand to massage my eyebrows. "I have no idea. Unfortunately, I'll have to speak with him again."

"Will you go to his house?"

"Ugh, now you sound like Hodgson. And Dr. Sanders. Just keep the champagne flowing. And let me see that letter, will you?"

Chapter 22

I should feel bad for him. I know that I should. If I were a better person, I'd be sympathetic to Mac for the miserable time he's having living with his grandmother again. Instead, Poppy and I toasted over his tears. He *should* be miserable. I certainly was. He was planning now on moving out of the city, to his cousin's farm, and I hoped he would step in poop every single day.

"Cheers to that," Poppy laughed, her words slurring together. "The idiot. He thought he was having a hard time in London? Ha! He'll get run out of Willowshire again in no time flat."

"Where will he go then?" My words were also slurring together a bit. I cleared my throat. "I mean, what happen lasstime?" I shook my head. "No. No, he sssuffers. We shh—we shhhould eat. Are you hungry? I'm hungry!"

"Cake." Poppy said. "I want cake."

"Oh golly, cake sssounds d'lishus."

She pointed to herself. "I will. I will order it. Because I know. I know what cake is best cake."

I nodded. Poppy was right. "Don't tell Marco, though. Because you do. You do know what cake is. Is best. But he. He thinks *he* knows. But he doesn't know."

She shook her head as she reached for the phone. "He doesn't know anything."

"He knows pie," I said in defense of the chef's honor. "Good pie. And Jim. He knows Jim."

"Who is Jim?"

"I don't know. I'm not Marco." My eyes felt crossed and the lids heavy. I widened them as far as I could and tried to look only at Poppy. The walls were tipping back and forth, which was strange.

Poppy ordered a seven-layer chocolate cake to be delivered post haste to my room, and when she hung up the phone, missing the receiver twice, she stood up and clapped her hands, missing bringing her palms together only once. "You know who else likes cake?"

"Everybody."

"Right. And. Russell."

My wide eyes were dry. I held them closed for a moment, but when I opened them, they were too small again. "Who? Oh! Oh *Russell*. We shh—we shhould. Invite him to have cake with us."

She held out her hand and wiggled her fingers. I made my eyes as wide as possible so I could see where her fingers were because the walls weren't staying still, and it was throwing off my vision. Hand in hand, the two of us stumbled to my front door. It was curious how much of my own furniture was in the way between us and the front door. There was the couch to contend with, as well as the rug, and then the table in the entrance. Monroe slunk into my bedroom and out of our path while Presley watched us with his ears up and his tail wagging.

He barked.

"Shh," Poppy and I said together.

"That's too loud, baby," I said. "We will be right back and then. Then? Uh."

"Dinner," Poppy said. "We will feed you. Dinner."

"Yes."

"Yes."

Presley's little pink tongue lolled out of his tiny mouth, as if he understood what we were bribing him with. I barely understood myself. Poppy and I managed turning the handle and opening the door; both were a bit tricky as we were holding hands and standing side by side in the small hallway. The hardest part was when we made it to the lift and began calling elevators.

The first lift boy was not Russell.

"Get out of here," Poppy said, waving our joined hands.

"We are looking for Castillo," I said to the poor young man. "Russell Castillo."

He apologized and closed the lift. We rang for another. The same young man returned. He was sweating. "I'm sorry," he said. "I'll just switch lifts with him, all right? Give me half a moment."

The door closed and the lift descended. I turned to Poppy. "How long is half a moment, exactly?"

"I have no idea. How long is a moment?"

I shook my head. That was a mistake. The entire hallway space tilted on its side. I closed my eyes and breathed through my nose. "Poppy? Is the building falling over?"

"No. Sturdy as ever."

"That's good."

After what felt like several long moments, the elevator doors opened, and it was the one and only Russell Castillo inside. He grinned. "Good evening, ladies. How may I help you?"

"We have ordered cake," I announced. "You are hereby cordially invited to dine with us. On it. The cake."

"Yes. I ordered it," Poppy clarified. "Because I know cake."

"Shhhhe does." *S*'s followed by *h*'s were hard to say, weren't they? It was hard to know when to stop saying them.

His grin widened, brightening up his whole face. "You two have been drinking?"

In unison, Poppy and I each held up our thumbs and forefingers to show that we'd been drinking only a little bit.

"I wish I could," Russell said. "Really. But I'm working."

"I'm the boss," I said. "You can be off for the night. I will call Mr. Shhharpe. Cake is a priority, after all."

Russell grimaced. "No. Thank you, Miss Murphy. I'm sorry, Poppy. I can't. You two have fun though, okay?" And then without further conversation, he closed the lift doors on us.

"He closed the lift doors on us!" Poppy shouted.

"Shhhhhh," I said, holding a finger over my lips. "There are guests up here!"

She slapped a hand over her mouth. "Sorry," she whispered under her palm. "He keeps. He keeps. Not." She groaned. "You know!"

"He won't go on proper dates anymore." I guided the both of us back to my room.

"Or improper," she said.

I shrieked out a laugh in sheer surprise.

"Shh!"

Now it was my turn to slap a hand over my mouth. "Sorry." The door was unlocked, and we went back in my room as easily as we left it. "Maybe he's got a wife," I said. "You have to be careful about that. I dated a baseball player once, and I didn't know he was married until our third month together."

Poppy let go of my hand and lay down on the couch. Presley wound his way through my legs, but I didn't trust myself enough to pick him up, so I sat down on the floor and let him climb up into my lap. He set his little paws on my chest and licked my chin until a knock at the door had him barking.

I yelled for the bellhop to enter and told him to help himself to a dollar from the bowl of small cash at my entry table once he'd positioned the cake cart in my dining room. Poppy hadn't ordered one slice of seven-layer cake; she'd ordered the entire seven-layer cake.

"Golly, Poppy," I said, widening my eyes so I could look at it properly. It was a bit trembly around the edges as it sat perfectly still. "You shhhhould sleep here tonight. Not safe to drive anyway, and walking is. So far. Stay here and we will eat all the cake."

"If we eat this much cake we might die."

"Yes," I said. "But what a way to go."

Chapter 23

I ate so much cake that the pain from my stomach offset the bubbles on my mind. I somehow went to bed without washing my face! Changing my clothes—no problem; but washing off mascara? Ha! Drunk and full Evelyn could not be bothered.

In my defense, I was exhausted and grateful for the break the champagne had given me from my thoughts. There were simply too many things to worry about.

Mac, being miserable. I wasn't worried about that, but I was thinking about it a lot.

Lois Mitchell, falling into my lap in her final moments.

Her husband, eating at my bar.

Wally and his flowers.

Colin and his music.

Ruth, Prudence, and Veronica and their sales pitch. With me as one of their salesgirls, they stood to earn quite a bit more money than they ever had before. Potentially anyway. I'd have to throw parties and convince people to buy the jewelry, which, yes, I could do, quite easily, in fact. I didn't want to join their team, but I wasn't above pretending to join in order to get in their good graces and discover which one of them was the killer.

If one of them was the killer.

What if I was doing all this but it had simply been an accident on Marco's part? He or one of his Jim's might have added shrimp to the salad dressing because of—who knows?—chef reasons. I didn't think shrimp got added to salad dressings, but anchovies were a type of seafood and they certainly left their mark on Caesar salads. Lois Mitchell, the determined sales leader, giving her underlings a stern talking to, had then eaten the dressing, choked on her swollen tongue, and died. Wouldn't that be egg on my face. My unwashed face! Why wasn't I still asleep? Sleep had been blissful, a complete disconnect from all these stupid thoughts, but now there was a noise.

Presley was barking.

I sat up, alert at once. Presley was barking in the middle of the night. It sounded like he was in the living room. He'd never, in his entire doggy life, barked when there wasn't someone worth barking at.

"Poppy," I reached over and shook her awake. She was drooling on the pillow her brother used to use. "Poppy, something's wrong."

"Hmm?" She wiped her face. "What is it?"

"Call the front desk." I threw the covers off and grabbed my lamp, unplugging it with one hard tug. At times like these, I wished the baseball player were still in my life, or at least his bat. Squaring my shoulders and clutching my lamp, I moved into the dark living room. The moon was shining from outside the balcony doors. Presley stood in front of someone, every bark propelling him off the ground.

A man was on my patio.

It was hard to see him, haloed as he was by the moon, but there he stood, in an all-black outfit, a dark ski mask over his face, gloves on his hands.

My mouth went dry, and my ears got all clogged up by my pulse. I felt the vibration of Presley's barking but could no longer hear it. My heart throbbed and thumped, squeezing tight and letting go, sending me into a spiral of lightheadedness. The lamp slid in my loosening grip.

He waved at me with one of his gloved hands, his leather fingers twiddling in the air.

I did the only thing I could think of and screamed. I screamed for all I was worth, as loud as I could, until the guests to my right started pounding on our shared walls.

The man set something on the patio floor. His dark, featureless head tilted toward his shoulder. His eyes weren't visible, but he was watching me. Appraising me. He pressed his hand to where his mouth should be and blew me a kiss before fleeing down the fire escape.

Poppy came running into the room, holding two slippers like weapons.

My voice gave out. I panted for breath, the lamp slippery in my hands. "There was," I gasped, "a man! Oh, Presley!" I set the lamp down and gathered him up. He was still barking, but it changed to whimpering when I held him. "You saved us!"

Monroe lounged on the couch, unfazed by all the ruckus.

Poppy turned on a light. "Not hard to see what he was after," she said, gesturing to the costume jewelry still on my table, visible from the balcony doors. "This is that reporter's fault, mark my words."

I approached the doors, afraid to open them lest he be waiting to spring inside. It was hard to see exactly what he'd left on the floor, but with my nose pressed against the glass and my eyes squinted, I could make it out. There, on the ground, was a bright red pocket square. The Gentleman Thief's calling card.

Chapter 24

Pinnacle Security was promptly dispatched to my room. One man took Poppy's and my statements—and gave Presley a treat, pulled from his trouser pockets; why he had a dog treat in his pants I do not know, but good on him for showing initiative. Another man went down my fire escape to see if he could catch sight of the mystery man. The police arrived soon after, putting the dropped pocket square into evidence and sending out an alert to be on the lookout for a man in all black leaving the Pinnacle.

It was exhausting, and all I did was sit on my couch and hold Presley while he ate his trouser treat. I did have to explain what happened at least three times, the last of which was to the elder Mr. Sharpe, and having to repeat myself is one of my biggest annoyances in life, so, perhaps that was the reason.

I could have also been so tried because of the amount of champagne I had consumed the day before. It was an awful lot of champagne, after all.

Mr. Sharpe fretted as he paced about the apartment in pajama pants and a suit jacket.

"What are you even doing here?" I asked him, my head aching. "You're never working this early."

"I, um . . ." He cleared his throat. "Yes. You're right. I—hmm."

"Oh." I glanced around to see how intently the security men were listening. They did not seem to be paying us any mind whatsoever, but one can never be too careful. "Did you have to stay late again to balance the books? And then you decided to sleep in an empty room instead of going all the way home to simply turn back around again?"

"That's exactly right, yes," he said. "Your father is on the West Coast, currently. In California. I fear it's too early to inform him of what happened."

I set Presley down on the cushion and stood, reaching out to take hold of Mr. Sharpe's arm. "You leave Daddy to me. You've been working so hard. Go on now and get some rest before the hotel wakes up." I walked him to the door but leaned in close to whisper before opening it. "Will you let Henry know what's going on and invite him to breakfast for me?"

"Of course." He cleared his throat and said, louder, "You get some rest too, Miss Murphy. See you shortly, I'm sure."

I pinched his sleeve between my fingers before he made it out of the room. "One more thing, Mr. Sharpe? Do you know if any of Lois Mitchell's friends have returned to the Gold Room since she died?"

He shook his head. "No. I can ask around."

"Please, and thank you."

After he left, Poppy asked the security if they planned on moving into my suite with me, to which the two men did not have an answer beyond mumbling that they were just getting ready to leave now anyway, wished us a good night, and out they went.

The two of us collapsed on my couch. Presley spun around between us before his feet spread out at all angles and he flopped down, rolling over to offer us his fluffy belly. We both rubbed it.

"This has been a long day," I said. "And it's barely even begun! Can we go back to bed until breakfast?"

She checked her watch. "It's five. I don't see why we can't grab another hour of sleep or two. But even though I'm exhausted, Ev, and I've got a headache like the dickens, I don't think I can sleep after all that excitement. I thought we were going to have to fight for our lives with your lamp and my slippers!"

I laughed, rubbing my puffy eyes with my fingertips. "Maybe I'll soak in the tub for two hours and read a book. I've got a new Christie here somewhere."

"Don't look now," Poppy whispered, "but the cake we left behind is still here. It's staring at us."

Half of a seven-layer chocolate cake sat on the metal cart the bellhop had rolled it in on, leaning over and drooping sadly to the right. I laughed again. "Better clean it up before Presley finds it. If I never eat cake again—well, that's not fair. I plan on eating cake again. Maybe tomorrow."

"Not today."

"Definitely not today. Henry should join us for breakfast, I'd guess by seven. And then Hodgson will be in around eight. I'll have to catch him up on events. I can't believe the Gentleman Thief tried to rob me! Here, at the Pinnacle! The audacity of that burglar, I swear."

"The burglar? More like the reporter! She told everyone about the jewels on your coffee table and the same night, the jewel thief tries to break in? That is not a coincidence, Evelyn."

"You can't possibly think they're working together."

"No, I don't. But I do think she hates you, and she knew what she was doing when she mentioned it. She wants to see the Pinnacle continually attacked for God knows what reason. The thief hits your room? Well, there's another front-page headline for Miss Dottie, *Times* Reporter."

I chewed on that thought for a minute. While I didn't think the dislike was personal, per se, it did seem like Dottie had it out for the Pinnacle, and me by extension. "You may have a point. Fortunately, my ferocious guard dog protected the hotel's honor for the time being."

"Do you want me to track down your father's number on the West Coast?"

"Oh, heavens no. I'll tell him about it at Christmas."

Poppy furrowed her brow. "In a month? You'll tell him about the robbery in a month?"

"It wasn't a robbery," I insisted. "It wasn't even breaking and entering. He was on my balcony. He took nothing. He didn't even make it inside! That's hardly news to share with Daddy. Besides, even if he did get in, the only jewels out here are costume. The real ones are in my closet."

As I said it, I realized how close I'd come to losing all my real jewelry. Diamonds and pearls and emeralds, some of which I'd inherited directly from my mother and my grandmother. "I'll move them to the hotel's safe today, I think."

"Good idea. The sooner the better."

"Not before I've had a long bath and a hearty meal. Something with no sugar in it. Or frosting."

Poppy groaned. "Or alcohol. I've got paracetamol in my handbag. Grab you one?"

"Please. Thank you."

She got up, fetched her bag, and dug around for two white pills. "I don't think you should be staying here alone for the time being, Evelyn. There's no telling if that thief might come back."

We shared the headache medicine, and she sat back down. Monroe slunk over to see what we were doing and stared at us for a moment before hopping onto the coffee table, tiptoeing her way between the shining pieces of costume jewelry. She found a mostly empty spot and made herself comfortable, tail flicking against a bracelet.

"You're right," I said. "I hate to ask you to stay. I know you've got your own place now with Jennifer. But would you mind?"

She grinned. "Not in the slightest. I was going to offer if you didn't ask anyway."

"I'll only take an hourlong bath so you can have a soak before Henry gets here as well, if you want." With a deep inhale, I forced myself up, my muscles sore from the top of my head to the bottom of my feet. "I won't even use the entire bottle of bubble bath."

"Is it lavender?"

"Of course."

"You're a doll."

★ ★ ★

Henry arrived at the same time as the food we ordered: a plethora of breakfast options sent up by Chef Marco, who had heard about the attempted break-in. There was a handwritten card with my name on it that simply said, *So you can have enough energy to do more than scream next time*, which was both thoughtful and rude, exactly as Marco always was.

"Darling, what happened?" Henry embraced me and kissed both my cheeks. "More trouble finding you, hmm? Poppy, how are you holding up?" He kissed her cheeks as well. "Darling girls, almost robbed. I heard all about it, of course, and not only from Silas. It's the talk of the hotel, and I only traveled two floors to get here."

I gestured to the table that Poppy had set. The waiter who had brought breakfast took last night's feast away, fortunately for the cake, that was starting to cave in on itself under the weight of all that uneaten frosting. "He didn't make it into the suite, thank goodness. And Presley. His bark alerted us to the intruder in the first place."

"What about the police? They haven't caught him?"

"Not that I've heard," I said. "Though I suppose I should put in a personal call to the chief. Hodgson will be in soon, and while he's not on the force anymore, he seems to have the inside scoop."

Poppy cut into her over-easy eggs, the yellow yolk running all over her plate and into her pile of roasted potatoes. "If I've said it once, I've said it a thousand times. This is entirely the fault of that reporter who talked about your jewelry in the first place and didn't bother to mention it was fake."

"To be fair," I said, "I didn't tell Dottie the jewelry was fake. I simply changed the subject."

"How are things going with that? Those women?" Henry added sugar to his coffee. "Have you found anything useful?"

As we dined on our eggs, toast, and sausage, I caught him up on the tea I'd had with the surviving Ladies Who Love to Sparkle. Henry helped himself to the French toast covered in strawberries and powdered sugar, but both Poppy and I were hesitant to indulge in that much sweet stuff again so soon. "I fear I'm no closer to figuring this out than I was the day it happened. Worse still, I need to speak to Mr. Mitchell, and I have no idea how to approach him. I've already offered him condolences. What else is there?"

Henry shrugged a single shoulder, his mouth curving into a half grin, because all good-looking men are required to grin like that. "I happen to know Mr. Mitchell. Not closely, mind you, but we've run in the same circles. He played football, was quite good at it before he retired. I can set up a casual meeting for you, Evelyn."

"Would you really, darling? You're the ginchiest."

He winked, pointed at me with his fork. "Takes one to know one, darling."

Chapter 25

Hodgson would be arriving shortly. I had decided to kill two birds with one stone and move all my real jewels into the Pinnacle's safe and then wait for him in the lobby to inform him of the night's events. It was too soon to ask him about the evidence he'd taken out of my fridge. Wally had suggested finding out exactly what the shrimp stock had been put into, to help figure out who put it there.

He never had told me what happened in his mushroom case. I needed to call and thank him for the flowers anyway, and I'd ask him about the case then, but it would have to wait. There were inherited gems to protect and a murder to solve, after all. If it even *was* a murder. All I had to go on was a bottle of something shrimpy. No motive and very little opportunity. It *could* be a coincidence.

My head was still fuzzy from the night before, and I was having a hard time directing my thoughts towards murder. But something in my gut was tingling, sparkling, like the fake diamonds in the necklace on my coffee table, and I couldn't ignore it. Something was off here, and not just the shrimp.

Dr. Sanders had suggested throwing a fundraiser for a charity as a way to pull myself out of the self-indulgent self-loathing

I'd slipped into upon Mac's departure, but perhaps I was better at solving murders than I was at throwing parties—which is saying something, because I am quite good at throwing parties. That's why Daddy had made me take the job as the Pinnacle's party planner in the first place. That and to learn the *value of a dollar*, whatever that meant.

I packed my jewelry up in a hatbox and carried it down to the lobby myself. Russell Castillo was noticeably absent in his post as lift boy. What was he up to at night? Why wouldn't he tell Poppy? Sometimes men are too afraid to outright reject women, so they hide from them instead. Maybe that's what he was doing? If that was true, then he was an absolute idiot. Poppy was stunningly beautiful, creative, and kind. She had an artistic eye and a knack for details and was excellent at ordering cake. I highly doubted he could ever find a better girl than Poppy Cooper, that was for sure.

"Miss Murphy? I mean, Evelyn." The thick Scottish brogue of the younger Mr. Sharpe stopped me in my tracks halfway to the Pinnacle's safe. I hadn't shaken the way his kiss on my hand had left me spinning, nor had I forgotten how he'd thought I was Poppy's assistant instead of the other way around. "I heard what happened last night. Are you all right?"

"Perfectly fine, thank you." I held up my hatbox and shook it gently, letting the tinkling jingle answer the question for me. "Simply taking precautions. But the hotel itself is very secure, I do hope you understand."

"Of course, of course." He grinned. "Don't want anything so valuable just lying about anymore, do we now?" His elbow bumped my own, and if he were anyone else, I wouldn't have noticed it was done on purpose. "Would you mind if I walked with you? I can carry your box, if you want."

"Not at all." I handed it over to him. "Actually, I wanted to pick your mind about something."

"The fundraiser?" He guessed. "Who is it for again?"

Oh, that infernal question again. Like I'm supposed to know all the details about the charity that I'm raising money for. "Hungry . . . children? Orphans. Hungry orphans? Listen, that wasn't what I wanted to talk to you about, though I am glad you're thinking of it. Don't be late on Sunday. We were talking about the paper, remember? About the Pinnacle's image. My image. You and I?"

"I recall, yes."

"Do you read the newspaper a lot?"

"I like to keep up with the times, so to speak."

"I read the newspaper a lot."

"Good for you."

I tapped my elbow against his side. "Do you think it's strange that Dottie, the reporter who has been so publicly against us, talks about my jewelry in her article and that very night the Gentleman Thief tries to break into my room?"

Colin looked at me from the corner of his dark eyes. "You don't think she's the Gentleman Thief, do you?"

"No, no—not the thief, but maybe someone who tips him off? I don't know. I hadn't even thought about the possibility they could be connected until Poppy brought it up."

Colin furrowed his brow. "Who?"

"My assistant? Poppy? The one you thought was me?"

He chuckled, shook his head. "Oh. Right."

The way he said those two words struck me as funny, like he really didn't remember who she was, which didn't make sense, considering the way he'd been pining after her. "Maybe the Gentleman Thief and Dottie are working together. She gives him tips and keeps his name in the papers. These criminal types often like to see themselves as celebrities. They like the notoriety, the infamy. In return, he targets people with connections to the hotel, so she can keep making the same argument."

"What argument?"

"That the Pinnacle is dangerous."

Colin sighed. "I don't know, Evelyn Murphy. That's the sort of conspiracy that only takes place in detective novels."

"Yes, sure, but I love detective novels," I said. "And sometimes the things that happen in detective novels occur in real life first. That's where the authors get their ideas from."

He stopped outside of the room where the safe was kept, the security guard manning the entrance watching us from his seat at a small desk. "So, you think a man and a woman really devised a plan to trick her rich friend into marrying her boyfriend so they could then murder her together on a cruise ship on the Nile and take her money as their inheritance?"

My heart skipped a beat. I reached for the pendant of Saint Anthony around my neck and held on tight to the silver medallion, cool between my fingers. "You read Agatha Christie?"

"'Course I do. She's brilliant."

The strangest thing happened. I giggled. I twirled my hair around my finger and *giggled* at Mr. Sharpe's son. The man I'd only yesterday warned his father to be careful of, because he was simply too charming for anyone's own good. "Don't get me wrong. I adore Poirot. But I've always been more of a Marple fan myself."

His dark eyes tracked me up and down, his mouth curving into that incredibly annoying half grin that for some reason only made me giggle more this time. "I can tell. Hey," he said, nodding at one of the security guards, "can you take this in for Miss Murphy, please?"

"Sure thing." The guard accepted the hatbox as if he were being handed a newborn infant. "We'll lock this up right away, Miss Murphy. Want to watch?"

The vault wasn't anything particularly impressive, but I did want to make sure the jewelry was properly locked away, so I nodded. "Mr. Sharpe?"

He held out his arm, and I took it with another stupid, unstoppable giggle.

The guard pulled out his key ring and opened the first of the two doors, Colin and I following behind him.

"You know, Dad wanted me to work on security. But I'm much better at music than at guarding. A noble profession, sir, and you do it well," he said to the guard nearest us, who nodded in response.

The other guard grinned at us over his shoulder as the second door swung open. "Here it is, Miss Murphy, Mr. Sharpe. Our very own set of Moslers."

They were big steel boxes stationed side by side, like metal armoires, alone in a white room with no windows and incandescent bulbs buzzing overhead.

"Two?" I asked, my nose wrinkling even more. A lot of twos when it came to our security measures.

Two locked doors; two security guards out front, responsible for one key each; and two bank employees who came by every evening to collect the cash. That didn't seem wise, considering the thief on the loose. How easy would it be for someone to sneak past our guards and our locks? Not very easy, of course, but it could happen. What could we do differently? I'd have to bring it up with Mr. Sharpe. We needed stricter safety measures, especially if my mother's jewelry was going to live inside the room from now on.

The guard who opened the second door responded. "Yes, miss. One for guest storage and one for the hotel's cash. We watch the bank men who come in here every night, miss. Us and Mr. Sharpe or one of them desk boys. Keeps 'em honest."

Forcing my nose to relax for once, I smiled and dropped the subject. In my opinion, staying honest in a group depended on who you were with, but the safe, under constant guard, was a much better option for my mother's jewelry than my second bedroom.

The guard holding on to my hatbox of goods turned the knob to a certain number. Then he turned around. The second guard turned the knob to another number. Colin and I looked at each other as the guards repeated this process three more times. Then they set my hatbox inside, on the top shelf of the safe; shut it tight, the metal reverberating in the near empty room; and spun the lock.

"Ain't no Peter Man getting in here," said the first guard. "Not even with all the gelignite in the world."

I kept smiling. "Marvelous. What . . . what is gelignite?"

"It's an explosive, miss," the second guard said. "A lot of these safecrackers just blow up the safe to get inside. Ends up damaging what they're trying to steal—and them hurting their own selves half the time."

Colin tsk-tsked. "That hardly seems smart, does it? Ruining jewelry or money or your own face just at a chance of making a payday?"

With a shrug, I said, "Depends on the payday and the person in need of funds. Thank you, gentlemen. I appreciate all you do for us."

The guards followed us out of the room, taking the time to lock both doors.

"I've got to get to the lobby," I told Colin. "I'm expecting someone."

He nodded and walked with me out of the hallway, the two of us casually strolling toward the Pinnacle's lobby. "For what it's worth, I don't think that reporter's got anything on you, Evelyn Murphy," Colin said. "She's riding your coattails for some notoriety. She'll find another target soon enough."

"I hope so. Dealing with murder is one thing. Dealing with bad press is another."

The door to his father's office was shut tight. I wondered if he'd made it to work yet after informing Henry of the night's events.

Colin set his hand on top of mine. My fingers warmed underneath his touch. "You're not meeting the square who stood you up the other night, I hope."

"No. And Wally isn't a square. He also didn't stand me up. He was at dinner with me. He just got called away before we could finish eating."

Something like joy, except more self-serving, crossed his handsome face. "Did he now? I wonder, did he ever tell you who called him away?"

Nose wrinkling yet again—it would be the death of me, or at least of my wrinkle-free skin—I stared at his profile through narrowed eyes, that tingling intuition sparking like fireworks in my belly. "Do you know who called him away?"

"You could say that."

I stopped walking abruptly, using my hold on his arm to stop him too. "Did you call him away?"

Colin smiled up at the ceiling instead of at me, his Adam's apple bobbing in his throat. "Now, what gave you that idea?"

"Look at me this instant, Colin Sharpe!"

He did, his tongue wetting his lips. "I'm looking at you, Evelyn Murphy. I'm always looking at you."

I dropped my hold on his arm to better wag my finger at the tip of his nose. "You called my date away!"

"I just wanted to spend time with you."

"Were you ever . . . did you really confuse Poppy with me?"

Colin reached out and grabbed my wagging finger, held my hand in his. "I needed some way to get you to notice me. Nothing else had worked."

I ripped my hand out of his. "So, you lied? You pretended to be interested in someone else and disinterested in me to get my attention?"

"Did it work?"

My mouth twisted into the deepest frown I could manage, and I stormed off, mad at him, mad at myself. Because—gosh darn it, darn him, darn his lopsided grin—it *had* worked.

Chapter 26

The lobby was busy, but Hodgson wasn't one of the patrons checking in, out, or getting breakfast.

"Hmm." I took a turn around the fountain before approaching the doorman. "Excuse me? Have you seen Mr. Hodgson?"

"Yes, Miss Murphy," the doorman said, tipping his hat. "Good morning, Miss Murphy. Mr. Hodgson asked the same thing about you. I said I hadn't seen you yet today and that you were probably in your room. That's all right, isn't it?"

I realized that my expression was still the massively frowny one that Colin Sharpe had deserved. With a quiet exhale, I smiled instead, my eyebrows and lips relaxing. "Yes, that's quite all right. Have a good day."

The smile didn't last for long, because it was Russell Castillo who picked me up in the lift. Where had he been? And what had he been up to? I glared at him, and he nodded back, a hard swallow tensing his throat.

"Good morning, Miss Murphy. I just brought Mr. Hodgson to your floor. He was looking for you."

"Wonderful. I'm looking for him." Only the two of us road the lift to the top floor. My hands were fists at my sides. "You do know, don't you, that a masked man tried to enter my room last night? Where Poppy and I were both fast asleep?"

He winced. "I heard that, yeah. Scary world we live in these days, Miss Murphy."

I turned straight toward him, positively vibrating with anger. We'd invited him to join us for cake. He could've stayed on my couch. He could've been there for us when all we had was a lamp and a pair of slippers and a barking, five-pound fluff ball. But he'd had other, mysterious plans. "Isn't it strange," I said, thinking out loud, "that the very day you see the Taylors on their anniversary, after Mrs. Taylor shows me her new bracelet, they're robbed? Don't you think it's odd timing that while you could have joined us for cake, you were busy, off doing something else on the night I was robbed?"

"Almost robbed," Russell corrected.

"That's all you have to say for yourself. That I was *almost* robbed?"

Russell's dark eyes searched my face. The lift came to a stop at the top floor. "Sorry?" He tried.

"Something is wrong with you. I don't know what it is, but I'll find out. And if you're the man who almost broke into my suite, I'll make you pay for it every day for the rest of your life. And if you're not? Well, Poppy can do better than you." I stomped off the elevator. "I'm going to make sure she knows it too!"

Russell didn't even bother to call after me, to argue with me—nothing! Oh, these men! I needed more women in my life. But who? My cousin Martha was coming to visit over Christmas. That would be a welcome change of pace. The women in my life right now were all murder suspects, save Poppy, of course. She didn't even know Lois Mitchell, and she had been busy talking to Henry the entire time I was at the Ladies Love to Sparkle table.

My door was unlocked, and I found Poppy sitting on the couch while Hodgson paced my patio back and forth. The doors were wide open, and the cool fall breeze made my curtains flutter in a way that Monroe could not resist. She sat on the carpet with her tail flicking, her green eyes on the gauzy fabric floating in the wind.

Hodgson was shaking his head as he muttered to himself. He noticed me and stopped all movement, except for his eyes, which narrowed into disapproving slits.

I was in Trouble with a capital *T*. No mistaking that look. I'd seen it on Nanny's face enough times growing up to recognize I was about to have sweets taken from me for the next few days.

Considering how much cake and pie I'd eaten recently, that wasn't entirely unacceptable.

Poppy slapped her hands on her thighs and stood up. "I'll take Presley for his walk."

I grabbed her arm. "Please, don't leave."

"Oh, I'm leaving." She gently tapped her palm against my cheek. "Good luck!"

Poppy scooped Presley up and grabbed his leash on the way out of the door.

I tried again. "Please stay!" But she left.

Hodgson walked into the room with his nostrils flared and his hands on his hips.

I rolled my shoulders back. "This wasn't my fault."

"Were you ever gonna tell me someone almost broke in?"

"Of course. I was in the lobby waiting for you!"

"You don't think it's suspicious that it happens when I've reopened your mom's investigation?"

"No," I answered. "I think it got printed in the paper that I had diamonds lying about. Honestly, this is the reporter's fault. She should know the difference between costume jewelry and the real thing. Although"—I tilted my head in acquiescence—"they are good fakes."

He drummed his fingers on his chin. "I did read that article yesterday. No thanks to you."

"I thought you had plenty of nickels? A pocket full of nickels, you said, jingling all around."

His nostrils flared again.

I took a step back. "The article wasn't my fault either!"

"You invited her in, didn't you? You opened your mouth and spoke to her?"

"How was I supposed to know she was going to print what I said?"

Hodgson covered his eyes with his hand. "Unbelievable. Do you not realize that you could've been hurt?"

"If he got inside," I said, "I had a lamp."

"What does that mean? Never mind, never mind." He pinched his nose. "Just—just get Poppy Cooper to stay over for a while."

"Already done."

"Well. Fine!"

"Fine."

He tossed both arms up in the air. "The least you can do is see the nun with me!"

That abrupt change in subject took me by surprise, and I blinked a few times to gather my thoughts. "You still haven't spoken to the nun?"

"I've tried, Murphy. I've shown her your letter, your mom's case file. She says she won't give me anything. She'll only give it to you directly. And I don't know if you're aware of this, but it's difficult to go after the Catholic church, especially for a cop who doesn't even have a badge anymore."

I looked past him to the park outside my patio. The golden leaves of the treetops rustled in the wind. Monroe had curled up and fallen asleep in a patch of sunlight, the curtain stroking her back as it fluttered. If I called my father right now and told him what had happened, how would he react?

Would he have been worried for my safety? Would he have stopped what he was doing and patrolled the scene of the crime for any clues missed by the police? Would he have insisted I have someone else stay with me?

"Fine."

"How can you—" Hodgson stopped himself. "Fine?"

"Yes. Fine. I'll go. It's a nice day. I've got a new coat I've been wanting to wear. Can we wait for Presley? I'd like to take him with us."

Hodgson cleared his throat. "All right. That's—yes. That's fine."

"I haven't left the hotel since I visited Yonkers last month. You won't leave me alone out there, will you?"

He shook his head.

I smiled for real for the first time all day. "Have you had coffee yet?"

"No."

"You missed coffee for me? Why, Hodgson. We are friends, no matter what you say. Let's go to the café and wait for Presley there. I'll treat you to breakfast."

Chapter 27

Hodgson drove my Silver Cloud Rolls-Royce to the other side of the Park, about twenty minutes away. I'd never been to a convent before. I couldn't imagine my mother in one. I thought of her will and how she'd left me her race horses, and also left her horses a stipend that would provide for them all their lives, without me ever even knowing they existed.

"Did we ever find out where the horses are?"

He nodded. "In a country club about an hour outside the city—that's if the traffic is good. I haven't made the drive yet because I'm not sure what horses could have to do with her death."

"But she might've mentioned someone in her prayer journal."

"That's exactly right." He looked at me from the corner of his eye. "Do you want me to read it?"

I reached into my large black purse and scratched the fur between Presley's triangle ears. "Eventually. But I'd like to . . . I'd like to keep it for a little while, if that's all right."

He shrugged. "It's your money, Murphy. I've combed over her will, and I think we can rule out money as the motive, since you were the one who benefited the most. But I do want to talk to your father. Not because I think he's responsible," he said defensively at my outraged look, "but because he might be able to give me some names of people in her immediate social circle who might've been left out of the police file. The detectives in charge at the time did a good job following leads, but there really weren't many to begin with. Now, if this was some random attack—"

"I understand." Presley rested his paws on my chest and licked my chin. I took a deep breath. "You're earning your paycheck, Hodgson, and I'm grateful for how good an investigator you are but, I can only handle this conversation in small doses."

"Right. You've got your . . . issues."

I glared at him. "Issues?"

"Yeah. You know." He gestured at me with one hand, encompassing my entire body in his *issues* statement. Was he wrong? No! Did he have any right to point it out? Probably! But it was still annoying!

"Yes, Hodgson, I do know!"

"All right. Fine. We're on the same page."

"Fine!"

"Fine."

I paid attention to Presley and none to Hodgson, and of course turned up my nose so he could tell I wasn't paying attention to him, or else what was the point? Besides, someone needed to admire all the cast-iron facades on the buildings we drove past. He huffed and ignored me right back. We rode in silence except for the frequent honking commonly heard in New York traffic, of course, until we pulled in front of a four-story, palazzo-style mansion. Presley hopped back down into his purse, and I opened the door and climbed out of the car with the purse on my shoulder. Hodgson followed shortly after, taking the lead to the entrance. He'd been there before, multiple times, and several nuns knew him on sight and greeted him when we made it to the interior courtyard.

Groups of young girls being led by nuns were walking around as well, in matching knee-length blue skirts, high socks, white shirts, and navy-blue coats. Not a convent, then. A school. I waved at a few of them.

"Is this Miss Murphy?" a nun asked, offering me her hand, which I took. She was about my age, and her white veil suggested she was a novice. "It's nice to meet you. I'm Sister Emily. Sister Theresa Anne is in her office. Shall I take you to her?"

"It's nice to meet you too, Sister Emily." I said, completing our handshake. "That would be most helpful."

The three of us walked up a set of limestone stairs into a long hall with a massive ceiling, arches of heavy stone lining the way. Sister Emily knocked on a heavy oak door, and when a female voice asked, "Yes?" she replied, "The private investigator is back, Sister. He's brought Evelyn Murphy with him this time."

"Are you sure it's her?"

Sister Emily looked me up and down and smiled. "She looks just like the pictures in the papers."

"All right. Let them in."

Sister Theresa Anne was an older woman, only her pale, wrinkled face visible under her black habit, but her clear blue eyes sparkled when she saw me.

"It's definitely you," she said. She didn't stand up or offer her hand, but I felt welcomed all the same. Hodgson and I took seats in front of her desk. "You look like your mother."

My heart skipped. "Really?" I settled Presley's purse on my lap, and he poked his head up, ears swiveling as he took in the room. "I fear I look too much like my father."

She smiled bright. "No, no, you look remarkably like Gwendolyn. Your hair is blonder, though I don't think you come by that naturally. I spent a lot of time with her, you know."

Presley licked my chin. I could feel Hodgson's eyes on me, but I worried if I glanced his way, I'd break down and cry. He'd seen me cry enough for one lifetime. Certainly, almost more than any other person I'd employed, save Poppy, who was with me when her brother left. *The wanker.* "I didn't know. You were friends?"

She hummed. "Gwendolyn very seriously considered becoming a nun."

Without a single drop of water or a speck of food in my mouth, I managed to choke anyway, my tongue a useless muscle in my mouth as I coughed into my fist. Presley harrumphed and buried himself in the purse. Hodgson reached over and smacked me on the back twice, something I'm sure he'd thought about doing frequently in our time together.

"I'm fine," I snapped at him. Smiling at the Sister, I forced a lungful of air into my lungs. "What happened?"

"Oh, she met your father. It happens a lot in this line of work. You'd be surprised."

"I already am," Hodgson said. "Did she get a special outfit?"

I very gently poked Hodgson in the ribs.

"Ow," he said, snaking away from me. "What?"

Sister Theresa Anne ignored the exchange, her sparkling blue eyes on me. "It's why I pushed so hard to see you. I understand that you have certain limitations, and I'm proud of you for coming here anyway."

Proud of me? Rarely was that sentence spoken to me by someone of authority. "Thank you."

"Your mother didn't leave me a prayer journal," she said.

I looked to Hodgson, flabbergasted. Why force me out here if you had nothing to give me? Hodgson shrugged in response, equally amazed.

"She left me *all* of her prayer journals. About a dozen." Sister Theresa Anne pulled a cardboard box out from under desk and set it on top of her workspace with a quiet "Oomph." "She was very diligent in her prayers."

Hodgson scooted forward in his chair and ran his index finger over the leather spines of the well-worn notebooks. "Why didn't you give these to the police after she died?"

"They didn't ask for them," Sister Theresa Anne said. "In general, we don't hand items from our parishioners over to anyone after they've been bequeathed to us. However, I'm making an exception in this case because I think Gwen would have wanted you to have them, Evelyn. Especially now that you're a woman grown."

I was a grown woman with a dog in a purse in my lap, but sure, I understood what she was trying to say, even if I still felt like a child most days.

Hodgson picked up a notebook from the middle and let it fall open in his hands. My mother's handwriting was neat and crisp in smudge-free black ink, and half of the page was covered in detailed sketches of flowers and birds. This was the closest I had been to her since I watched her casket slide into a mausoleum with her family's name carved into the stone. I reached over, took it from him, and closed it.

"May I keep them forever?" I asked. "Or do you want them back?"

"Please. They're yours. But if you'd ever like to visit, perhaps the two of us can chat about what you find."

The notebook was warm in my hands. My palms were damp, and my fingers shook. Presley nudged my wrist with his cold, wet nose, and I remembered to breathe. "Thank you, Sister. I'll do my best," I said, because I never liked lying to nuns and wasn't very good at lying anyway.

Hodgson and I said our goodbyes. He took the box and led me back to the car while I took Presley out of his purse and held him in my arms, burying my face in his furry little back.

"The books are not my mom," I whispered. "They're not. They're just books. Everything's normal."

Presley wiggled in my hold until he could push his nose against my ear, his snuffling breath tickling me out of my panic.

Hodgson set the box of my mother's prayer journals in the backseat of my Silver Cloud Rolls-Royce. "You tell me when you're ready for me to go through 'em, and I will, Murphy."

It wasn't a particularly kind or thoughtful thing for him to say, but my eyes welled with tears, and something warm filled my chest. "Thank you, Hodgson."

He tipped his hat. "I ain't openin' the door for you, though."

Tears spilling over my lashes, I laughed and opened the passenger door for myself.

Chapter 28

"Yoo-hoo, Evelyn!" A familiar Southern voice rang out in the lobby the moment I stepped in from the main doors.

Ruth was waving from by the fountain. She'd been sitting on the edge, a man beside her.

I waved back, and then the man was on his feet. He was middle-aged, balding, and pale, with light eyebrows and dark eyes. He took Ruth by the hand and led her over to me.

Hodgson swore under his breath.

"Will you take the journals up to my room, please?" I asked him. "This is one of the ladies who, uh, sparkle."

He swore again, but walked away, supposedly to do what I'd asked.

Ruth was in the same blue dress she'd worn to have tea in my suite. The man next to her was in a comely suit, but it had to be several years old; there was noticeable wear in the elbows and knees.

"Hi, Evelyn," she greeted, flushed. "This is my husband, Nathaniel. Nathaniel, this is Evelyn Murphy, the girl I was telling you about."

I reached for the pendant around my neck without realizing it, the cold metal reminding my fingers they had something to do. I offered him my hand. He looked at it for a beat too long before finally shaking it.

"Miss Murphy," he said, "I have a bone to pick with you."

His Southern accent was even thicker than Ruth's.

"Do you?" I giggled. "Why, whatever is the matter, Nathaniel?"

"Every time I let Ruthie come here, it's always a mistake."

Ruth bristled, her frankly enviable chest heaving. "Nathaniel? *Really?* Let's do be serious."

He grunted. "Fine. Every time Ruthie comes here, something bad happens. That we can agree on, can't we?"

"No," I said. "No, we can't. I understand her first visit was cut short by tragedy but—"

"Nobody's crying over that woman's death," Nathaniel said. "It ain't a tragedy she's gone. I thought it would be a relief. But no, you invite Ruthie back here and buy some more of that . . . that . . . useless junk from her, and now she's back on the wagon. Buying more and more, calling round to the pastor's wife to see if she'll join the circus."

My brow furrowed. "Is it *on* the wagon or *off* the wagon?"

"That don't matter," he said with another dismissive wave of his hand. "The point is, I got the pastor himself complaining about what Ruthie's doing. And then? She comes here a third time and returns home drunk as a skunk. The pastor and his wife were there to witness it."

Ruth's light and pleasant flush had turned into full-blown patchy redness. She feathered her bangs with her fingers and cleared her throat. "I was enjoying tea with my friends, Nathaniel."

"Tea," he scoffed. "She told me you kept the champagne flowing, Miss Murphy. That might be all well and good for people like you who don't have any responsibilities, but Ruth is a mother. She's a wife. She's got a house to run. She doesn't have time for this jewelry nonsense, and she doesn't have the luxury to get drunk on a Thursday afternoon."

Ruth vibrated where she stood. Her husband hadn't looked at her once since he'd started in on me.

Could he have slipped into the Gold Room somehow? He certainly wasn't sad Lois Mitchell was dead. *I need those results back from the police.* The last thing I wanted to do was anger a suspect so badly they would never agree to see me again, or they'd keep their wife, another suspect, from seeing me again.

So, I smiled, and held out my arms. "Let me apologize. I fear the Pinnacle looks quite bad right now in your eyes, and I'd like to make that up to you." I hoped he didn't notice I was making it sound like the Pinnacle was apologizing instead of me, since all his complaints were about me, specifically. He was wrong, of course, but that had never stopped anyone from being angry before. "Are you two hungry? The diner offers a wide variety of classic American food. You can't go wrong with their burger and fries. Or if you'd like, we have a beautiful bar with its own menu. Steaks and mashed potatoes. That sort of thing. It's perfect for a date. What do you say? It'll be my treat."

Ruth's patchy redness was seceding. "Nathaniel? We haven't been on a date in so long."

He made a show of checking his watch, a deep frown on his wide face. "Humph. It's a little early for drinking, Ruthie."

"The diner also has wonderful milkshakes," I said, a musical lilt to my voice.

"Please, Nathaniel? Won't that be lovely? Just the two of us?"

"Fine," he groused. "If that's what you really want."

I gave them both giant smiles. "Excellent. Right this way."

★ ★ ★

Hodgson had set the box of my mother's prayer journals on the coffee table where the jewelry had been, with a note saying he'd be in his office, if I needed him.

I didn't need him. What I needed was for this not to be happening. I wanted to solve my mother's murder, but every thought of her was painful. How could I do anything with a knife in my brain?

Monroe hopped up on the table and gave the notebooks a good sniff before slinking over to me, meowing. I picked her up. "Hello, gorgeous," I said, resting her on my shoulder, enjoying the feel of her warm purr. Presley trotted into the kitchen, shortly followed by the sounds of water splashing out of his bowl and on to the kitchen floor.

This wasn't such a bad life. It was little, but it was mine. How would it have been different if my mother were still here? Would I be globe-trotting like my father? Would I have wanted to settle down and raise a family, like she did? Would she have put me in that school with the nuns for teachers instead of the tutors Daddy supplied for me? I'd know a thing or two more about horses, that was for sure.

There was a knock on the door, followed by Henry's voice calling, "Darling? Are you home?"

I set Monroe on the couch and let him in. He was wearing brown slacks, a blue shirt, and a tweed sports jacket. "Why, darling," I said, kissing his cheek, "don't you look sharp."

He fixed his lapels, grinning widely. "Thank you. I'm headed over to our mutual friend Theodore Mitchell's house."

"The husband!" I clapped my hands in glee. "That's wonderful! Are you surprising him, or is this a planned visit?"

"I called to offer my condolences, and he invited me over for drinks and to watch the game."

"Oh." I furrowed my brow. "What game?"

Henry said, "You know, I didn't ask."

"Football?"

"I believe that football is on Sundays. It's most likely baseball."

"Did he say who was playing?"

"No, he said only *the game* was on. Huh." Henry's brow furrowed now. "Come to think of it, he might've said 'the fight.'"

I held the pendant of Saint Anthony. "He's going to fight you?"

"No, of course not." He chuckled. "It's boxing. Or baseball. One of the two. Either way, I'll get in there and ask him if he killed his wife."

"Oh no! No, no, no, you mustn't." I took Henry's arm and guided him toward the couch. "You can't simply ask someone if they committed a crime. You have to talk around it. Do you understand?"

"I'm an actor, Ev," Henry said. "I can pretend to be a detective as well as you can."

I dropped his arm to plant my fist on my hip, and began tapping my toe on the ground. "What was that?"

He patted me lightly on the top of the head. "Let me try again, shall I? You, Evelyn, are marvelous at finding things but dreadful at lying. I'm good at lying but would lose my head if it weren't attached to my neck. That's why I came down here in the first place. We should go together. As a team. Sniff him out, the two of us. What do you say?"

My first thought was no. I'd already been out of the hotel to see the nuns with Hodgson, and it was the first time I'd left

Pinnacle property since I'd wound up in Yonkers on my own. But out of the corner of my eye I could see the box of my mother's journals, and being left alone with her prayers felt worse than leaving with a friend. And he was right, both of us had our own strengths and weaknesses that could balance out this investigation.

If it *was* an investigation. Because there was still a chance, however small, that Marco was wrong about an ingredient somewhere in his kitchen, loathe as I was to admit he could be at fault.

"All right. Let me get ready."

"Darling, your outfit is perfect."

I shook my head. "I don't need to change. I need to leave a note for Poppy and grab my lockpicking kit."

Henry laughed and reached for my hand. "He's inviting us into his home, remember?"

I squeezed his fingers before letting him go and returned to my to-do list. "That's exactly why I need the kit! Oh, we will have to find a driver."

He winked. "I've already got Little Tommy lined up. Big Tommy was unfortunately unavailable."

The Tommys were part of the hotel's valet team and had been for some time. They'd made it through all the hubbub last month, what with the death in the Pinnacle's garage and all. "Maybe he's in the fight?"

"Now, wouldn't that be something? He's got the build for it. And the temperament."

"You'd think missing one eye would be a hindrance in boxing."

"You'd think it'd be a hindrance in his valet work as well, but that seems to be going along swimmingly enough."

Chapter 29

The street that the Mitchell house was on was lined with ten turn-of-the-century brownstones, all sharing one roof. Each one had ten concrete steps to climb, and each had with a perfectly manicured tree standing sentinel at the bottom of the steps. At the end of the row of houses stood another house, close to the ten but alone, with its own roof. It was only two stories and only required five steps to climb to the entrance, and instead of a tree at the bottom, there was a shrub. It rustled in the breeze, and so did my hair, my cheeks stinging in the cold air. Mr. Mitchell's housekeeper opened the brownstone's door.

"Hello," Henry greeted, flashing his movie-star grin. "I'm Henry Fox. Mr. Mitchell is expecting me. This is my dear friend, Evelyn Murphy."

"I think we've spoken over the phone." I offered her my hand after reluctantly pulling it from my coat pocket. "Thank you for your help in contacting Mrs. Mitchell's friends."

She stared at my hand for a moment before taking it in her own, her fingers calloused and warm. "Mr. Mitchell doesn't know about that."

"He won't hear about it from me."

"Or me." Henry took her hand when she let go of mine. "Scouts honor."

The housekeeper sighed, nodded once, and stepped back so we could enter. "May I take your coats?"

Henry helped take off mine before he removed his own, handing them one by one to the housekeeper, who hung them up in Mr. Mitchell's hall closet, next to a set of skis, a black sweater, and a light brown tweed Dior coat from this year's fall season. I wondered if Mrs. Mitchell had even had a chance to wear it before her unfortunate passing.

The housekeeper closed the door, snapping me out of my thoughts, and led us to the Mitchells' living room, where sounds of a television emanated.

"I didn't know you were in the Boy Scouts," I whispered, bumping my arm against Henry's.

"Oh. I wasn't. I told you, I'm an excellent liar."

I laughed. "At least you lead with your strengths, darling. Are we playing a couple for Mr. Mitchell?"

"Why not?" Henry offered me his elbow. "I'll be your date for the evening if you'll be mine."

"Anytime you want." I kissed his cheek. "You lie, I'll snoop."

"The perfect date."

The housekeeper waved us in.

Mr. Mitchell was sitting in an armchair, a cigar in his mouth and a glass half full of beer in his hand. "Henry, my good man. And Miss Murphy, what a surprise. Have a seat, Henry. There's a bar cart over there, Miss Murphy. I'll take a scotch. What do you want?"

He was asking Henry. I was the one to serve them, apparently. Normally when I served people, namely, my father, it was my choice. But this was expected of me, which made me hate it immediately, which made me picture getting him his scotch and then dumping it in his lap. But that would mean getting kicked out of the house and losing the opportunity to snoop.

Instead, I smiled completely and totally naturally at my friend, who swallowed so hard his entire throat bobbed.

"A scotch as well, Ev—thanks."

I approached the bar cart as Mr. Mitchell blew out a big puff of smoke, the minty, smoky cloud blockading my way until there was no path but forward. It stuck to my clothes and inside my nose, and I kept smiling. The perfect guest. *Would you really think little old me would snoop through your belongings the moment your back is turned? Not if I pour this scotch into a heavy glass and serve it happily!*

"Game just started and we're already down by one," Mr. Mitchell tapped his ashes into a glass tray. "Can you believe it?"

Henry shook his head. "Bunch of bums."

"A buncha bums! That's right. Thank you, Sweetheart." Mr. Mitchell and I traded his beer for the scotch. I put it on the cart and then handed Henry his drink before making my own, which was really an excuse to use the bathroom in a few minutes.

That, and, if my hands were busy, I couldn't strangle anyone for calling me "Sweetheart." *Sweetheart.* Of all the degrading, demeaning nicknames and—

"Sweetheart, could you add some ice, please? I thought I said I wanted this on the rocks."

He had not said he wanted it on the rocks. But I apologized anyway, took his glass back to the bar, and added a few ice cubes. "And please," I said, "call me *Evelyn*."

"Thank you, Evelyn." He sipped his drink while watching baseball on the TV. "It is nice to have a woman's touch around the house again."

I highly doubted his wife was even buried yet, but I smiled and nodded and sat down next to Henry. He reached over and gave my knee a squeeze in solidarity.

This was going to be a long baseball game. And I was remembering one time when I'd attended a game my boyfriend was pitching, only to find his wife already in my seat.

★ ★ ★

I sipped at my drink, carefully sneaking some of it into the base of a nearby potted plant when Mr. Mitchell was wrapped up in the game. After an inning and a half, I asked him where the powder room was.

Mr. Mitchell lit a new cigar. "Down the hall and to the right. Door should be open."

"Thank you ever so." I threw Henry a glance over my shoulder.

He cleared his throat and, when I was no longer in the doorway, said, "You'll have to excuse her. She dated the pitcher."

"Really? Huh. My wife and his wife were friends."

"Right. Yeah, well, that's why they aren't dating anymore."

There was a long pause before Mr. Mitchell went, "Oh!" and barked out a laugh. "What a *dog*. Good for him!"

I shuddered in revulsion and tiptoed down the hall. Hopefully that excuse gave me a few extra minutes beyond what he'd reasonably expect. I did go into the bathroom, making a big show of shutting the door. After checking my hair in the mirror, I opened the hidden door in the medicine cabinet. There was a toothbrush, a half-used tube of toothpaste, an almost empty jar of Pond's cold cream, and a pink moisturizer from Oil of Olay.

Hmm. No Erno Laszlo. Maybe she kept it in the master bathroom? There was no makeup here either, and Mrs. Mitchell had been wearing rouge, lipstick, and false lashes at the lunch, where she died. In my hotel. She fell right into my lap, and her husband was drinking and smoking cigars and watching one of my exes play *baseball*.

Poor Lois Mitchell. Married to a man like that. I'd positively haunt my husband if he were half as cavalier before I'd even been entombed.

Carefully, I cracked the door open and crept down the hall. One door was locked, and after hearing both men cheer from the living room, I decided to come back to it later. The next door was open. A bedroom. A guest bedroom, by the looks of it, the lone bed surrounded by boxes that said "Ladies Love to Sparkle" on the sides. I opened one, unsurprised to find costume jewelry inside. As quickly and quietly as I could, I hurried up the stairs. There were more rooms up here, all of them unlocked. One of them was the master bedroom. Two massive dogs were lounging in it, spread out on the king-sized bed in such a way as to make the mattress look tiny.

The raised their heads and looked at me, their big eyes drooping.

"Oh, little babies," I cooed quietly. I let them sniff my fingers and then scratched behind their ears. "What good boys you are. I'll get out of your way in a minute, I promise."

That promise received a long, wet lick from one of the dogs, so I assumed I was given permission and resumed my snooping. Mrs. Mitchell's vanity was covered in cosmetics and skin-care products. I took half a second to look them over, and while I didn't see a single thing from Erno Laszlo, Lois had been a voracious user of brands across the board.

I needed to get to the locked room, and quick. Down the stairs, I peeked into the living room. Henry noticed me. Mr. Mitchell was half asleep in his armchair, his face flushed from the alcohol, the cigar end smooshed in the center of the ashtray.

Henry raised his eyebrows.

I shook my head.

He nodded, and I took that to mean that I still had a few minutes before we had an issue with my timing. My lockpicking kit—well, the lockpicking kit that Mac had given me, but I was no longer thinking about Mac—was hidden safely in my longline bra. Perhaps too safely. It took a least a minute to retrieve it. But once I had it, opening the lock took no time at all.

I exhaled, proud of myself. The first time I'd picked a lock it had taken forever, and I had been a sweaty mess in the end. Isn't it funny how, once you do one hard thing, the next time you have to do the same hard thing, it isn't as hard?

"Like leaving the hotel," I could hear Dr. Sanders say. I ignored her voice inside my head and moved into the only locked room in the house. An office. Judging by the massive mahogany desk and football paraphernalia, I judged it to be Mr. Mitchell's own. Why did he need an office when he was a retired athlete, and his wife ran a business?

She'd had the spare downstairs bedroom, I suppose. Maybe they'd shared the desk. On top was a large black leather book. I opened it up and found their banking information. While the Mitchells weren't poorly off, they certainly weren't pulling in Daddy's numbers. Mr. Mitchell had a small payout every month, whether it came from football retirement or investments I wasn't sure, but Mrs. Mitchell was bringing in more every month. The amount fluctuated, from one hundred to four hundred dollars, but it was more than Mr. Mitchell's income. I rifled through the drawers. At first there wasn't much but unanswered correspondence, some fan mail of Mr. Mitchell's, a list of ladies' names—some either crossed out or with a diamond next to them. There were far fewer with the doodled diamonds than those crossed out. Both Ruth and Veronica were crossed out, whereas Prudence had a diamond.

In the bottom drawer, on the very top, was Mrs. Mitchell's life insurance policy.

The payout was such that even if she only earned her smallest amount every month, she would earn more in six months than the life insurance would pay.

There goes money as the reason, I thought. What were the three that Hodgson had listed that were really six? Lust, love, revenge, money, true belief . . . oh, and to hide evidence. What reason could Mr. Mitchell have to kill his wife if not for money? Did he have a secret lover? Had Mrs. Mitchell?

Footsteps padded down the stairs. I pocketed the paper with the list of women's names and hurried out of the office, locking it behind me.

The housekeeper caught me with my fingers on the doorknob. She walked off the last step, brow furrowed, her lips between her teeth.

"Miss Murphy?" she whispered. "Were you in Mr. Mitchell's office?"

Direct questions were the worst. Lying made my tongue expand in my throat and my nose itch. "Well, I needed to use the bathroom."

She took my hands. Hers were warm and calloused, and they held mine tight. "Miss Murphy, you help people. Right? People who . . . people who have been killed?"

"I don't know if I *help* them," I said. "After all, they're dead. But I've had some luck recently in finding murderers, if that's what you're getting at."

She looked over her shoulder and then, in an even quieter whisper, asked, "May I speak with you tomorrow? It's my off day."

I glanced at the living room door. Henry and Mr. Mitchell were talking in low voices. "Are you in danger?"

"No. Not me. Please. Will you speak with me tomorrow?"

This was incredible luck. An inside scoop, so to speak, into the domestic life of the Mitchells. *Take that, Dottie.* "Yes. Of course. Come to the hotel and ask for me at the desk. I'll be around."

She squeezed my fingers, flashed a smile, and then released me.

When I made it back to the living room, Mr. Mitchell's half-lidded eyes dragged away from the screen and to my face. I grimaced performatively and held my stomach. "I am so sorry, darling, but I'm not feeling well."

Henry groaned as he stood. "My good man, it was nice to watch at least part of the game with you. But you know how women are these days."

"Of course." He waved a lazy hand. "Gotta get her home safe and sound. Safe and sound, Sweetheart."

He sounded almost as drunk as Poppy and I had been the other night.

"I'm sorry for ending your fun early."

He shrugged a shoulder. "Wasn't much fun, to be honest."

Henry shook his hand, the other man never even rising from his seat, before taking me by the arm and assisting me toward the entrance.

"Did you find anything?" he whispered.

I nodded. "I'll tell you about it in the car. Do you think Small Tommy stayed close?"

"Sure, he's a professional. Here—our coats." He opened the hall closet and pulled mine out first, draping it over my shoulders, before reaching for his own. While he busied himself with his winter gear, I let my fingertips trail over the practically brand-new Dior coat Mrs. Mitchell would never wear again.

There was a lump in the pocket. I reached in and pulled out a red pocket square.

Chapter 30

Henry gasped. A deep throated, warbly gasp.
"Shh!" I shushed.

He pressed his lips shut tight and nodded. I pocketed the piece of fabric, storing it safely with my stolen paperwork, and the two of us quickly hightailed it out of the Mitchells' home. Small Tommy was waiting for us at the curb. He opened the door so we could slide into the back of the Rolls.

"Did you see the outfit in the closet?" Henry asked me. "Was it the same one the man who tried to rob you was wearing?"

"Oh." I wrinkled my nose and attempted to picture both outfits. Were they the same? They were similar. What I'd noticed most was the way the Gentleman Thief wagged his fingers at me, studied me, blew me a kiss. What had his outfit been? "The robbery was—"

Small Tommy opened the driver door and slid inside.

Henry nudged me and mouthed, "Shh!"

I glared at him but obeyed. He was right. We didn't need more ears on this than necessary. Accusing a man of Mr. Mitchell's caliber was gossip big enough to spread like wildfire throughout the employees of the Pinnacle. Simply because I had never heard of him didn't mean that no one had, and even if he was completely unknown to all, who could resist listening to information that followed the question, "Did you hear about the Gentleman Thief?"

"*He ate in our hotel with the owner's daughter, he did!*" they'd say.

"*Yeah, and that was after his wife collapsed right into Miss Murphy's lap!*" someone else would offer up.

Besides, as I was about to say to Henry, I had my own suspicions about who the thief was, and he was way closer to the Pinnacle than I cared to admit. It would look terrible in the paper if I was right. *Especially* if I was right. An employee of the Pinnacle using his position to pick targets? Dottie would spin it into somehow being my fault. Like I created the thief out of my own boredom.

She'd be wrong, of course. Murder was so much more interesting than theft. Both were more interesting than galas, and—*oh no*! When was the gala? In two days?

Oh, golly. Thank God for Poppy. Had my analyst advised that throwing a gala for the benefit of others would be beneficial to me in my time of grief? Yes. But it was Poppy who had really run with it, so I could keep right on pouting. It was why I paid her so well.

I didn't even know the cause the gala was supposed to benefit. The pets of hungry children or something. Probably wouldn't be something to brag to my analyst about, come to think of it.

We made it to the Pinnacle and hurried up to my room. The man I suspected was the thief was nowhere to be seen, or at least wasn't in the lift that took us to the top floor. Suspicious? Or simply part of his job?

Presley spun around in circles when I walked through the door, before launching himself at my shins. Henry's energy was similar, as he locked the door and immediately burst into speech. I scooped Presley up in my arms and tried to decipher the words Henry was saying between his shallow breaths.

"And did you see the ski mask? Was the thief wearing a ski mask? I can't believe this—I know him! I know him, and he's stealing things from rich people! Like Robin Hood!" He gasped again, that deep, warbly sound. "Like Robin Hood!"

"Henry, darling, please." Presley licked my chin. "Whoever is stealing from the rich is nothing like Robin Hood. Robin gave back to the poor in his community, remember?"

"Who's to say that the thief isn't doing just that?" Henry bopped my nose before collapsing on the couch. I kept standing, facing him, because if I sat down, it would be the coffee table and its occupants in my line of sight.

Monroe came over and wound herself around my ankles, but when I set Presley down to pet her, she slunk away. "Then why would he rob me? When I'm about to throw a gala to help the poor or whoever it is for—I don't remember. Wounded soldiers?"

Henry shrugged, not knowing the cause or recipients of my benefit gala either. "Perhaps it's because you're the richest person in Manhattan currently? Unless Mr. Rockefeller is in town, I suppose."

"The Vanderbilts are here for the holidays," I said dismissively, waving my hand. "I'm down on the list until they summer in the French Riviera. That's only if you're not counting Daddy's money, of course."

He hummed in sarcastic empathy. "Of course."

"While I admit that Mr. Mitchell having a ski mask in his front closet and his deceased wife having a red pocket square in her coat is interesting—"

"He's also about the same build as the Gentleman Thief, don't forget. And you'd have to be athletic to do the kinds of things he does to break into people's homes."

I glared at him without heat and kept going. "The ski mask was next to a set of skis, so maybe, just maybe, he likes to ski. Being that he is athletic."

Henry rolled his eyes.

"Besides, I have a pretty good suspect for the Gentleman Thief."

He sat up, annoyance replaced by intense interest on his movie-star face. "Let's hear it. Who is it?"

Clapping my hands together, I took a deep breath, rolled back my shoulders, and readied myself for the big reveal. "Russell Castillo."

Now there was only confusion on his face. "Who?"

"Russell? Russell Castillo?"

Henry shook his head.

"Poppy's current beau? The lift boy!"

"Oh!" Henry chuckled. "I call him 'Cute Tattoos' in my mind."

I bobbed my head from side to side. A fairly accurate nickname, all things considered. "He's the right height and build, sure. But not only that, he witnessed Mrs. Taylor showing me the new bracelet she got for her anniversary, and that very night that bracelet was stolen from their home."

"That could be a coincidence," Henry said. "Same as the skis and the ski mask in Mitchell's closet, though I think the man's pocket square in Mrs. Mitchell's coat is a really big clue, and I don't know why you don't think so."

"Because why would it be in *her* coat if her husband was the thief? Does she carry them around for him? It's more likely she was having an affair that—oh!" It was my turn to gasp. "That would be motive for Mr. Mitchell to kill her."

"So now you think he's the murderer?"

"I don't know!" I forgot about everything else for a moment and sat on the couch next to him, my mother's journals making themselves known instantly. I grabbed a pillow and held it over my face. "I find lots of strange items, Henry," I said. "Sometimes I put murder weapons in my pocket. That doesn't mean that I'm a murderer or having an affair. Not that I have anyone in my life I could betray."

Henry wrapped his arm around my shoulder and kissed my temple. "You will."

I huffed out a laugh. "That isn't the only reason I have to suspect Russell."

"Who?"

"'Cute Tattoos.' The night I was almost robbed? Poppy and I invited him back here to have cake with us, and he refused and wouldn't tell us why."

"I'm new at this sleuthing thing, darling, but that doesn't seem like a clue to me."

"No, it isn't. But it is suspicious. And when you have enough suspicious things, you can add them together and make a clue."

Henry's brow furrowed. "Is that true?"

"Doesn't matter if it's true—it's what happens."

He blew out a breath between puffed lips. "I wonder what your lawyer friend would think of that statement."

"Oh." I placed a hand on my forehead dramatically, as the situation called for drama. "I forgot to call him and thank him for the flowers. He sent me those flowers." I pointed at the bouquet on my dining table. "Aren't they lovely? He got called away early from our date, and you'll never guess who called him."

"Cute Tattoos?"

"No! Colin Sharpe."

Henry sat back, aghast. "Colin needed a lawyer?"

"No! No, he faked an emergency that required Mr. Feretti's immediate attention so that *he* could spend time with me instead."

Henry nodded, a smile tugging at the corners of his lips. "That's sort of adorable, darling."

"No, it isn't," I lied. "He even pretended to confuse Poppy and me, pretended like he thought she was the owner's daughter. Pretended to like her and not even notice me, just to get my attention! It's sneaky and underhanded."

"Which is why you like it." He gently tugged on my hair. "If he was a perfectly fine, upstanding man, like your lawyer, you wouldn't be interested."

I rubbed my eyes and left my hands on my face, my cool palms a relief against my warm cheeks. "What is wrong with me? I only like men who are bad for me. And I can't find happiness organizing a fundraiser for people in need, but only in snooping around and solving murders."

"You're entirely too close to your dog," Henry added. "You only wear designer clothing, and typically only once. You refuse to admit that your true shoe size is half a size bigger than you buy. You continue to wear purple, even though it both washes you out and makes you look like you haven't slept in days."

My tongue pushed against my cheek. "Are you done?"

Henry opened his mouth as if to continue, but then he saw my expression and nodded instead.

"I'm going to go take a bath," I announced. When I stood, I tossed a pillow at his head. "And you are going to leave. I'll see you at the gala on Sunday. Wear a purple tie," I said, "because I intend on wearing a purple designer gown."

Henry wisely kept his mouth closed.

Chapter 31

The next morning, I handed Presley over to a jumpy Mr. Mullins. I don't know why he was so afraid of my little dog. Sure, he bit Mullins's ankles whenever he had the chance, but they were such small teeth! Presley rarely ever drew blood.

Hodgson was eating at the café. He waved me over to his usual table when I spotted him. We hadn't planned on meeting, but it wasn't exactly an unusual occurrence. The man had a *usual* table, after all.

"Glad you're here, Murphy."

"Uh-oh. Why?"

"I heard from the lab last night." He wiped his napkin over his face, his omelet more than half gone. "What I'm sure will come as no surprise to you, given how often it happens—twice, if I'm not mistaken, in a matter of weeks too—but *your* fingerprints were found on the bottle containing shrimp stock."

I licked my teeth. "Wonderful. Now—"

"Not done." He held up a finger while he guzzled down the rest of his coffee.

"You don't need to eat or drink this fast," I said. "I'm not paying you by the hour. You're salaried, Hodgson."

He glared at me over his mug and, if anything, drank it faster. "There was a second fingerprint not belonging to you on the very bottom of the bottle. They haven't been able to match it to anyone yet."

I nodded. That was something, at least.

"Last bit. Shrimp stock residue was found in the champagne glass, not in the salad. Which means it wasn't in the strawberries either."

I sighed in relief. "Thank goodness. She *was* murdered, then."

"That's . . . good?"

"It proves Marco didn't kill her by accident, so, yes. Considering the alternative, good. But also, terrible." I scrunched my eyes closed, feeling a throbbing headache beginning to form in the middle of my forehead. "I should've saved all the champagne glasses, and not just hers."

"Yeah." He ate the last of his meal. "You should've. Then we could've known if it was only in her glass or not. Guess that's why it's best to save the police work for the actual police, hmm?"

"The actual police think this was an accident."

He shook his head. "Not anymore. Not since the results came back. They're now investigating it as a homicide."

Another sigh of relief had my headache easing. "Good. That's good. I'm meeting with Mr. Mitchell's housekeeper today, which I'm sure will make you happy."

"You still don't think he did it?"

"I don't know. It sure seems like Mrs. Mitchell promised those women a lot for their money, and they'd yet to earn a penny back. Worse, they've gone backward. But I did *not* enjoy being in his presence yesterday."

"Why were you with Mr. Mitchell yesterday?"

I filled Hodgson in on the adventure Henry and I had both had watching what turned out to be a baseball game. I left out the part about how the pitcher was once known to me on a personal level. "I found this," I said, and from my handbag pulled out the documents I'd stolen from Mr. Mitchell's desk. "I intend to ask the housekeeper about it."

"What do these diamonds mean?"

"That's what I plan on asking about," I said. "Only one of the Ladies Love to Sparkle women I've interviewed has the diamond next to her name. The other two are crossed out."

Hodgson said, "Huh."

"That's not all." I then told him what I'd seen on Mrs. Mitchell's life insurance policy.

"It's not a lot," he admitted, "but I've seen people killed for less."

A bleak statement. "I got a look at their bank accounts, though, Hodgson. She was bringing in at least one hundred dollars a month, sometimes up to four. She made more in a year than the life insurance paid out. I don't know much about how regular people live, but more money is better than less money, isn't it?"

"As a general rule of thumb, yeah." He handed the papers back. "There must be some other reason, then. A mistress. Maybe she had a boyfriend."

My nose wrinkled. "Actually. That . . . hmm."

"What?"

I scooted my chair closer to his and leaned in close, my voice dropping to a whisper. "Henry and I found a red pocket square in Mrs. Mitchell's coat pocket. Not unlike the one the Gentleman Thief leaves behind. Henry surmised that Mr. Mitchell might be the thief."

"And what? He killed his wife because she found out who he was?"

"That's one theory. But what if Mrs. Mitchell had been dating the Gentleman Thief?" The thought of Russell Castillo and Lois Mitchell together crossed my mind's eye. They weren't a very good match, but I could see how a wealthy older woman might attract a handsome young man looking to heist jewels. "Or at least maybe she was interested in him? And Mr. Mitchell simply snapped. As far as one can snap while executing a complicated murder like the one we're suggesting he pulled off."

"Yeah, usually in that instance it's strangulation as a cause of death. But maybe this guy is smart. Calculating. How did he seem to you last night?"

"Drunk. And a bit of a Neanderthal."

Hodgson sat away from me and waved over a waiter. I requested my usual and, once I had my cappuccino in front of me, told Hodgson about my suspicions regarding Poppy's newest boyfriend.

"That is suspicious," he said. "He won't even tell Miss Cooper what he's up to?"

"Not a word."

He tapped his index finger on the table over and over, his eyes narrowed at the middle distance. "It's probably another dame. Miss Cooper seems to have a problem with only dating men who, uh . . . well. You remember."

I stuck my tongue out in disgust. Not long ago, Hodgson and I had walked in on Poppy's ex beau canoodling with the shop attendant here in my very own hotel. It had been a memorable sight, the same way it's easier to recall nightmares than regular, or even happy, dreams.

"The simplest answer is often the correct one, is that right?"

Hodgson nodded. "Exactly."

The Mitchells' housekeeper wandered into the lobby with a dazed look on her face, her wide eyes slowly taking in the scene around her while her fingers twisted around one another nervously. I waved, but she didn't respond. She seemed to be noticing everything, which was keeping her from noticing anything.

Hodgson turned to see what I was waving at, and then tossed his napkin on the table. "Let me know what you learn. I'll be in my office. I've almost got it completely un-trapped, by the way."

I arched an eyebrow. I highly doubted that.

"I'm still waiting on those journals, Murphy."

"I know." I finished my cappuccino. "You'll get them."

Chapter 32

After tipping the waiter, I approached the Mitchells' housekeeper. She noticed me, finally, and her awed expression changed into one of relief. I held out my hand. "Please, forgive me, I don't believe I caught your name yesterday."

"It's Susan. Susan Beyers. Thank you for meeting with me."

"Of course." I was delighted she had offered. Most of the time I had to trick people into talking to me. About murder, I mean. "Are you hungry? Do you want coffee?"

She shook her head. "I had breakfast already, thanks. And I don't think I'll be here very long."

"All right. Here." I led her over to an empty couch near the bank of pay phones. None were currently in use, so we had the area to ourselves. "Have a seat."

We sat together, side by side, and she took a deep breath. "I don't know what to say."

"Well. I suppose we should start with what you wanted to tell me last night."

"I'm worried about Mr. Mitchell."

I patted Susan on the hand. "Of course. He just lost his wife."

"No. I mean, yes, right. But his drinking. It's . . . it's gotten out of hand. He doesn't stop except when he sleeps. I'm worried he'll kill himself if he keeps going at this rate."

With a furrowed brow, I assessed the housekeeper. She was dressed modestly, in a sensible gray dress that covered her from throat to feet, a black overcoat, thick black gloves. Her hair was neatly brushed and styled, and though she didn't wear makeup, her face was bright, and her eyes were keen. She didn't seem the type to make up stories out of a longing for dramatics to unfold around her. "I see. He was rather . . . overserved when I was there yesterday. Has he always been like that, or is it just since Mrs. Mitchell's unfortunate passing?"

She shook her head. "He's always been a drinker, but never a drunkard. It used to bother Mrs. Mitchell."

My nose wrinkled. I noticed it and tried to straighten it. The stupid thing has a mind of its own whenever my mind is working on being smart. "Did they argue a lot?"

"I don't know what you mean by 'a lot.' They never shouted, Miss Murphy. Nothing ever got broken. Nobody ever got hit. I'd worked for families like that before, where you walk around on eggshells, nervous all the time, because the mister was an angry drunk or the mother got mad if the child wet the bed. The Mitchells were nothing like those families. But sometimes I'd walk into a room to clean something up or bring them the mail, and there'd be this . . . tension in the air, you understand?"

I nodded. "Were the moments of tension always related to his drinking?"

"No. He didn't like the way she spent money. Well, she'd laugh and say she'd earned it, she could do with it what she wanted. And then he'd laugh and poor himself a drink and say that it was his body, and he could put it in what he wants. Then"—she shrugged and held out empty palms—"they'd be right as rain for a while. No more tension."

"Hmm." I still wasn't sure why Susan had felt the need to tell me about this, but asking outright seemed ill-mannered. "Do you think that Mr. Mitchell would be capable of hurting Mrs. Mitchell?"

She hesitated before answering. "He isn't an angry man, Miss Murphy."

And that wasn't really an answer to my question. "Is that why you wanted to see me? Are you worried about the police focusing on him?"

"The police?" Her eyes went round. "No, I'm not worried about that. Or else, I wasn't until now. I thought her death was an accident."

"The last I heard, the police were looking into the possibility of foul play."

"Oh no." She closed her eyes and made the sign of the cross. "Oh, poor Mrs. Mitchell. She never hurt anybody."

I had a list in my pocket that suggested otherwise. I pulled it out and showed it to Susan. "Can you tell me a little about the markings? What do the diamonds mean?"

If she had any problem with the fact that I'd essentially stolen her employer's property, she didn't make it known. She looked over the list and handed it back. "It's like a promotion. If you've moved enough product, you become a Diamond Leader."

"So, the people who have diamonds have sold a lot of Ladies Love to Sparkle jewelry?"

She nodded. "Or they bought a lot. Mrs. Mitchell had a couple ladies like that. They buy a lot of jewelry to sell later, and simply buying enough can make you a Diamond Leader. Some women buy a lot for that reason."

"Why? What happens when you become a Diamond Leader?"

"You get further up the ladder," she said. "The whole system is set up like a ladder, and the higher you get, the more money you make."

Prudence had a diamond sketched next to her name. But when I'd spoken to her, it sounded like she hadn't made any money yet. "How high up the ladder do you have to be before you start earning money?"

"I don't know," Susan said. "Whatever rung Mrs. Mitchell was on was good, though. She made a lot of money."

And she spent a lot of it too, if what Susan said about the arguments the Mitchells had were true. "Do you know if either of them ever entertained friends of the opposite sex?"

"You mean, like, an affair?" Susan looked as if I had suggested she was the one cheating on a spouse. "Never a hint of that from either of them, Miss Murphy. No, ma'am. They had friends over for dinners, stuff like that, but always in even pairs."

I did my best to smile. "Thank you ever so for your help, Susan."

"Of course," she said. "And if you need anything else, don't hesitate to ring. The sooner this is solved, the sooner Mr. Mitchell may find peace and put the bottle down. I like my job, Miss Murphy. The pay is good, and the hours are better. I won't be able to do it if both of them are dead."

Chapter 33

The conversation with Susan answered some of my questions but raised more. Prudence was a Diamond Leader, but she had bought herself that rank, so it didn't exactly erase her from my suspect list. If anything, it only made me underline her name. She'd spent more than the other ladies. But Ruth's husband hated Lois Mitchell, disliked the entire business. He seemed a far more likely candidate than Ruth, but if it was him, wouldn't Ruth have said something? Wouldn't she have noticed her husband was the Jim passing out the champagne? Had they been in on it together? I didn't know enough about Veronica. I needed to fix that as soon as possible.

Mrs. Mitchell's Ladies Love to Sparkle list of had more women than the three she'd brought with her to lunch at the Pinnacle. Could one of them have broken in, spiked her champagne, and left before I'd seen her? But, no. The waiters were men, as well as the cooks. Unless she was very heavily disguised, it had either happened at the table, or a Jim had done it.

Wouldn't Mrs. Mitchell have recognized her husband? Had he stayed in the kitchen and sent out the champagne? But then, how had the murder weapon ended up in the Gold Room?

My head ached. I walked into the elevator with a nod toward the lift boy and then winced, pressing my fingers to my temples. I should go and talk this out with Hodgson, but I didn't want to. I didn't want to talk to anyone. I wanted to take a hot bath, put on my silkiest pajamas, order room service, and read a Christie novel with my cat on my lap and my dog at my side.

Poirot would've figured it out by now. So would have Marple. Marple would be twinkling, saying how Mr. Mitchell reminded her of so and so from the village, and oh, that Ruth, she was just like the butcher's wife who did such and such. I spent a lot of my time observing people. I knew that the most likely candidate was Lois's husband, but I also knew that money—or the lack of it—was a great motivator for murder. Revenge, in this case, instead of greed.

It had to be revenge because killing her didn't give anybody more money. Not Ruth, Veronica, Prudence, or even Mr. Mitchell.

Unfortunately for my plans, Poppy was pacing in my suite. She reminded me so much of her brother at that moment that my heart burned. I swallowed hard, took a deep breath, and headed to the kitchen for some water.

"Poppy, are you well?" I filled a glass in the sink. "Last-minute gala preparations stressing you? Worry not. I'm great at details when I set my mind to it. I'll order us something yummy from the kitchen and—"

"I would love for you to plan your own party, Evelyn—that would be wonderful, but that is not why I'm upset!" She hovered in the doorway, her eyes narrowed and her hair wild. "I'm upset because Russell didn't come to work today."

"Ah." I frowned politely before sipping at my water. "He isn't the most reliable individual, is he?"

Her mouth and eyes formed three perfect *o*'s. "'The most'?" she repeated, her voice trailing off. "Are you loony? I've always known you were rather shambolic, Evelyn, but I put that down to eccentricity and not to being positively off your rocker!"

I didn't know what some of those words meant, but I knew enough of them to know I was being insulted. I covered my heart with my free hand. "I beg your pardon?"

"You ran him off!"

"What are you talking about?" I brushed past her into the living room. Presley was waiting for me, his body wagging with the force of his happy tail. "It isn't my fault he doesn't show up when we invite him to spend time with us. Just like it isn't my fault that he witnessed the Taylors tell me about their new purchase and then the very same night, when we don't know where he is because he won't tell us, they're robbed."

Poppy stomped after me. "You always do this, Evelyn! You think the worst of the boys I date. You thought Burrows could be a killer, for god's sake!"

I scooped Presley up and held him close. "I was wrong that he could be a killer, but he was a philanderer, which is a memory I will take with me to the grave, unfortunately."

She tugged at her hair. "You weren't even the least bit interested in Colin Sharpe until he expressed interest in *me*!"

"It wasn't so much that he expressed interest in you, darling. That's only natural. You're young and gorgeous. It's that he thought I wasn't who I am."

Poppy continued on as if I hadn't spoken. "And now you think Russell, my Russell, could be a *thief*?"

"I merely found his behavior suspicious and asked him to explain himself, which he would not do. I hardly ran him off. I certainly didn't fire him."

"You told him he wasn't good enough for me, and you'd do everything in your power to make sure I knew it."

I flinched, embarrassed. "Did I say that? Are you sure? Those exact words?"

"It doesn't matter what the exact words are, Evelyn. You think he's the thief, don't you? The one that's been in the papers?"

"I think it's a possibility, yes. And if it's not that, then it's something else. He's clearly up to something, Poppy—you must see it. If he isn't the thief, he's got a girlfriend. Or a wife. You must be very careful about wives, you know."

Poppy ran her tongue over her teeth. "That's how it is, is it? If he's interested in me, then something is wrong with him. Is that right?"

"That's not what—"

"You said, if it's not that, it's something else. Didn't you?" She curled her hands into fists at her side. "I can't believe that you're this selfish, Evelyn. I really can't."

She delivered that dagger straight to the heart before leaving my suite without so much as a look back. The glass of water trembled in my hand. Selfish? Me? Sure, I've been known to bouts of selfishness. But I'd been working on it. Getting better. Doing my best to learn about the people who work in my father's hotel beyond how they serve me. I was *trying*. And maybe I was focused on my grief over losing a relationship that I'd thought would last for the rest of my life, or on solving the murder of the woman who'd been poisoned in front of me. But I was improving.

I was. I knew I was.

Wasn't I?

I was afraid to call Henry, unsure whose side he would take now that he and Poppy were such good friends. And I just knew

Hodgson would only sigh and cover his eyes and say, *"Murphy"* in that disappointed way of his. I didn't have anyone else. Not really. Not since Mac left.

Presley followed me to the couch. I sat down, unblinking, my eyes burning. It wasn't until Presley jumped onto my lap that I realized I was still holding a now empty glass. The water had done nothing to settle my insides. I placed it on the coffee table, next to the box that contained my mother's journals.

I stared at them as tears filled my eyes, clouded my vision. They beaded on my lashes before a blink sent them spilling down my cheeks.

I reached for the nearest journal and opened it up to the first page.

My mother had written my name in her perfect, swirling cursive handwriting.

The dam broke. I sobbed.

Chapter 34

Reading further proved impossible. Every time I tried to read a page, my eyes welled up with tears and spilled on her words and drawings. With short, painful breaths, I reached for my phone and called the number I was only supposed to use during emergencies.

"Hello?" Dr. Sanders's voice was upbeat and pleasant.

I responded by sobbing directly into the receiver.

"Evelyn," Dr. Sanders said. "Evelyn, take a deep breath, please. There you go. Another one. Hold it in. Now, let it out slowly. Good. Are you calling me because of the death in your hotel or because of the reporter writing negatively about you?"

I wiped my face on my sleeve. "Neither. I'm calling you about my mother."

"Oh!" Dr. Sanders cleared her throat. "Oh. I see. Yes. Okay. Honey"—that last word was not directed at me—"will you take the kids out to play? Anywhere. I need an hour. Evelyn? I'm ready. What . . . what would you like to talk about regarding your mother?"

Sniffling, I told her about my journey, with Hodgson, to the nuns in the mansion and the retrieval of a box full of journals my mother used to write her prayers. "Is that odd, that she wrote her prayers? I've never written a prayer in my life. Is this something I am supposed to be doing?"

"Some people find they focus better on words written instead of words thought," my analyst replied. "Do you want to tell me about the journals?"

"I don't know," I said. "I've only looked at a page. She's got drawings in them too. Birds and flowers. She was talented. Mostly it . . . every time I try to read them, I start crying, and I don't know what to do."

"That is hard." Dr. Sanders hummed. "Mr. Hodgson said he'd read them for you?"

"Yes. And I appreciate that. But these are my mother's and—anyway, I'm very good at finding things."

"That is true," she said. "It sounds like you already know what to do, Evelyn."

I closed my eyes and focused on my breathing, because she was right. I did already know what to do.

"And you left the hotel?"

"Twice," I said. "Twice I left, thank you for asking. It was fine. I survived it, but I didn't like it."

"That's probably what it'll be like reading her journals," Dr. Sanders said. "You won't like it, but you'll survive. How . . . how are you feeling about your clothes, lately?"

I looked down at my outfit. "Fine?"

"I mean, do you remember we talked about how you focus on your appearance because of your anxiety?"

How could I forget? "Yes. I remember. I also said that I don't see the problem with that. It seems like a perfectly healthy way to control at least something in my life."

Dr. Sanders hummed again. I hated those hums. Those hums meant I was wrong, but she wasn't going to tell me I was wrong, because I was supposed to figure that out for myself. "Have you ever thought about letting your hair grow out into its natural color?"

I moved the receiver away from my face so I could stare at it belligerently. "I beg your pardon?" I asked the device in my hand. Huffing, I stood up, spun around, sat back down again, the cord tangling around my middle. I stood up and spun the other direction to free myself. "Are you . . . what? And what else should I let go into its natural state? Should I stop wearing bras? Should I stop wearing girdles? Should the Pinnacle fire the staff and hire monkeys instead?"

"It was only a question." Dr. Sanders had a smile in her voice. "One you've answered quite definitively. Was there anything else you wanted to talk about, Evelyn?"

There were plenty of things that sprang to mind, chiefly among them the fight I'd had with Poppy. But that would involve having to tell my analyst I was wrong about something, and I didn't need to hear any more of her hums or ridiculous questions anytime soon.

Fortunately, I was spared from lying by a knock on the door. "I am sorry, Dr. Sanders, but someone is here."

"All right. We have a meeting next week."

I rolled my eyes. I hated in-person meetings with Dr. Sanders. And now that I'd left the hotel on murder business, she'd ask me why I couldn't leave it to see her, and then I'd either have to lie or tell the truth, and neither of those options was great when talking to Dr. Sanders. "See you then."

★ ★ ★

"One moment!" I called to the visitor, taking a second in the kitchen to splash water on my face. Presley thought this was also a good idea and began to splash around in his water bowl.

Saying his name in a disapproving tone did nothing to hinder his good time, so I picked him up and took him with me to the door.

Veronica waited in the hallway, looking very small in an oversized coat.

What luck! I needed to meet with her again, and here she was. I was getting good at this investigating thing. "Veronica, hello. Good to see you. Are you by yourself?"

She nodded, dimples popping around her smile. "I hope this isn't a bad time?"

"Not at all. Do come in."

She scurried inside, eyes wide, blinking as she took in my suite for the second time. It was unchanged since she had been here before, so I wasn't sure why she was in such awe. Setting Presley down, I offered to take her coat.

"My assistant isn't here right now," I said. "If you'd like something to drink, I could call room service."

"I'm fine, thank you."

Splashing noises came from the kitchen.

I smiled anyway. "Shall we sit?"

Veronica nodded and rushed to the couch, then hesitated. I sat down and patted the spot next to me. She perched herself on the edge of the cushion.

"Veronica? Are you all right?"

"Yes, sorry. Nervous." She chewed on her bottom lip. "I'm trying to be brave."

Was she going to confess to Lois's murder? Wow. Solving crimes kept getting easier and easier.

She closed her eyes, took a deep breath, and then came out with it. "I'd like you to join my team!"

That was not the "confession" I was expecting.

"I'm sorry. What?"

"My Ladies Love to Sparkle team." She opened her eyes and smiled wide, dimples popping. "Miss Murphy—Evelyn. You'd be marvelous at selling our jewelry, and I just know—I just *know* I could be a mentor to you in this business. I could teach you how to sell."

As a general rule of thumb, I try my best not to pity people. People don't like to be pitied. Understanding someone is a lot more helpful than pitying them. But I couldn't help the flash of pity that struck me as I sat beside her.

"Really? I thought you and your friends wanted me on all your teams? A joint-effort sort of thing?"

Her smile faltered. "That was the original plan, but I've been giving it some thought, and I think that you would benefit the most from a more one-on-one approach."

"I see." Well. Time to practice lying. I wish I were better at it. Maybe if I was in motion? If I didn't have to look directly at the person? "I'm going to get some water. Are you thirsty?"

"Oh. Uh."

I left the living room, and Veronica shortly followed.

"Water," she said. "Sure. Fine."

While rooting around in the cupboards for two glasses—and not the cupboards that contain my books that Hodgson is so fascinated by—I said, "I'm still thinking about joining, but if I do, I promise, you'll be my first call."

I heard her harsh exhale of relief. "That would be wonderful, Miss Murphy. My husband, he works so much. And having you on my team? He might be able to be home more often."

How would killing Lois give her more time with her husband? Unless it had been done in revenge for Lois not allowing Veronica to earn as much as she'd been promised.

After filling up both glasses at the sink and handing her one, I leaned against the counter and relaxed, my lies completed successfully. "I was wondering about the teams," I said. "Who is in charge of Mrs. Mitchell's team now that she is no longer with us?"

"It reverts to the person who convinced her to join. The owner of Ladies Love to Sparkle."

All the money that Lois earned monthly reverts to the owner? That sounded like motive to me.

"Does the owner live in New York too?"

"No. No, he's in California."

There went the *means* part needed for a viable suspect. "My father is in California right now," I said. *Wouldn't it figure if the two of them were friends?*

"I've never been myself," she said, "but I hear it's lovely."

"There's a Pinnacle Hotel out there as well," I told her. "I haven't been since I was little, and I don't really remember it."

Thinking about the Pinnacle in California made me think about my mother, which made me think about all the journals on my coffee table. "Veronica, I'm so glad you stopped by, but I have a full afternoon."

"Of course." She put her glass in the sink. "Thank you for seeing me."

Presley helped me lead her to the door. "It was my pleasure," I assured her.

Chapter 35

Two journals, a bath, and a cup of tea later, I hadn't found a single clue, but I was feeling better. Reading what my mother had written about her hopes for me, that she'd routinely prayed I would be happy and healthy and know that I was loved, settled my nerves in a way nothing else ever had. One of the journals covered her meeting my father and how she wrestled with whether to encourage his pursuit of her. Whether she was meant to be a nun.

What an odd thought. My mother: a nun. Well, I certainly wouldn't exist if she had chosen that path. She might even be alive right now.

So far, I'd read about my birth, my infancy, and my parents' courtship, in that order. I wasn't sure they would be beneficial to Hodgson in any way, shape, or form, but he wanted to read them all, so I set them aside for him to go through next.

Maybe writing down my thoughts would help me, the same way it had helped my mother. It was worth a shot. I picked up a Pinnacle pad and pencil from beside my living room telephone and made a list.

1. Mr. Mitchell: no discernable motive for killing his wife
2. Prudence: spent the most money with no return on Ladies Love to Sparkle
3. Ruth: no money earned whatsoever
4. Ruth's husband, Nathaniel: the entire endeavor was an embarrassment to him
5. Veronica: needs money the most and is the most desperate to cut her friends out to turn a profit

I held the pencil between my nose and puckered lips, in thought. Should I cross Veronica out? If she needed the money so badly, there was no way she'd kill her mentor. She'd be desperate to tie herself closer to her, if anything. But didn't her coming here alone and trying to recruit me solo show that she was not beyond behaving dubiously?

I exchanged my notes for my tea and puzzled over the murder some more. It was in the champagne—the shrimp was in the champagne. *Why didn't Lois notice? Wouldn't you taste shrimp in your drink? Why did she keep drinking it? Why didn't she ask for another one?*

There was a knock on the door. I had a cup of tea in my hand and Monroe on my slippered feet, so I called, "Come in!"

Poppy walked in.

I almost dropped my cup in surprise. "Didn't expect to see you so soon," I said.

"It's nighttime." She straightened her posture. "And I said I'd stay with you while the thief was out there, didn't I?"

My lips trembled. "You . . . you're not going to leave?"

She crossed her arms tight over her chest and shook her head. "Not today."

"Oh, Poppy!" I stood up so fast Monroe hit the ground on all fours. She meowed and haughtily strode away, but I paid no mind, running over to Poppy, room-temperature tea spilling on to my fingers. I wrapped my arms around her stiff form as best I could. "I'm so, so sorry. You're my friend. I trust your judgment."

I pulled away, wiped my face with the sleeve of my robe. "I trust you. If you say he's innocent, I believe you. Please forgive me."

A smile broke across her face. She brought me into another hug with a laugh on her lips. "That's exactly what I wanted to hear, Evelyn. I forgive you. Now"—she patted my shoulders and stepped back—"wait here one moment, okay? Don't go anywhere."

"Okay."

Poppy left my suite, the door clicking shut behind her. She'd told me I couldn't move, but never said anything about finishing my drink. Which I did. There was a lot less of it after my run from the couch.

The door opened again, and Poppy entered, dragging a blushing Russell Castillo behind her. I set my empty cup down on the nearest table and looked him over. I'd never seen him out of the Pinnacle green. Cute Tattoos was an apt nickname, as he had even more of them on his tan arms, visible now in his white shirt with the sleeves pushed up to his elbows.

"Tell her," Poppy said.

Russell shook his head.

"Go on. You can trust her. She's my best friend. Evelyn, you promise you won't laugh?"

This was quite a promise to make when I had no idea what was about to be presented to me. But she had called me her best friend, and I would've done just about anything she asked. "I promise."

He scratched his forehead, left his hand on top of his head. His eyes were locked on his feet. Presley was there, so maybe he was looking at my dog, who was sniffing his ankles delicately and without all the gruff noises Mullins usually got. "I have a second job. Outside of the hotel, I mean. Way outside."

"I see," I said, though I didn't.

"It's a stable outside of the city, so the trek is a little long, and I end up sleeping out with the horses most of the time, to be honest. It, um . . ."

"You're cleaning horse stalls?" I asked. "This is marvelous news. I have recently come into an inheritance of horses."

"I am not cleaning, no." He grimaced, and his hand traveled to the back of his neck. "I have a particular job. With the, um . . . the male horses."

I looked to Poppy for answers. She had none.

Smiling, I apologized softly. "I don't understand. What is that you do?"

"I work with stud horses." He blurted it out, his tan skin taking on a rosy undertone. "I help the stud horses do their job of getting mares pregnant."

My mouth fell open. I snapped it closed when I felt a giggle form in my throat. With a light cough, I said, "Excuse me one moment," and turned around. Facing my balcony door, I took several deep breaths, in and out, shaking my hands at my sides. I had promised I would not laugh. *I promised. My best friend. She called me her best friend.* I would not laugh. I would not laugh. One last deep breath, and I turned to face them. Russell looked like he wanted the floor to cave in and take him with it, while Poppy was watching me with narrowed eyes, her bottom lip between her teeth.

"Do you like your second job? I only ask because I can put in a good word with the boss for you to be next in line for a promotion and a raise."

"I like working with animals," he said. "I wish I didn't have to travel so far to do it. And the actual job is, uh . . . not my favorite. But I can barely support myself on my pay as a lift boy, let alone—well. Let alone someone else."

It was Poppy's turn to blush. They were pretty early on in their relationship for that sort of future talk, weren't they? But, I supposed, it was better to be prepared for these things then left unaware.

"I'll see what I can do. Thank you for telling me. I apologize for thinking more nefarious activities were taking place."

Poppy beamed at me. She looped her arm through Russell's and popped up on her tiptoes to kiss him on the cheek. He still seemed embarrassed, but less mortified than he had been a minute or so ago.

"How long do horses live, Russell?" I asked. "My mother bequeathed some to me, and I have no idea if they're alive or not."

He shrugged a shoulder. "Maybe thirty years. I heard of one that lived to be fifty, but that doesn't happen too often."

"Really? Thirty years?" I picked up Presley from where he sat between us on the carpet. "My mother's horses might still be alive." I lost myself in thought as I kissed the top of Presley's furry little head. My mother's horses were mine now. They had known her. Would they like me? It was another connection to her that I desperately longed for. Daddy was so stingy with details. Mom had been an only child. I hadn't seen my cousin Martha's parents in years. My father's sister surely knew my mother if she'd inherited all of Mom's clothes, but I'd never asked.

Martha would be here soon, with Mom's clothes in tow. Hopefully she wasn't bringing any jewels with her, what with the thief still on the loose. Her parents were still in Texas, and Martha had moved back home after finishing up her schooling in Arizona. It was kind of her to bring my mother's clothes to me. I'd have to give my aunt a ring and thank her for the opportunity.

I sighed. "I don't know what to do now that you're not the Gentleman Thief. It means he's still out there. Worse, it means that Henry is probably right."

"Right about what?"

"The identity of the thief. It just . . . it makes no sense to me." Hodgson had said it was always the husband. Had Mrs. Mitchell found out that Mr. Mitchell was the thief, and worried she might expose him, had he killed her? He certainly hadn't kill her for money or, according to their housekeeper, for revenge. And Hodgson had said that hiding evidence was a common enough motive for murder.

But it didn't *feel* right. Besides, I still hadn't completely ruled out the women who were working for her either. Something was fishy, and it wasn't only the shrimp stock.

"Two crimes to solve," Poppy tsked. "And a gala to throw. No wonder you're so tired, Evelyn."

I swore. "I forgot about the gala. Tomorrow, is it?"

Poppy nodded, laughing quietly.

Inspiration struck like lightning. A plan straight from the heavens and into my brain. "We have to invite them! All the suspects! The three women and Mr. Mitchell!"

"Where? To the gala?"

I started pacing, my mind going faster than my mouth. "I found the murder weapon, didn't I? And no one knows it yet. It wasn't in the papers. I'll tell them all that I've found it and that it's safe in Hodgson's office. And whoever tries to steal it back is the guilty party. And if it is Mr. Mitchell, like everyone seems to think it is, and he *is* the Gentleman Thief, well, he won't be able to resist sneaking into room 1313."

Russell shook his head, deep frown lines appearing on his forehead. "Oh no, Miss Murphy. That room is *haunted*."

I winked at him. "Exactly."

Chapter 36

My purple gown was stunning. Absolutely breathtaking. From Balenciaga, it was a royal-purple floral lace pattern, with a high–low skirt that showed my legs yet trailed dramatically behind me, three-quarter-length sleeves, a high neckline, and a dangerously low back. I paired it with nude hose, black gloves, and black stiletto pumps and admired myself.

It did wash me out a bit.

But I was in this too far to admit Henry was right, darn him. Darn all men while we were at it. I doubled up on foundation under my eyes to hide the purple parts and rouged my cheeks. Vaseline went on the cheekbones and on top of white eyeshadow to add sparkle. I darkened my eyebrows and applied a full set of false lashes—something I did not often do because I didn't like the feel of them—because I'd invited Dottie from the paper, and I wanted to be camera ready. My lips were red, of course, and this was my favorite part of the process, because I borrowed it from Marilyn the best I knew how. I lined them in red first. Used a darker shade of red on the edges and a lighter shade of red in the middle before adding a touch of Vaseline directly in the center.

My hair was last. I was still stinging a bit from my conversation with Dr. Sanders and frowned at my perfectly bleached roots. Just because I took great care in my appearance to assuage my anxiety didn't make it a bad thing. She hadn't said that it was bad, of course, but she'd suggested I stop paying so much attention to my appearance. The nerve of some people, I swear. And where did she get off offering that kind of advice? Because I pay her? Ridiculous.

My mother had been a natural blonde. That was part of the reason why I'd started using peroxide on my hair all those years ago. I didn't want to look as much like my father as I do. I wanted something of my mother to cling to. Dr. Sanders was right, and my appearance was something I could control in an uncontrollable world. Giving it up was terrifying. Like the entire building would begin spinning, off-kilter, and I'd be stuck in the center, unable to get out. If I stopped bleaching my hair, if I let my natural brown color come in, I wouldn't look like her at all.

I'd be my father's daughter, through and through.

I removed the pin curls I'd kept in overnight. Counterclockwise pin curls in the back, clockwise pin curls near my face, standing pin curls on the top of my bangs. I rubbed a little pomade on my fingers and combed them through my newly loose hair. I brushed it out before using a small comb to set my bangs in a pageboy style, spraying the whole thing down with hairspray. Since this was a gala and I was in a beautiful gown, I pulled back a side section of my hair and held it in place with a sparkling comb, one I'd picked up from Ladies Love to Sparkle, actually.

The Ladies were my guests tonight. I hope they noticed. I wanted them confused and nervous and unsure of where I stood. They were more likely to make mistakes that way.

I needed all my suspects nervous and therefore willing to act out.

The door opened and my heart dropped for a second, but Presley didn't bark, so I took a deep breath and waited for my heart to return to its proper spot.

"Darling?" Henry called. "It's our time to shine. Are you decent?"

"In here!" I answered from my second-bedroom-turned-closet. Presley waited by the door with his tail wagging and jumped up on Henry's shins the moment he entered the room. Henry scratched him behind the ears.

"I'd pick you up, old sport, but I don't want dog hair on my suit. It's my best one."

"You look dashing, darling," I said appreciatively. Since Colin's arrival, Henry wasn't the most handsome man I'd ever seen in real life, but he was a narrow second. With his blue eyes and square jaw and thick head of dark hair, and his perfect silver screen–ready smile, he was the best date I could ask for at any event.

But he wasn't who I wanted. Who I wanted didn't want me anymore. I was grateful for the time Henry spent with me all the same. He had donned black slacks and a jacket, a white dress shirt, and a snazzy purple tie. "I had to call around to find this, I hope you know," he said, waving the end of it in my face. "But I'd do anything for you, darling."

I stood up and kissed the air near his cheek, not ready to have my lipstick smudged. "You're the ginchiest. Are you ready for the gala?"

"I'm always up for a bash," he said, and flashed me a checkbook. "Less for the trap part. Who . . . who are the suspects again? I mean, besides the husband, who I think you and I both agree is the most likely suspect and also the thief."

"There could've been any number of reasons for Mrs. Mitchell to have that pocket square in her coat. Perhaps she had allergies?

A cold? She was sad? I had one that Hodgson's wife made in my possession for a while, remember?"

Henry held both my hands. "But why else would he kill her?"

"I have no idea." I sighed. "Any of the women? Easy: revenge." Ticking them off on my fingers, I gave Henry a rundown of my suspects. "Prudence has spent the most money earning her way up the ladder. She used the money her husband left her to do so. She was the most comfortably off of the three, but maybe that's changed with this new business endeavor. Ruth was lonely without her family nearby and after her children grew up, but money was also tight, and she thought she'd found a way to solve both things. Her husband was getting frustrated with their money only going in one direction, and embarrassed by her attempts to make her business work. And Veronica? Veronica desperately needed the money. Her husband was out of work. Their kids are young. She thought the ladder was her way out, something to dig them out of the hole they found themselves in, and it only dug them deeper."

"Could one of the husbands have done it?" Henry asked. "They knew that their wives were going to be at the lunch. Maybe one of them dressed up as a waiter and poisoned her drink?"

I pulled away from him and gave myself one more look in the mirror, checking my teeth for lipstick. "Anything is possible, darling. That's why I was sure to invite them *and* their husbands to the party. *And* Mr. Mitchell."

"You don't have any idea, Ev?" Henry asked, sounding worried.

I smiled at his reflection. "Now, why would you think that? I'm being careful, that's all. Miss Marple always says you have to be certain of these things. And tonight? I'm certain we're going to catch the killer. I'm also certain that this gown is gorgeous, and you haven't complimented me once."

"You're beautiful." Henry laughed. "You're positively radiant. The most beautiful creature on Earth, even wearing a color that doesn't suit you."

"Better! What bag? Black clutch with silver hardware or purple evening bag with the gold chain?" I held them up for him to see.

"The clutch," he said. "A nice contrast to your dress. Are you ready, now? I'm sure they're all waiting for you. Making a speech, aren't you?"

"I did plan on welcoming everyone, yes, and introducing the . . . owner? Of the charity? What are they called?"

"I don't know. CEO? What is the charity for again?"

"I—oh! I know this one!" I snapped my fingers, the sound soft because of my gloves, but no less satisfying. "Unwed mothers!"

Henry applauded. "Well done, darling. You've remembered the beneficiaries of the gala you're throwing. I'm so proud of you."

After dipping into a quick curtsey, I bid goodbye to Presley. "Be nice to your sister. Wherever she is." Knowing Monroe, she was napping somewhere that was both warm and inconvenient.

I took Henry's arm and gave him a squeeze, excited enough I could hop in my heels. "Let's go spring a trap!"

Chapter 37

When we reached the middle of the grand stairs, a flashbulb went off. I blinked the lights out of my eyes and scanned the audience below. The room was full of guests, and Colin was already playing music. Canapés and champagne were being passed around on silver trays by waiters wearing black slacks and white shirts. The camera was to the right of the stairs, and Dottie stood beside the man holding it. I smiled brightly at her and waved.

She arched a perfect brow and waved back.

"You invited the press?" Henry asked, his hand on my back and a smile on his face as the photographer took another blinding picture. "Does Silas know?"

Mr. Sharpe—senior that is—had a strict no-press rule that Henry and I broke frequently when we pretended to be more than friends. Mac would often assist in this rule breaking, sneaking in a photographer through the back doors for a few bucks. As it turned out, I didn't need Mac's help. Not for bringing the press in, not for picking locks, not even for leaving the hotel. I did all those things on my own.

Well. Not entirely on my own, of course. I had left the hotel twice since Mac's departure. Once with Henry and once with

Hodgson. And Poppy brought the press into the Gold Room. But Mac hadn't needed to be here for any of it.

"Yes." The two of us started walking again. "Part of the plan, darling. Have to clear the Pinnacle's name, you know," I said.

"And yours too."

"And *mine* too, darn it all." I was steps away from Dottie when Poppy swooped between us, Russell at her side.

"Evelyn, here." She thrust a small card in my hands. "I've got your speech written. And I need you to meet Mrs. Leslie, the chairperson, before you introduce her."

I took the card with a smile, giving it a quick glance. It seemed simple enough, introducing the chairperson and the charity to our guests before Mrs. Leslie asked them to open their wallets. I was going to completely ignore it and instead spook my suspects, but I couldn't tell Poppy that with the reporter nearby. "Thank you ever so, Poppy. I'll be with you in one moment. Dottie, might I have a word with you?"

"On the record?"

"Of course."

She pulled her notepad out of her pocket and licked the tip of her pen. "Whenever you're ready, Miss Murphy."

"Yes. Thank you. I've solved the murder of Mrs. Mitchell and figured out the identity of the Gentleman Thief."

Her dark eyes went wide. "Pardon me?"

"Did I say that too fast?" I glanced at Henry, but he shook his head.

"I understood you perfectly, darling."

"I'll say it once more. Are you ready? I have solved the murder of Mrs. Mitchell and figured out the identity of the Gentleman

Thief. The Pinnacle is safe once again. You have my permission to print that. Word for word."

Dottie scribbled down what I said, but her eyes were still wide. "Who?" She asked. "What? How?"

"Ah, yes, you're definitely a reporter. I see that now. And all those questions will be answered before the gala is over, if you'll stay."

Dottie huffed. "I'm not going anywhere," she said, and it sounded like a threat.

"Wonderful. Oh, and this lovely comb? It's from Ladies Love to Sparkle. You can print that too. Poppy? Is Mrs. Leslie ready for me?"

She nodded. "Right this way."

I took her arm and grinned at her date. "Mr. Castillo. You're looking handsome this evening."

"Ah, thanks." He nervously ran his hand over his head. He was in a black suit that almost fit him, and a black tie that fell a little longer than it should. "Wasn't planning on going, so I had to be resourceful."

Poppy grunted. "It's Mac's," she said. "He didn't take it with him, the idiot."

There were a lot of things he hadn't taken with him. I shook my head, shook that thought away. I couldn't think about Mac anymore. He was gone, and a murderer was here in this room. I had to *focus*.

Among the crowd and yet not quite in it, a bit off to the side and yet not so far as to be apart, was an older woman with a fierce bun and thick black glasses, surrounded by three younger women. All of them wore beautiful dresses, their hair styled in soft curls, their makeup done in colors that complemented their skin tones. I glanced at Poppy, who gave a nod. We'd treated all of them to a day at our spa, then. Good. That was a good idea that I wished I'd had, but I was grateful for my assistant for having it on her own.

My second thought, which came right on the coattails of the first, was how much they reminded me of the group of ladies I'd met exactly one week prior, in this very room. But though the older woman's bun was fierce, her smile was open, and she shook my hand.

"Miss Murphy, I can't thank you enough for hosting us! I'm so excited. This is a better turnout than I could have hoped for."

I gave a look around the Gold Room. There were a little over a hundred people. It wasn't a full room, but certainly not an empty one either. Given the short amount of time we'd had to put it together, plus the time of year, I was happy with the attendance. "It's not bad, is it?" I offered my hand to the next woman in line and introduced myself.

"Please, excuse me." Mrs. Leslie laughed nervously. "Where are my manners? Miss Murphy, allow me to introduce three of our mothers." She did just that, introducing me to women who were not that much older than I was. One, I learned, had lost her husband in the Korean War. The other had become a mom for the first time at age fifteen. And the last was not only a single mother herself but was raising two of her younger siblings.

My plan had been to use my speech to make the killer nervous. To announce to the room at large the discovery of the murder weapon. I wanted a big show of it, something positively Poirot worthy. But these women didn't need me putting a dark mark on their evening.

I thanked them all for coming, and they thanked me for having them, and then I asked Mrs. Leslie to the small stage set up around Mr. Sharpe's piano. Colin nodded at me as he played, and he eased off his tune. The guests who were dancing came to a stop, and the room applauded. Poppy handed me a microphone.

I wasn't normally nervous in front of a crowd. In the middle of one? Not my favorite place. But in front of a crowd, I could handle myself. Usually. Now, though, with my plans for my speech thrown out the proverbial window, my palms were damp. I wrapped my fingers around the microphone and held on tight, the cord hitting me in the thigh.

When I cleared my throat, it echoed in the room. Whoops. *That's okay. Lots of people clear their throats.* I rolled my shoulders back, took a deep breath, and smiled. "Hello, everyone. My name is Evelyn Murphy. I'm your hostess for the evening. Before I hand the microphone to someone more worthy of the time, I'd like to thank you all for coming to support these mothers. As many of you know, I lost my mother at a young age. I miss her every day."

The crowd of at least one hundred people was watching me. Faces were hard to distinguish, but toward the right, my three main suspects plus one husband stood together, silent and staring. Veronica's husband hadn't been able to get off the boat on short notice, then. Near the bar was Mr. Mitchell. I was glad to see he'd attended as well. He stood with his elbow on the bar top, a drink in his hand, and was very clearly talking to the bartender. The same bartender who had played piano for Colin the other night.

Hodgson was in the back. He saw me looking at him and raised his glass. He'd lost his son in the Korean War, just like this woman had lost her husband. Now she was left alone with a child who would not remember his father. Loss was everywhere I looked.

Mrs. Mitchell, for all her faults roping women into a business where they almost certainly could never turn a profit, hadn't deserved to be murdered. She was still someone's daughter, someone's sister, someone's friend. She didn't deserve to meet her end here, in the Gold Room, at my side.

I cleared my throat again, blinked away the stinging sensation behind my eyes. "So, I would like to say two things. First, and most importantly, to Mrs. Leslie and her group of mothers: your children appreciate you and love you. Thank you for all you do for them, and the sacrifices you make daily. Second, to everyone else: I plan on matching the cumulative total of donations raised tonight."

Mrs. Leslie and her women gasped.

"So, please, open your wallets. I know some of you are itching to drain Daddy's savings a little."

That got a small, polite laugh.

"Ladies and gentlemen, please welcome Mrs. Leslie, the director of our featured charity."

More applause this time. I handed the microphone over, left a kiss in the air near Mrs. Leslie's cheek, and walked off the stage. Colin Sharpe watched me from his seat at the piano. I could feel his gaze on the back of my neck, goose bumps running down my spine. Over my shoulder, I met his dark gaze with a soft smile.

Pity he was busy. I'd love to dance with him again.

Chapter 38

After listening to Mrs. Leslie talk about her charity, I approached the bar. Henry and Mr. Mitchell were talking, with Mr. Sharpe hovering nearby. Er, the older Mr. Sharpe. Henry's Mr. Sharpe, not my Mr. Sharpe.

Not that Colin was *mine*, of course. Just because I wanted to dance with him didn't mean he was mine. He just wasn't Henry's, is all.

"I'm glad you made it," I said to the older Mr. Sharpe. "I'm assuming you're off the clock?"

He raised a hand and rocked it from side to side. "I'm staying sober," he said, "but I am attending."

"By any chance, did you ever find out if any of Mrs. Mitchell's friends or her husband attempted to gain entrance to the Gold Room?"

"As a matter of fact," he said with a smile, his mustache twitching, "I learned all of them have been back to the Pinnacle. Some of them, multiple times."

"I knew that," I dismissed. "I'm asking about the Gold Room."

"I'm sorry to say we don't employ guards stationed in front of the ballrooms to make a list of all who enter or exit."

Licking my teeth, I did not blurt out the first response that came to mind. Instead, I swallowed it down and chose the second option. "I knew it was a long shot," I said. "I appreciate you trying all the same. One more favor? Perhaps you can keep an eye on my Henry?

"Henry, darling?" I continued, looking toward him.

Henry stopped talking to Mr. Mitchell and turned around, smiling at me. "Yes, darling?"

I kissed the air by his cheek, still fearful of smudging my lipstick. "I fear I must continue socializing, but Mr. Sharpe here will make sure you're taken care of."

Henry raised an empty crystal glass.

Mr. Sharpe sighed but waved the bartender over and asked him to fill it up.

"You know the drinks are free," I said.

"It's more fun to have someone else order it for me," Henry replied.

With a shake of my head, I moved around him. "Mr. Mitchell? May I steal you away for a moment?"

He drained his drink before offering me his arm. I took it with an appreciative smile. "I am happy to see you," I said.

Mr. Mitchell nodded. "It's good to get out of the house. I almost didn't come. At home with my dogs? That's where I'm happiest. I'm afraid my housekeeper urged me to go. She was right too. Being out in a crowd like this is a good reminder that, well, life goes on."

I squeezed his arm. "As unfortunate as it seems sometimes. Here we are. I believe you know everyone?"

We'd walked up to the group of Ladies Love to Sparkle, who hadn't spread out into the Gold Room, but congregated together in a four-person circle.

"Almost everyone," Mr. Mitchell said and offered his hand to Ruth's husband. "I'm Theodore."

"Nathaniel. Hello. Nice to meet you. Sorry for the circumstances, of course."

The group made room for us, and we scooted into their circle. Behind Prudence's gray head, Hodgson caught my eye. I nodded once, and he turned and left.

"I wanted to thank you all personally for coming," I said, looking each and every one of the potential killers in the face. Ruth, perhaps urged on by her husband, who was sick of the spending without any return, and embarrassed by how they looked in front of their fellow churchgoers. Veronica, so desperate for money that she had approached me on her own. Prudence, who had spent more than anyone to climb the rungs of the ladder and had yet to see a penny of it come her way. And Mr. Mitchell, who was The Husband, and that was often reason enough. "I have some—well, we will call it good news."

Ruth's ice-blue eyes sparkled. "What is it, Miss Murphy?"

"Evelyn," I corrected. "Please. We are all friends here." I made a show of taking a deep breath. "Recently, I was in this room, and while the staff was cleaning the floors, I found a small bottle that . . . well, it smells like shellfish." That was the truth, so it was easy to say. Next came the hard part. I looked downcast at the floor in the middle of the circle, hoping my posture and lack of eye contact would hide the lie. "Now, it's still in this hotel, so we haven't been able to run tests on it. But the chief of police is coming by this evening to collect it personally, and they'll be able to tell if it contains anything that Mrs. Mitchell was allergic to, as well as collect any fingerprints on the bottle."

"What sort of a bottle?" Prudence asked, which surprised me. Not the question—I'd been expecting that. But that *she* was the one to ask.

"I've been advised not to give out specific details." That's what Hodgson had told me to say. He called it "guilt knowledge" and said to leave those details as something only the killer would know.

"And you, you don't know what's in it?" Mr. Mitchell asked.

"Not yet." I put a hand on his shoulder to be sympathetic and to give my lying hands something to do. "But the chief of police has promised me that they'll put it to the very top of their lab's list. We will also need all of you to head to the station this week and leave your fingerprints on file."

Veronica fixed her hair, which had been perfectly in place. "Why do you need our fingerprints?"

"It's precautionary," I said. "Simply to rule you all out as suspects so they can start looking for the real killer. Because I know, in my heart"—I put my hands on my heart to emphasize my point—"that all of you here are innocent."

Ruth's husband shifted on his feet. "But it could also be nothing, right?"

I made my eyes wide when I looked at him. "What do you mean?"

"Whatever is in it might not be what killed Mrs. Mitchell, I mean. Sorry, Theodore."

Mr. Mitchell hung his head.

"That's true. However, we do have Mrs. Mitchell's stomach contents to compare. If they are the same thing, in the bottle and in her stomach, well then. We've found the murder weapon. But you are right. This is simply the first small step toward finding justice for your friend. I wanted to tell you now, though, so that perhaps you can find a little peace in the knowledge that this *will* be solved." Once more I met each and every one of their gazes. "I promise you."

"Real justice would be firing your chef," Mr. Mitchell said. His head was still down, but he stared at me from under his lashes. "I see he's still working here."

I licked my lips, considered my words very carefully. Hodgson and I had also discussed the possibility of them still blaming Marco. Guilt Knowledge. You could only make an argument that Marco was responsible for Lois's death if the shrimp had been found in the food. Marco doesn't pour champagne, and he certainly doesn't deliver it to the tables.

"I suppose that depends on the results from the bottle, Mr. Mitchell," I spoke slowly. "But that is something I will take into serious consideration. Please, try and enjoy your evening. I'll see you all very soon." I let that last sentence linger before walking away, back toward the bar. But Henry and Mr. Sharpe were no longer there, and I didn't want to be seen doubling back, away from the group that I wanted to start sweating, so I ordered a gin and tonic from the bar.

I was more of a champagne drinker, but I needed *something* to make my leaving more believable.

"Miss Murphy?" a man said behind me.

I glanced over my shoulder before committing to a full spin around. "Wally!" I wrapped my arms around his neck in a hug. "It's good to see you! I'm so happy you could attend."

"Of course." His arms shuffled at his sides before they settled on my waist. "I, uh. Happy to be here."

When I let him go, there was a blush staining his cheekbones. The music changed to "I'll Be Seeing You." I did not have to look up at the stage to know that Colin was aware I was hugging Wally.

"Once again, let me apologize for having to leave early the other night, Miss Murphy."

"It's Evelyn." The bartender handed me my gin and tonic, and I took a sip, shivering as it burned its way down my throat. "Anyway." I stuck my tongue out with the hopes the air would cool it. "I owe you an apology for not calling after I got those beautiful flowers. I've been a little busy as of late."

Wally fixed his tie. "I can tell. This is a lovely party you've thrown, Evelyn."

"Poppy handled most of this. No, I mean, solving that murder I told you about?"

"Shrimp?"

"Shrimp." I sipped my drink again, but it was too strong, and I set it down on the bar. "It should be wrapped up tonight, though! Perhaps we could get together again soon?"

"Really?" He grinned so wide I could see all his teeth. "I'd like that."

He was the right choice for me. A good one. A smart man that my father would approve of, with his own money and his own career and his own family history.

"Wonderful! Could you, um . . . Would you be willing . . . Hmm."

Wally took a step closer. "What is it, Evelyn?"

"I need your help. Tonight. Unrelated to having a future date, so there is no obligation on your part to participate."

"Why don't you tell me what it is, and then I'll let you know if I'm available to participate?"

Spoken like a true lawyer. I leaned in close and gave him a very brief overview in the softest voice I could manage, looking over his shoulder the whole time to make sure no one was listening.

Wally nodded. "I can do that."

"Wonderful. Fifteen minutes, and then head up to room 1313. Knock three times and tell Hodgson I sent you."

When he reached between us to fix his tie again, I beat him to it, adjusting the Windsor knot to fit more comfortably at the base of his throat. "Wally," I said. "You're the ginchiest."

He was the perfect man for me. If only I could convince my heart of that.

Chapter 39

I left both my drink and Wally at the bar, so I could do a lap around the room, on the lookout for Chief Harvey. He was step two in my little plan. I'd barely made it to the dance floor when someone placed their hand on my back.

"Care for another dance, Evelyn?" asked a man with a Scottish accent.

I rolled my eyes, lest he realize I'd been thinking about nothing else since I introduced Mrs. Leslie and saw him playing. "I suppose one dance couldn't hurt. But I *am* working, Mr. Sharpe."

He grinned and kissed my knuckles. "Me too."

A glance toward the stage confirmed he'd swapped in the bartender from the other night. "I did wonder why the music had suddenly improved. Perhaps I should've hired him for this evening instead?"

Colin wrapped his arm around my waist and pulled me close. "You're a terrible liar. You do know that, don't you?"

"I've been told." I held on to his shoulders and allowed him to lead. The music was slow, and we swayed together, so close I could feel his breath on my cheek. He smelled like cigarettes, and it made me think of Mac, and I did not want to think about Mac anymore. "How long do you have?"

He shrugged, and my hands moved with the motion. "As long as it takes."

"As long as what takes?"

He danced us away from the crowd, toward the hallway that employees used for quick access to the kitchen.

"Colin," I laughed. "What are you doing?"

"What I've wanted to do since I first arrived at the Pinnacle." His smoky breath filled my nose as he pulled me even closer, his warm lips pressing against mine in a soft chaste kiss.

I frowned when he pulled away. "Colin?"

"Yes, Evelyn?"

"Would you kiss me again?"

Colin's smile lit up his entire face, the first time I'd ever seen anything but that standard crooked grin of his. "I'd be delighted."

He kissed me again, longer this time, and less chaste. When we broke apart, he was still smiling, red lipstick smudged over his mouth.

I sighed. "Well. That's disappointing."

"I . . . I beg your pardon?"

I let go of him and then reached for his hands, removing them from my waist. "I thought there would be sparks. I was expecting there to be sparks. Unfortunately"—I shook my head—"I felt nothing in either of those kisses."

His mouth fell open. Colin's forehead wrinkled, and he took a step toward me, and then one back. "You can't be serious."

"You said it yourself. I'm a terrible liar. It isn't your fault. You are handsome and clever and charming. It seems that I'm still hung up on my previous beau. And there just isn't anything either of us can do about that."

"I could try again?" His crooked grin made for a valiant effort at returning. "One more try?"

"No. Twice was quite enough. Now, it's time you get back to work, isn't it? I'm very busy. I'll see you around?" Without waiting for confirmation, I turned and headed toward the main part of the Gold Room. A waiter came out of the kitchen carrying a tray of champagne, and I took a glass. "I don't like gin," I told him.

He nodded at me once, a confused look on his face, and hurried ahead of me.

Behind me was Colin, sputtering. "Evelyn?" He called. "Evelyn, come back! I can try again. Evelyn? There were sparks for me, Evelyn! There were sparks for me!"

I sipped my champagne as I searched for Chief Harvey. Colin would have to wait.

★ ★ ★

Chief Harvey was not difficult to spot in his blue uniform, hat awkwardly tucked under his arm. To my surprise, he was surrounded by the women Mrs. Leslie had brought, Mrs. Leslie herself giggling and blushing as she spoke to the chief of police. Chief Harvey held a drink in his hand, but it was obvious by the amount of champagne in the glass he'd had less than a single sip.

"Hello, ladies," I greeted, inserting myself into their group. "Are you enjoying yourselves?"

"Very much, thank you again," Mrs. Leslie said, smiling bright, her eyes wrinkling at the corners. She should let her hair down. Literally. The tightness of the bun aged her unfairly.

"Would you mind if I stole Chief Harvey for a moment?"

Mrs. Leslie shook her head. "Please. Is everything all right?"

"Everything's peachy," I assured. "Chief Harvey?"

He offered me his arm that wasn't holding the hat and I set my hand on his elbow, careful of his drink. "Don't like champagne, Chief?"

"I don't like to drink when I'm on duty," he replied. "Even if I'm technically not on duty right now."

I smiled at him as I steered us to the middle of the dance floor. "It's very kind of you to indulge me."

"I have to say, Miss Murphy, that this seems particularly dangerous. If you were anyone else, I'd advise against it."

But I wasn't anyone else, was I? I didn't know if he was talking about the two previous murderers I'd help bring to justice, or the fact that my father and I donate quite regularly to the policeman's union. But I didn't ask for verification, because no matter the reason, I was getting my way. "Don't you worry about a thing, Chief. Miss Marple does things like this all the time."

"Who?"

We were in the middle of the room now, so I stood in front of him, and began moving my hands around in conversation. I wanted to be seen, so my gestures were probably bigger than they needed to be. Chief Harvey ducked his champagne glass a second before my fingers smashed into the side. Liquid spilled on to his hand.

"Sorry about that, Chief." My hand motions got smaller. "I was going to explain who Miss Marple is, but, I feel like now is the opportune moment for me to slink away. Sneakily, of course. The bartender will have napkins, and then I think Mrs. Leslie might have a night open for dinner this week."

He blushed at my words and then went full red at my wink. With that, I gave a casual look around me and started, ever so carefully, through the crowd. Colin was no longer in the hallway where I'd left him, but he wasn't on stage either. In fact, the bartender had gone back to tending bar, so there wasn't any music at all.

I frowned but kept going. I was in too deep to back out now. Poppy would have to handle it without me.

CHAPTER 40

Pretending to sneak around was more difficult than I'd thought. Part of me wanted to press myself against walls and peer around corners, even though I knew I was being trailed from behind. But I didn't want to spook my killer. I *wanted* to be followed, so I acted like who everyone thinks I am: ditzy and clueless. I strolled into the lobby while humming "I'll be Seeing You," stopping occasionally to skip and play with my purple skirt. I greeted the lift boy with a loud "Hello!" and an even louder "Floor thirteen, please!" Then I dug around in my purse as the elevator door closed so I had an excuse for not looking up.

Maybe I was as ditzy and clueless as people suspected. I hadn't figured out a motive at all. And if this didn't go right, I might not ever know why. Technically, motive wasn't a necessary part of the legal process. A prosecutor only needs means and opportunity, which I had. Mostly. This would solidify things. It had to, or we would have absolutely nothing. And what could a prosecutor do with nothing?

I shook that worry off. *One step at a time.* I had a plan. And maybe it *was* ditzy, thought up by a clueless girl, but nobody else had one. The elevator stopped on the thirteenth floor, and I took my time wandering over to room thirteen, still digging around in my purse like I was looking for a key. I "found" it, held it up with a smile, and unlocked the door, leaving it cracked open as I stepped inside and got ready, hoping the scene was set.

Putting trust in others to do something so important—like Poppy throwing the gala—was new to me. But it was good too. Unless it turned out badly. And then I'd never trust anyone ever again! Except Poppy. *Best friend.* And she wasn't interested in me romantically and never asked me for money and didn't need to use my name to distract the press from her personal life. She stuck around even when I made her angry.

She called me her best friend.

In the darkness, the door creaked open. I held my breath and waited. Someone was inside, but they hadn't fully entered the room yet. The lamp lights on the hall table flickered. One went out. The other began to rise off the table.

The intruder sucked in a breath and stepped inside. The door slammed shut behind them. The floating lamp crashed, and the lights went out. Blinded, the intruder spun around and reached for the doorknob, only to find the door locked, wedged closed.

Their swallow was audible in the quiet of the room as they turned toward the suite again. The dining table, covered in Hodgson's paperwork, started to shake, slowly at first, and then harder. The notebooks and files began to slide, some of them hitting the carpet. But one began to float in the air and hover, the pages covered in scribbled ink rapidly flipping forward, only visible by the thin light of the moon coming in from the torn blinds of a single window.

The intruder backed away, heel catching on the broken lamp. A light came back on, but not from the lamps, broken or otherwise. It seemed to come from inside the mirror above the hall table and it did not illuminate the room, but instead showed a reflection. Not of the intruder, but of a man, his face covered in red streaks, his lips blue, the skin around his eyes black.

The intruder jumped away, finally in the middle of the room. Their feet triggered the ropes, and the net laid on top of the floor the intruder stood on was sucked up toward the ceiling.

I reached for the non-broken lamp and switched it on, smiling at my guest. He hung inside the net like a squished and angry bear, his legs curled into his waist, one arm stuck above his head.

"Hello, Mr. Mitchell. I've been expecting you."

Chapter 41

"Wally, would you join us, please?" The net holding Mr. Mitchell swayed back and forth as he tried to untangle himself, pretzeled up inside as he was. All he achieved was to wind up with his right cheek pressed against the diamond-shaped mesh of the net so hard it would leaven an imprint for hours.

"This won't take very long, Mr. Mitchell," I assured him as the lawyer appeared from behind a curtain. He'd been in charge of lifting the notebook off the table with a filament wire. The flipping pages had been an excellent touch, one I wasn't sure how he'd managed. "This is Mr. Feretti of Feretti, Feretti, Feretti, and Feretti. He is one of the finest defense attorneys, not only in Manhattan but in the country as well."

Even in the dim lamp light, the blush on Wally's cheekbones was evident. "Thank you, Miss Murphy."

"Mr. Mitchell. *Theodore.*" I took a step toward him. His eye, split behind the rope, followed me. "We know you killed your wife."

He opened his mouth, or at least tried to, his tongue awkwardly hitting the frayed knots. I held up a finger. "There is no use arguing it. You followed me up here to retrieve the missing bottle. You couldn't risk the fingerprint on the bottom being a match. In fact, the day that we had lunch together, you'd come over to search for the bottle, isn't that right?"

Mr. Mitchell didn't answer.

"That's all right," I soothed. "You don't have to talk. Your actions speak loudly enough. I told five people I was handing the evidence over to the chief today, and you're the only one who followed me. That's enough for any prosecutor to weave a convincing story, isn't it, Mr. Feretti?"

Wally cleared his throat. "That's correct."

"The most important part of any court case, Theodore, isn't the evidence or the eyewitnesses. It's the *story*. And your story paints quite a picture. That's where Mr. Feretti comes in." I motioned to my lawyer. "He can help you. He can, but you have to come up with something he can use in front of a jury. Because, Theodore, husbands killing their wives? It happens all the time. But a thief breaking into the homes of the wealthy and stealing their valuables? Oh, they'll fry you for that. They'll say it's because of Lois, but it is purely revenge for making them feel unsafe for even a moment."

Theodore closed his eyes, his breathing shallow.

"What is his story right now, Mr. Feretti?"

Wally, one of the smartest men I'd ever had as a friend, understood exactly what I needed him to say. "The prosecutors will say you were bored in your retirement, and you used your athletic skills to steal priceless jewels from innocent citizens. And that when your wife found out and threatened to expose you, you killed her."

I raised my chin, feeling rather proud, and maybe a bit smitten, that Wally had known the exact angle I was pursuing. Maybe there was a future where he was by my side.

Theodore shook his head, the trap swaying as he moved. "That's not true."

"You've got to give me something I can work with." Wally held out empty hands. "You came up here looking for the evidence, Mr. Mitchell. That's damning. The only motive the jury will believe is that it was to keep your wife from revealing your nightly escapades—"

Theodore swore. "I ain't no thief! I killed my wife, yes, but not because of some Robin Hood nonsense. I'm not stealing from the rich. I'm not stealing from anybody!"

"Hmm." I made a show of tapping my index finger against my chin. "I almost believe you."

He snarled at me, his hand turning white from lack of blood flow while his face was increasingly more purple. "I snuck into your damn kitchen. Wasn't hard—all you need is a suit. I made some shrimp stock at home, didn't take long, but the only thing I could carry it in was that damn skin-care bottle I found in Lois's trash. Stupid thing slipped right out of my pocket." He closed his eyes and growled. "That good-for-nothing chef doesn't even look at your employees, did you know that? He called me 'Jim' and yelled at me to get back to work. So, I took a tray of champagne, I put a little bit of shrimp stock I made into each glass, and then I gave it to another Jim and told him to deliver it to the table."

None of the women were big champagne drinkers, and I had been sitting right there with them. If it had tasted off, odds are they would have been too reserved to complain in front of me, or worried that it wasn't off at all and that they just didn't know any better. I had the inkling Lois herself fell into the latter group. She'd have been too worried to be perceived as someone who wasn't sophisticated enough to appreciate the finer things for her to complain about a drink that I was drinking, although mine had been delivered by a different "Jim" altogether. She wanted so badly to fit in with the wealthy, but she never quite could. Just like her home, which was in the right neighborhood, on the same street as all those other grand homes, but which wasn't as grand as the rest.

And the women wouldn't think to do something that Lois herself wasn't doing. If she'd only said something, spoken up, not just assumed that since I was drinking champagne, it was the *same* champagne—she might still be alive.

Wally shook his head. "Admitting the means of the murder doesn't wipe away the prosecutor's story, Mr. Mitchell, and you won't find any leniency when it comes to this. Miss Murphy is right. They will say you're getting the death penalty because of the murder, but it'll be because of the thefts."

"I didn't steal a damn thing!"

"Then *why*," I said, stepping forward, eyes wide, "did you kill your wife?"

"That business changed her!" The trap rocked so much it looked like it would fall from the ceiling. Wally grabbed my elbow and pulled me back. "It changed her. She used to be a perfect wife. Meek. Thoughtful. Apologetic, even, because we always wanted kids. I always wanted a son. And she never could carry a child to term. She tried to make up for it by being the sweetest wife possible, sweeter than honey.

"Once the money came in, she got it into her little head that she was as smart as me. Even smarter. She started arguing with me about every decision, acting like she had a say in how the money was spent. I couldn't live like that. It's my money, it's my house, and it's my wife."

His words struck me. I stood there beside the hanging trap, Wally's shoulder in front of mine, as if to prevent the man in the net from approaching me, despite the fact he was quite entangled in the net. "Well," I said, "she *was* your wife. And it *was* your house. And it *was* your money. But you'll never enter your home again, Mr. Mitchell, and your money won't be your money for much longer."

Hodgson appeared from the underneath the table while a uniformed police officer came out of the second bedroom.

"Theodore Mitchell," the officer said, "you're under arrest."

The veins in Mr. Mitchell's throat were throbbing, so purple as to be black. His Adam's apple bobbed when he swallowed. "You're gonna help me, aren't you? Mr. Feretti? Tell a story, I mean?"

Wally shook his head. "A husband killing his wife because of the fragility of his ego isn't a story I'm interested in telling, Mr. Mitchell. Good luck to you."

Chapter 42

The officer handcuffed Mr. Mitchell, whose skin coloring was rapidly returning to normal, though there was fire in his eyes, and diamond-shaped imprints from the mesh net marked his face. "Miss Murphy," he said. "My dogs."

He was a cold-blooded killer who had enacted an incredibly complicated plan to kill his wife in public while making it look like my kitchen staff had offed her accidentally, but I couldn't fault him for the concern for his pets.

"I'll handle it," I said, making a mental note to get a hold of his housekeeper. Would she be able to care for the dogs herself? They were *big* boys. I couldn't take them in. Presley and Monroe would never let me hear the end of it.

He nodded in acknowledgement and allowed the officer to walk him out the door, where Chief Harvey was waiting. He tipped his hat. "Miss Murphy, I believe that's yet another plaque I owe you."

I waved a hand as if to wipe his words out of the air. "It's no bother, Chief. I'm always happy to help. Speaking of. Did you get Mrs. Leslie's contact information?"

The chief blushed something fierce, mumbled something incoherent, and left. I shrugged and turned to Wally and Hodgson. "Men never know what's best for them. Daddy is the same way."

Hodgson rolled his eyes, and Wally opened his mouth to say something, but Mr. Sharpe and Henry walked into the suite. Henry in full makeup, wiping fruitlessly at his skin with a wet hand towel. "I usually charge for that kind of thing," he said.

Mr. Sharpe's expression was pinched. He held a flashlight in his hand, and he was smacking himself in the opposite palm. "Miss Murphy."

Uh-oh. I'd heard that tone of voice before. I inched closer to my lawyer and my private investigator. "Yes, Mr. Sharpe?"

"When did you have that two-way mirror installed?"

Another step away. "That two-way mirror?" I indicated the mirror above the broken lamps. "The one that Henry used to scare Mr. Mitchell?"

"Yes, that one that uses the false wall and hidden hallway that the mob built in during Prohibition."

I bumped into Wally's shoulder. He put his hand on the small of my back. I glanced at him, and he nodded, giving me a lawyer's permission to answer the question at hand. "I believe that I was, um . . . it was around eight years ago."

Mr. Sharpe's mustache twitched in a most unfriendly fashion. "You were only thirteen yet you were able to hire a contractor to install a two-way mirror in a guest suite without my knowledge?" The mustache twitch moved down his entire body. *"How?"*

"Oh, Mr. Sharpe." I giggled. "A magician never reveals her secrets."

But he was on a roll. "Why haunt this whole room? Why . . . there were never any ghosts. It was always just you! *Why?*"

"Well, the net was very obvious," I said, with a pointed look at Hodgson.

He raised his hands, showing the bandages on his fingers. "I did the best I could in the time frame I was given, thank you very much. All I had at my disposal was not enough rope and Miss Cooper's newest infatuation."

"I wanted to spook him enough to walk onto the net and trigger the trap without realizing what he was doing." Wally was still touching the small of my back, and I found I didn't mind it. I smiled at Mr. Sharpe. "It worked, didn't it? Great job, Henry! You knocked it out of the park."

He took a bow.

Mr. Sharpe pressed the bulb of the flashlight against his forehead. "Years we've left this room vacant. *Years*, Miss Murphy."

"The occasional haunting is good for business," I said.

"*You* were haunting it!"

I blinked at him. "I don't see your point. Wally?"

He shook his head. "It's essentially the same thing, Mr. Sharpe."

Mr. Sharpe looked very much like he wanted to argue that it was *not* essentially the same thing, when Henry took the flashlight from his hands. "It's a shame, Ev. All that work, and he didn't admit he was the thief."

"I'm sorry. I must've forgotten to explain. That's because he's not."

"Then," said Henry, "who is?"

I stepped away from Wally and wrapped Henry in a hug. "Don't worry about that now. Please, I need you and Mr. Sharpe to return to the party. Wally, you too. I'm afraid I left Poppy all on her own for too long. Can the three of you guilt rich people into donating while I wrap up here with Hodgson?"

Begrudgingly, Mr. Sharpe left the room, throwing me a disapproving look over his shoulder as he went. Henry kissed my cheek. "I'll get those stingy hangers-on to open their wallets, Evelyn—you can count on me."

He was right. I always could. "You might want to stop at a bathroom on your way, darling. You've got a bit," I motioned at my under eyes.

He sighed. "There is no rest for the beautiful."

When he was gone, I reached for Wally's hand and gave his fingers a squeeze. "Thank you ever so for all your help, Wally. You're the ginchiest, and I mean that."

He raised my hand to his lips and pressed a gentle kiss on my knuckles. I smiled, held his eye contact, even giggled for good measure. But my heart sank, straight to the center of my stomach. He wasn't Mac. He'd never be Mac. But he was here, and Mac wasn't, and that had to be worth something.

"Wally, wait."

He turned around.

"You never told me what happened in your mushroom case."

He sighed, fixed his tie. "The husband was convicted for murder. The prosecutor laid out a story that he'd made a second dinner that he didn't tell his wife about, using the death cap mushrooms. He served her one meal and served himself the other. The jury bought it."

Hodgson sucked his teeth. "It's always the husband."

Wally inclined his head.

"One more thing, Wally."

"Yes, Evelyn?"

"How did you get the pages to flutter like that?"

He looked hard at the table. I followed his gaze, and so did Hodgson. After a while, Wally shrugged. "I have absolutely no idea."

"Huh." My nose wrinkled. "Maybe this room is haunted."

Chapter 43

Hodgson and I hurried into the lift and rode in silence to the lobby. Well. Until he opened his mouth, anyway.

"What did I tell you? It's always the husband."

I rolled my eyes. "Yes, yes. You were correct. For *once*. Congratulations."

"For once," he repeated in a huff. "Right. What is it you say all the time? *'Thank you ever so.'* Where'd you even pick that up? One of those novels you keep in your kitchen cabinets?"

I regretted rolling my eyes earlier, as now would've been a much better time to do so, but I worried if I did it too much it would lose its impact. "Marilyn Monroe's character, Lorelei Lee, says it in *Gentlemen Prefer Blondes*, if you must know. Now, go on and lecture me about how I don't have a personality of my own, I have to steal it from movie stars."

"Personality you've got in spades," Hodgson said as the lift doors opened, and the chaos of the lobby came into view. "What do I care if your style is copied from someone else's? As long as the paychecks keep coming, I say, thank whoever you want, however as much as you want."

I led Hodgson out of the lobby and past Mr. Sharpe's office. "Remind me to get you my analyst's phone number. Maybe you can talk some sense into her. She suggested that I let my natural hair color grow out. Can you believe it?"

"The nerve of some people," Hodgson said, sounding very much like he could believe it, and also like he didn't care about it at all.

I glared at him but didn't slow my pace. If I was wrong, then what? *What happens next? Do I go back to the party with my tail between my legs? Do I admit to everyone that I didn't know what I was doing?* I wondered. And if I didn't know what I was doing now, did that mean all my other successes as of late were flukes?

The first door into the vault was ajar, and the security guard stationed outside was nowhere to be seen. I picked up my pace to a run. Hodgson matched my hurried strides, reaching into his coat to pull out his gun.

We came up to the door, and he grasped my shoulder, shook his head.

I narrowed my eyes. "We still have a chance to catch him in the act."

"Then let the man with the gun go in first, yeah?"

Once again, I cursed my premature eye rolling. With a wide sweep of my arm, I stepped back and let him lead. Hodgson said, "Police," in a deep, authoritative voice before swinging the door open, his revolver extended and steady before him.

The lights were on inside the safe room, revealing two Pinnacle guards bound and gagged, and the safe door wide open.

Hodgson hurried forward to check on the men and clear the room, but I shook my head. "We have to go—now! We'll call for help as we run!"

"Run where?" He asked as the two of us ran out into the lobby.

"To catch up with him, of course!"

"With *who*?"

"The Gentleman Thief! Honestly, Hodgson, what do I pay you for if not to pay attention?"

Mr. Sharpe's secretary spotted us coming down the hallway. She flattened against the wall. "Call the police!" I yelled. "The guards are tied up in the vault!"

The lobby was bustling, as always, with new arrivals checking in, and guests checking out. Bellhops pushing golden carts laden with luggage filled the available space between the fountain and the employee lift. The fish tanks bubbled; the smell of coffee from the café that was open all hours permeated the air. And the doorman held open the main door for Colin Sharpe, checking out of work with, at his side, his usual bag that carried his bespoke tuxedo. Today, his bag was positively bulging, even though his bespoke tuxedo was still on his person.

"Colin!" I shouted, dodging a young child twirling around a doll. "Don't do this!"

He smiled at me over his shoulder, twiddled his fingers in a wave, and took off in a run.

"Stop him!" Hodgson yelled, but no one seemed to understand what he was yelling. In fact, the only thing people thought to do when they saw the two of us running as fast as we could was to dodge out of the way. At least the doorman had the forethought to hold the door open for us.

Colin was halfway down the sidewalk.

"He's headed for the subway," Hodgson panted. "Come on—hurry! If we lose him in the tunnels, we'll never catch up!"

"I'd like to see you run in these heels and say that!"

He wheezed out a laugh. "I bet you would!"

Colin made it to the station before us, weaving between people as he rushed down the stairs. He was so fast! *Athletic*, the papers had called the Gentleman Thief, and athletic Colin Sharpe was.

He made it through the turnstiles, and we still hadn't caught up to him. Hodgson dug into his pocket and pulled out a few coins, dropping them into the turnstile and then continued.

"Hodgson!" I called out. "Hodgson, I don't have any money!"

He grunted as he turned around and ran back toward me with his hand in his pocket. "You're one of the richest people on the planet. How do you not have any money?!"

"We left the hotel in a hurry, and I don't keep loose change, as a general rule. To prevent jingling, you understand."

He dropped in two more coins, and then the turnstile let me in, the line of people grousing in response.

A train was boarding. Far down the platform, Colin ducked inside. Hodgson ran at a breakneck speed, and I at a more break-ankle speed. A whistle blew, and Hodgson grabbed my arm and dragged me into the nearest open door, which closed a second after my skirt twirled inside.

This was not Colin's compartment. Colin was quite unreachable from us, in the compartment over, his bag of stolen goods in his hand and a smile on his face.

The train began to move. I swayed with it, nearly falling on my rear before grabbing a handle above my head and holding on tight. There were brightly colored cartoons advertising baseball games and a variety of household cleaners all around our compartment, while fans running down the center of the ceiling overhead moved the cold air. The chairs, something I would never sit on, were covered in an off-white material, while the floors were a strange orange color and sticky beneath my feet. Hodgson was staring back at Colin through the small windows of the doors separating us.

"Hodgson," I whispered, my breath shallow as my lungs recovered from the effort of chasing the thief.

"Hmm?" His breathing was rapid as well.

Colin, however, looked completely unbothered as he blew me a kiss.

"I've never been on the subway before."

"Congratulations, Murphy. You're a real New Yorker now."

Chapter 44

The train stopped and Colin was gone in a flash. Hodgson and I followed suit, but I was nervous he'd double back and wind up on the same train again. Even in a full tux, it was hard to keep an eye on Colin in the crowd. I thought I saw his perfect head of dark hair to my right, so I hurried toward it.

The head of hair was instead attached to a gentleman traveling with small children and a vexed looking woman, and no one in their immediate group was wearing a tuxedo.

I swore, spun back around to confer with Hodgson. But Hodgson wasn't at my side. The train pulled out on the tracks. I hurried up the stairs to get a better look, to see if I could spy Colin in a window or Hodgson on the platform, but there was only a sea of people pushing upward. I had to go with the current or get swept away.

The swarm forced me into a gigantic room. Honey-colored marble covered the floor, lit by massive glass windowpanes in the one-hundred-and fifty-foot-high vaulted ceilings. Barrel arches intersected the open expanse, interrupting the moonlight as it streamed down among us. People were moving, standing, lining up, buying tickets, hugging, laughing.

I forced breath into my lungs, people cursing me as they split around my unmoving body. "Penn Station," I whispered.

I'd been inside of it once as a child with my mother, though I couldn't remember why. We never rode the subway. But I was as mesmerized by it now as I had been eighteen years ago, clutching my mom's hand and staring, open mouthed, watching the sunlight cast shadows down on us.

"Miss Murphy," a familiar Scottish brogue purred in my ear, "what a surprise to find you here alone. No, don't think about screaming."

I snapped my mouth closed when something hard and cylindrical pressed into my side. Colin Sharpe's gun was hidden in the pocket of his tux, but I could still hear the click when he pulled back the hammer with his thumb.

"I'd prefer not to ruin your gown, Miss Murphy." Colin's nose traced the shell of my ear. "Though, I don't think purple is your color."

I twitched away from him, but he dug his gun deeper into my hip, keeping me in place. "What do you want, Colin? You've already got my jewels."

"Oh, my apologies. I thought I was obvious. I want *you*, Miss Murphy. Come along now, love. We're going to miss our train. Mind the step."

Chapter 45

With his right hand holding his case of stolen goods and his left hand hidden in his pocket, Colin dug the gun deeper into my side and pressed a kiss on my cheek. We were on a platform, waiting for a train to who knows where. "Keep smiling. Don't try and signal to anyone that something is wrong. I'm watching you very closely." His breath was on my neck. "Your rental detective didn't follow us. I'd wager he got all turned around and confused before you and I even bumped into each other."

I glared. "You're not going to get away with this."

"Miss Murphy. *Evelyn*. It wounds me that you would resort to dialogue found in one of your silly mystery novels. Surely you can do better than that."

Wind whipped in the tunnel as the train pulled in, my skirt tugging hard to the side. It came to an abrupt stop, and the doors slid open, passengers departing in a mad rush. I locked eyes with a woman, made a step toward her, but Colin kissed my cheek again.

"We're going to miss our train, love, and I don't want to be late."

He forced me inside and guided us to a seat. I did not want to sit in the subway. Standing had been bad enough, but at least I'd only touched a handle, and my gloves were far easier to remove than the dress I was wearing. But the gun at my side gave me little room for argument.

"Look, do you see? This is your great city." Colin pointed at a man sleeping on a seat a few rows away from us. He set his case of jewels on his lap and wrapped his free arm around my shoulders, brought his mouth to my ear again.

The tip of his nose sent shivers spiraling down my neck.

"We are barreling into winter," he whispered, "and do your wealthy care what happens to those without homes? To be fair, I don't care about what happens to this gentleman either, but I'm betting *you* will. If you act up in any way, or draw attention to us, I'll shoot him where he sleeps. And in the chaos, slip away."

I kept my eyes down so as not to accidentally make eye contact with anyone and draw Colin's ire. This was not a great predicament I found myself in. Away from my hotel, away from any help, stuck in a train full of potential victims for the thief I had tried to corner to use as leverage. But I wasn't afraid as much as I felt stupid. He held all the power right now, which made us all as safe as we could be, considering. He'd only start firing if he thought he was losing. And I had no intention of besting him now.

"Why work for the hotel?" I whispered back. "Were you always planning on robbing us?"

"Obviously." he said. "Hotels are great for jewels and cash. I prefer jewelry. Gems, gold, silver. Much harder for the police to track, especially after you melt it down. But I'll take cash if it falls into my lap. Hadn't been able to get a good look at the setup until that day you invited me in, and I've been biding my time since. I wasn't planning on striking today—that was your fault, you know. You . . . no spark—really? None?"

I shook my head. "None, sorry. I don't have a brother, but I'd imagine kissing you to be about as romantic as that."

Colin pulled away from me, a deep frown etched into his handsome face. "There was a spark there. I know it. I felt it."

"When we danced the first time," I admitted. "But I think as I got to know you more, it just sort of faded."

"You're a terrible liar," he said.

"Does it look like I'm lying now?"

Colin stared at me hard, his dark eyes tracking over my face. "Yes," he said with a crooked smile. "Yes, it does."

I rolled my eyes. Finally.

"There were other advantages of working for the hotel too." He sighed, tangled his fingers in my hair. "I could scope out potential targets. Though, the paper figured that out faster than I expected, which made me a bit nervous you'd put it together that it was an employee. Dad says you're smarter than most people think."

I shrugged the shoulder under his hand. "If I was so smart, I wouldn't be stuck here with you."

He nodded at the sleeping man. "There are worse places."

The train entered a station, colors streaking across the windows, and when it stopped, Colin shook his head. "Not yet, love." Passengers departed and new ones hopped on, but the man near us stayed asleep. Colin relaxed against me when the doors closed, and we began to move again, his head resting against mine.

"I didn't expect you to be as beautiful as you are," he admitted. "That threw a wrench into my plans. I started thinking of a future. A rich, beautiful wife. But you wouldn't even look my way. I had to get your attention."

"We've established the details of that particular plan," I groused. "Pretending to mix me and Poppy up."

"And it worked, didn't it? No spark indeed." Colin grinned. "This entire thing is your fault, you know that, don't you? If you had admitted you felt for me what I feel for you after our kiss today, I would've gone back to the piano. I would've continued my plan of wooing you. I wouldn't have felt the need to take out your security, crack the safe, and steal your jewels. Would've worked better for me anyway, because the bank had already come and collected the Pinnacle's cash today. I didn't know they came on the weekends."

He was staring straight ahead, his legs crossed at the ankles. The bag with my jewelry sat on his lap. It would be easy to swipe it, but then what? He'd taken his hand out of his pocket to hold on to me, but how long would it take for him to start shooting? Not long. What was in that bag was certainly not worth more than a person's life.

"If you were trying to woo me," I said, "and you were worried I'd figure out that a Pinnacle employee was behind the whole scheme, why did you keep up with the robberies?"

Colin sighed. "I have a *very* particular buyer. I thought I'd gotten enough to make him happy, but it turned out the jewelry in question was"—he lowered his voice to a growl—"costume."

Pieces that had been outside the puzzle I'd been trying to force together all week finally snapped into place all on their own. "The Mitchells," I said with relief. "She had your red square in her coat." It was going to be the death of me to have not figured that clue out. *Oh, perhaps that's the wrong turn of phrase to use regarding Lois.*

"Who?"

"The woman who died when you were playing piano."

"Ah. I thought she died in hospital?"

I answered that question with a nod, because he was technically correct. She'd been poisoned with her greatest allergen at the Pinnacle but had succumbed to its effects in a hospital bed.

"No great loss, let me assure you. That theft gave me *quite* a headache. They had these giant dogs too, but they were much scarier to look at then deal with. One belly rub, and they were silent as a mouse. Unlike that terror on four legs you carry around as if he were a child, Evelyn."

"Presley is a good boy," I agreed. "But you, Mr. Sharpe, are a scoundrel."

"Of course I am." The train began to slow, and Colin stood up, steady on his feet. He took hold of my hand and pulled me to standing, pressed a kiss to my knuckles as I swayed with the movement of the stopping subway. "You wouldn't like me if I wasn't."

"I don't like you now."

His crooked grin somehow made his eyes crinkle in the most charming manner. "You're a terrible liar, Evelyn. Don't ever change. Come on, now. This way. Mind the step."

We left the train with the rush of departing passengers. He was still too close and too armed for me to try to escape. Instead, I went with the flow of travel, his hand on my back the entire way. At the bottom of the stairs, Colin kissed my temple and whispered, "I'll be seeing you."

The hand on my back was gone. When I looked over my shoulder, so was he.

I spun around to try and find him again, but he had disappeared in the mass of people, some of whom were urging me upward.

"Excuse me." I tried to force my way downstream. "Pardon me. Excuse me." No matter how many steps I took, I made little progress, the push of traffic forcing me out of the platform.

It was with great regret that I walked into the station. My heart beat erratically, like I'd run up the stairs instead of practically being carried. A sign, hung on the walls, written in giant capital letters read, "WELCOME TO NEWARK."

"Oh, dear Lord." I covered my gaping mouth with my hand before realizing I'd touched so many different things on the train. Gagging, I peeled off my gloves. "He took me to New Jersey!"

Chapter 46

It is odd how little people want to help you when you have no money to your name. I tried, of course, to tell someone about Colin. Like a police officer, who was on patrol outside of the station.

"Hello!" My hands were clasped firmly in front of me, lest I touch my face with them again. "Yes. Hi. I was taken hostage by a jewel thief, and he's escaped."

The officer stared at me. He was in the middle of writing a parking ticket. He stared at me some more before returning to his parking ticket and placing it on the windshield of the unsuspecting owner.

"Hello, sir? I could use some assistance."

"Ma'am, if you were taken hostage, why are you roaming free right now?"

"Well, as I said, he sort of . . . escaped?"

"So, was he holding *you* hostage, or were you holding *him* hostage?"

I tugged at the pendant of Saint Anthony around my neck. "Yes. Okay. I don't normally like to do this but, I'm Evelyn Murphy?"

The cop took a step, but it was away from me, his ticket book still in his hand. "Are you asking me or telling me?"

"I was telling," I said. "Yes. Telling. I'm Evelyn Murphy, and I require assistance."

He started writing in his book. "Nice to meet you, Evelyn Murphy. I'm Matthew Grady, and I'm required to write these tickets."

I yanked so hard on Tony it was a wonder my necklace didn't break. "Can I at least get a ride back home, please?"

"Subway's behind you," he said, and kept going.

I looked at the station. It was indeed behind me. "But I don't have any money?"

He was too far away to hear me, or he didn't care anymore about what I had to say. Most likely the latter, if the way he started to hum loudly and off-key was any indication. Bucking up my courage and fixing my wind-blown skirt, I hailed a taxi.

One pulled up to the curb behind the row of ticketed cars, cigarette smoke billowing out of his open window.

"Hello," I greeted, coughing a little. "I need a ride to the Pinnacle Hotel."

"In Manhattan? Central Park?"

"The very same! I'm so happy you've heard of it. Now, I do not have any money-"

The taxi driver called me a rude name and peeled off, mud from under his tires spewing out to the sides and behind and all over my once wind-blown skirt.

Gasping, gagging, crying, I fluffed the purple gown out as best I could, wet mud dripping off the asymmetrical, floral lace. "But this . . . this is *Balenciaga*!"

Absolutely no one cared. People passed me on the sidewalk, snickering to one another or outright ignoring me. No one was going to help me. Not the taxi driver, not the police officer, not even the man walking by with his cat on a leash.

I had never seen a cat on a leash before. The cat was loving it, prowling down the busy sidewalk like it owned the place. It made me think of Monroe, waiting for me at home to serve her. Of Presley, scared and yet determined, barking a warning when the thief tried to enter my home. They needed me to save myself.

"Right." I dried my tears with my wrist, careful not to touch my face with my hands. "Okay." A deep, rattling sniff steeled my nerves. "I need fifteen cents to get on the subway. I can do that. I'm Evelyn Murphy. I can find anything!"

Just to be safe, I touched my pendant and said a quick prayer to Saint Anthony.

It took ten minutes and two blocks, but I found three nickels, a dime, and two pennies.

* * *

The ride to Penn Station was a lot less eventful than my departure. This was probably because I looked insane, covered in mud and crying, and people tended not to look directly at the outright zany. Back in Manhattan, if I told a police officer I was Evelyn Murphy, there was a better chance they'd know who I was and would give me a ride to the hotel. Or I should have enough coins left over from the New Jersey streets, covered in grime though they were—the coins, I mean, though the streets weren't that much better.

A plop of mud dropped from my skirt and onto my foot. I closed my eyes and prayed, *For the love of God*. Fortunately, the crowd that had been so anxious to force me up and down stairs earlier gave me a wide birth now as I ascended into Penn Station.

It was still as grand as I'd remembered it was as a child, but there were marks of time scuffing up the place. The granite columns were covered in peeling plaster, and splotches of pink granite scuffed up the honey marble floor.

My plan to find a police officer worked perfectly. The moment I stepped into the main waiting room, one took me by the elbow.

"Evelyn Murphy?"

"Yes?"

"I found her!" He shouted that to the room at large. I noticed there was a collection of other officers huddled in a group not far from us, Hodgson in the center, and they all turned toward us at my locator's holler.

Relief fell over Hodgson like a blanket. His shoulders sagged forward, his chest inflating with air, and then he hurried toward us.

Soon, I was in the center of the police huddle. I ran my fingers through my hair to freshen up.

"Miss Murphy," Hodgson said, which caught me off guard. He never used "Miss" anymore. Granted, most of the time we were talking alone, and now we were surrounded by strangers with weapons. "What happened?"

"Oh, Hodgson, it was *awful*." The tears I had forced down at the sight of that cat on a leash, walking his owner, came back full force, clouding my vision. "He took me to New Jersey!"

Chapter 47

The police officers left us in order to continue their search for Colin. Apparently, an APB had been put out for both of us, but I didn't know what that stood for, and I was too tired and dirty to learn anything new.

"Did you get a look at his gun?" Hodgson asked me before the cops left.

"No, he kept it in his pocket."

"Armed and dangerous," one of them said. "Got it."

Then they were gone, and the two of us were alone in the incredibly busy Penn Station.

"Can you please take me home? I am in desperate need of a change of clothes."

"Aren't you upset?" He asked. "All your jewelry—your mother's jewelry?"

"Oh. I'm sorry. I forgot I didn't share that part with you. I switched all the jewelry in the safe with my Ladies Love to Sparkle purchases. Except for the tiara. He'd seen that one, so he was expecting it, and the Ladies didn't sell any tiaras."

Hodgson leaned away from me. He spun around in a circle, pushing his hat up his head with his fingers as he scratched his forehead. "Murphy, *you*?" Another circle. "Murphy, you *knew* he was the Gentleman Thief?"

Guilt shot through me, though I wasn't sure why. Something I'd have to ask Dr. Sanders about later. "I *guessed* it."

He covered his eyes with his hand. "I'm afraid to ask, but *how* did you guess it?"

"He talked about the paper a lot."

His second hand joined the first in covering his eyes. "What?"

"When I first read about the Gentleman Thief, I theorized that whoever it was enjoyed the notoriety. That's why they left their calling card."

"So you figured it was Colin Sharpe who was robbing rich people because he talked to you about the paper? The paper that you read every single day?"

I twirled my fingers into the cleanest part of my gown I could find. "He wanted to be sure I was seeing the articles written about him. And, I don't know, I had a feeling he was up to something. It *did* seem like the thief was connected to the hotel in some way, though at first I thought it was a totally different employee. The way he courted me was strange too: at first dismissive, and then he was overly romantic."

Hodgson dropped his hands, but only to turn them into fists on his hips. "And from that you deduced he was the Gentleman Thief?"

"I guessed! I had an inkling. An inkling isn't proof. So I . . . annoyed him on purpose at the party today to see if he would strike. And he did. Good thing too, because I made sure the bank came and took the cash out, or he really would been making off with quite a payday." I giggled. "Oh well, at least he gets the tiara out of it."

Hodgson shook his head and sighed. "Let's get you home. Maybe we'll swing by that doctor of yours, have your head looked at."

"Really! I feel much better now that I'm not in New Jersey." I shuddered. "An absolute beast of a man, to treat a lady that way."

Hodgson's eyes narrowed. He studied me as if there was going to be a quiz about my face soon.

"What?"

"You *like* the cretin."

Nervously, I laughed and stepped away. "No. Of course not! He's a thief and a liar, and when he kissed me, there was absolutely no spark."

"He kissed you?"

"Twice." I winced. "But it was . . . fine."

Hodgson shook his head. "You're a terrible liar, Murphy. You know they're going to find him, right? He'll be in jail before the night is over. You'll have your fake jewelry and your real tiara by breakfast."

"I doubt that very much. A shame too—I never even got to wear that tiara. But I do think we'll be seeing him again."

"You think or you hope?"

I swatted his arm. "Right now, the only thing I hope for is a hot bath. Which train takes us to the hotel?"

He sighed again. "I'll just hail a taxi."

"Okay, but I don't have any money. I had to find loose change on the street to get here, Hodgson!"

"Maybe that'll teach you not to leave home without jingling."

"I'd rather still be in New Jersey. Here." I handed him my remaining coins. "For you. For your trouble."

Hodgson flipped the coins over in his palm with the nail of his index finger. "Why is this penny green?"

Chapter 48

The next day took three cups of coffee before I was able to dress. Presley and Monroe were happy with my laziness, content to stay in bed all day. Monroe preferred my chest, but Presley was happy on the pillow that used to be Mac's, belly and tiny legs in the air for me to scratch between refills.

I didn't really want to leave my suite, but I had plans, so my outfit for the day was a simple pair of gray slacks, a pink blouse, and tan flats. I didn't bother with makeup, and I ran a quick comb through my hair, pinning it back and taming it with pink barrettes. I hadn't curled it after my bath the previous night, and it had taken on a life of its own.

There was a knock on the door, and I opened it with a smile. "Good morning, Hodgson. Coffee?"

"It's nearly noon, Murphy."

"That's why I said, 'Good *morning*,' as it is not yet *after*noon. Poppy, Henry, and your dear friend Russell are on their way for lunch. Can I entice you to stay?"

"I've had enough of your social gatherings to hold me over for a while. You gonna give me the box or what?"

I stood back and waved him in. Presley trotted out of the bedroom to meet him, twirling around his ankles. Hodgson begrudgingly bent down to scratch the tiny Pomeranian behind the ears in greeting.

With a loud, cleansing sigh, I picked up one of Mom's journals and put it back into the box. "I've only read the first three," I said. "But I think it's time you took over from here."

He nodded and didn't say anything as I looked over each of the dozen journals, taking in my fill of the sight of them, before stacking them in the box the nun had given us. My mother had spent time on each one of these pages, her handwriting across every inch, her hopes and her worries spelled out in black ink. She'd been a person, a real separate entity, existing outside of my memory. Her own individual. I struggled to remember even the sound of her laugh.

"Hodgson," I said, "I had trouble sleeping because I was thinking about yesterday."

"New Jersey?"

"What? Oh no. Well, a little bit. But I was thinking specifically about Theodore and Lois Mitchell."

"I was thinking about them too as I rebandaged my net wounds." He raised his hands and wiggled his fingers, and sure enough, about three of them were bandaged.

"Why did he kill her?" My thumb traced the spine of a journal. "He said it was because she started having opinions about the money she was earning. That's such . . . that's such a stupid reason, I can't get it to make sense in my own head. I *knew* he killed her. I knew it, but I couldn't figure out *why*, and talking to him didn't help at all, even though Wally and I were able to get that confession."

"Good thing too," Hodgson said. "That fingerprint on the bottom of the bottle was Mrs. Mitchell's, and the only thing that proves is the killer took it from her house. A good defense attorney could argue Mrs. Mitchell poisoned herself. Without him following you up there and confessing, there wouldn't be a case."

Monroe jumped up from out of nowhere and onto the back of the couch. I paused in my ritual to scratch down her back. "We talked about motives, remember? Revenge, love, money. Hiding evidence. True belief. Where does this fit?"

Hodgson spread out his arms as if he intended to embrace an invisible giant. "Not everything fits into little boxes that you can check off, Murphy. My time spent on the force, or before that, fighting in the War, I've seen people do horrible, inexplicable things. Nothing surprises me anymore. Sometimes . . . sometimes a man, or a woman, will just snap. There doesn't have to be a real reason, Murphy. Mr. Mitchell, he viewed his wife as a *thing*, not as a person. And if she's just an object, well, then, she's disposable. She upset him when she started making more money than him. So"—Hodgson shrugged, his arms still outstretched—"he got rid of her."

With another sigh, I grabbed my mother's last journal off the coffee table. "You'll give these back to me when you're done?"

"They'll be in my office," Hodgson said. "The one I've spent all morning putting back together after your most recent and most definitely final haunting. You can come and get them whenever you want."

"I'll want them once her killer is behind bars." I slapped the journal against my open palm to sell my statement. A loose sheaf of paper fell out, drifted to the floor. Wrinkling my nose, I plucked it off my shoe with two fingers. It was folded in thirds, and longer when opened than the paper in any of the journals.

"What is it?" Hodgson asked.

I tried to figure that out with another glance over the paper. They were English letters, but none of them made up a single

English word. "I don't know. It is my mother's handwriting, but it doesn't make any sense."

Hodgson took it, his eyes wide at first and then narrowing to slits as he read and reread it.

"Why would she write a letter in gibberish?" I held out my hand to take it back.

"Because she didn't," he said. "This isn't gibberish, Murphy. It's code."

"Code?" I repeated, incredulous. But there were six numbers on the top right corner: 122243. The day before the day she died. The paper fell from my fingers and Hodgson snatched it out of the air. "Now why . . . why did my mother write a letter in code the day before she died?"

"Yeah." Hodgson put it in the box on top her journals. "Yeah, that's the question, ain't it?"

Chapter 49

Pinnacle Heiress Makes Bold Statement

Evelyn Murphy attended a gala in the Pinnacle's Gold Room wearing a purple gown that stunned the crowd—but not as much as her conversation on the record with this reporter. "I've solved the murder of Mrs. Mitchell and figured out the identity of the Gentleman Thief," she proclaimed mid-twirl. The Times can report that Evelyn Murphy, socialite sleuth, has done it again. Mr. Mitchell was arrested on first-degree murder charges for killing his wife, Lois, the woman lunching at the Pinnacle for her last meal, after Miss Murphy convinced him to confess to police. Colin Sharpe, the son of Pinnacle hotel manager Silas, has been identified as the Gentleman Thief who struck fear into the hearts of Manhattan's bejeweled aficionados over the last few weeks. He is on the run and presumed dangerous. See below.

A very handsome picture of Colin's very handsome face was in the corner of the article, below the fold. The picture of Henry and me on the stairs, in our coordinating purple, made it to the front page. It wasn't in color, which was for the best. No one would see our coordinating purple, which was a shame, but they also wouldn't see how washed out I looked.

I tried to hide my smile as I tucked the paper under my plate. "I wasn't twirling."

"I seem to remember a twirl or two," Henry said.

"I most certainly did not twirl. Did I, Poppy?"

She swallowed her mouthful of pineapple upside-down cake. "Um." She said. "I . . . was otherwise preoccupied."

Russell nodded sagely. "She got up and played piano after Sharpe's son split."

"Why, Poppy!" I said, "I knew you were an artist, but I had no idea you could play piano!"

"That's 'cause I can't." Her grimace revealed all her teeth. "But by then everyone was more than a little tipsy and didn't seem to mind."

A boyish grin lit Henry's face much better than the torch in the two-way mirror. "It was terrible, darling, absolutely terrible! People were donating hand over fist in a desperate attempt to get you to stop playing."

Poppy hid her face behind her fork. I burst into laughter.

Russell patted her on the shoulder. "The point was to make money for those mothers, and it doesn't matter how it happened."

Henry wobbled his hand from side to side as if to say, *"It matters a little."*

The four of us were in my suite, eating lunch sent up by Chef Marco, who did not care he had ever been under suspicion for Lois Mitchell's death, and so therefore was not offering his thanks by the decadent spread of sandwiches made with fresh bread and homemade strawberry jam, along with a variety of other meats, cheeses, and fruits. He said so himself in the note he wrote and sent along underneath the silver pot filled with cream for the coffee.

Monroe was far too interested in the cream. I shooed her off the cart and picked up the still warm carafe. Splashing noises from the kitchen indicated that Presley was enjoying his own lunch. Perhaps a little too much.

"Thank you so much for your help," I said. First to Poppy, and then to Henry and Russell too. I refilled all our cups of coffee. "Poppy, you ran the entire gala and did a marvelous job. None of it would have happened without you. Russell, you helped Poppy with the gala, and you helped Hodgson with the net. He never would've finished on time if you hadn't stepped in to help. And Henry, you helped scare Mr. Mitchell into the trap itself!"

"Happy to do it," Henry said. "Any time you need me to play a ghost, darling, count me in. Especially as I find myself rather in between gigs at the moment."

"Henry, is Mr. Sharpe doing all right? I haven't seen him since we trapped Mr. Mitchell."

He took a big sip of the coffee I'd poured him. "He's disappointed, of course," he said, smacking his lips. "But Colin is a grown man. There's only so much Silas can do at this point."

"Oh, and Miss Evelyn?" Russell cleared his throat. "I called my old boss at the stables, and they'd be happy to take Mr. Mitchell's dogs. The horses love to play with dogs, especially big ones like those Great Danes."

"That's wonderful news!" I went to sit down again, but there was a knock on the door. "You three keep eating. I'll be right back."

No one had stopped eating, so following my order was not difficult. I expected another round of food from the certainly not grateful Chef Marco but was instead greeted by a giant bouquet of flowers with feet.

The feet were a bellboy's, and he handed over the bouquet, vase and all, and readily accepted my dollar in thanks. There were at least four dozen red roses in a heavy crystal vase, wrapped in a red bow. I hauled it into the living room, panting the entire way.

"Should've let the bell hop do that," Russell called from the table.

I huffed in response, setting the flowers on my currently empty coffee table. There was a note tucked inside, and I was unsurprised to find it was from Wally.

"Your lawyer beau?" Henry asked.

I tucked the note back into the flowers. "He wants to take me to the theater this weekend. I'll have to buy a new dress."

"Oh, how terrible for you," Henry drawled.

With a roll of my eyes, I took my seat at the table. "At least he—you know." I twirled my spoon in my fingers. "Mr. Mitchell killed his wife because she started earning more money than him. There are very few young men in the world right now who have more money than I do. Wally has his own money. Not as much as my family, but he comes from money, and maybe that's enough? Maybe that'll be enough for someone to love me for myself?"

Henry put his hand over mine, steadying the spinning spoon. "Darling, you've always got us."

Poppy nodded, leaning over in her seat to wrap me in a one-armed hug. "We're here for you, whether you have all the money in the world or you end up as poor and as destitute as the rest of us."

There was another knock on the door. "I'll get it," I said.

Henry raised his cup of coffee. "Who wants to make a little wager? More food from a definitely not grateful Marco or from a definitely not desperate lawyer?"

"It's food," Poppy said. "Without a doubt."

"I bet it's candy," Russell added. "Which is food, but it'll be from the lawyer. He's trying to marry Miss Mur—Evelyn."

Giggling, I swung open the door, fully expecting the bellhop to be there with roses that had fallen out in his travels to the top floor. The giggle froze on my lips, stuck in my throat, blocked air from entering my lungs.

Malcolm Cooper stood in the hallway. Mac! With his gray eyes and his unruly hair and his perfect jaw, covered in enough stubble to be considered a full beard now. Today's paper was tucked under his arm, and the bag he'd packed and taken when he walked out on me in Yonkers was by his feet.

"Hi, Ev," he greeted, and his deep, lyrical voice swept over my body. "I'm back."

I shut the door. The room was tilting, and I hadn't had a single sip of champagne. My chest tingled, and the tingling spread down my arms and legs and up to my head. My vision blurred. My hands ached. I held on to the wall for support, walked on wobbly knees toward my friends.

"Darling?" Henry asked. "Are you all right? You look like you've seen a ghost."

THE END

Author's Note

The line that Lois Mitchell uses, saying that anyone who fails at her business is lazy, stupid, greedy, or dead, is a direct quote from a man by the name of William Penn Patrick. Now, Mr. Patrick didn't start his multilevel marketing business, Holiday Magic, until the early 1960s, and while that does make Lois's use of it a bit anachronistic, my thinking is that he might've said it before he started Holiday Magic, but he just didn't write it down until the 1960s. Anything is possible with fiction if you're okay with lying.

He also went on to create Mind Dynamics, so I don't feel too bad playing a bit fast and loose with the timeline of things here. I hope you enjoyed the spirit of the story as it is written! And do not google Mind Dynamics unless you're prepared to lose an entire weekend.

Acknowledgments

Many, many thanks to:

- My wonderful agent, Madelyn Burt.
- My incredible editor, Faith Black Ross.
- The phenomenal team at Crooked Lane Books.
- Amara Jasper, for her exceptional ability to bring Evelyn to life.
- Kashmira Sarode, for this beautiful cover.
- My family and friends for their support and understanding.
  - Paul, I love you a lot. Possibly too much. I should get out more.
  - Sam, Avery, Eloise, Madeline, and Margaret, you're all so amazing, and I'm so proud of you.
  - Mom and Dad, you got the dedication for this book, and you're welcome. But Dad shares my love of learning very specifically about multilevel marketing schemes, so it seemed extra fitting.
  - Doug, Kim, Stephen, and Reed, you're great and you should know it.
  - Jordan, thank you for being a friend.

- Leira and Ayesha, thanks for sticking around after all these years.
- My friends at Sisters in Crime and, especially, my cohorts at Citrus Crime Writers, I'm grateful for your support.
- And *you*, of course, for reading. You're the best and your hair looks amazing.